fakers

A
Canaan Island
NOVEL

OTHER BOOKS BY
Meg Collett

THE FEAR UNIVERSITY SERIES

Fear University
The Killing Season

END OF DAYS SERIES

The Hunted One
The Lost One
The Only One

DAYS OF NEW SERIES

Speaking of the Devil
Full of the Devil
Better the Devil You Know
Devil in the Details
Give the Devil His Due

NOVELLAS

Little Girls and Their Ponies

fakers

A *Canaan Island* NOVEL

MEG COLLETT

Fakers
© Copyright 2016 Meg Collett
www.megcollett.com
All Rights Reserved

This book or parts thereof may not be reproduced in any form, stored in a retrieval system, or transmitted in any form by any means without prior written permission of the authors, except as provided by United States of America copyright law.

Cover Design by Najla Qamber Designs
Editing by Jessica West (www.west1jessedits.com) and Red Road Editing / Kristina Circelli (www.circelli.info)

The following is a work of fiction. Names, characters, places, and incidents are fictitious or used fictitiously. Any resemblance to real persons, living or dead, to factual events or to businesses is coincidental and unintentional.

ISBN-13: 978-1500814816
ISBN-10: 1500814814

For those who struggle with a darkness.

1

The Jeep ran over the curb and came to an indelicate stop. An impressive assortment of surfboards on the roof rattled as the engine cut off. Neighbors walking on the quiet road lined with Bradford Pears and white-picket fencing slowed to catch a glimpse of the new owner of 22 Gardenia Street, their eyes narrowing at the large U-Haul poking out into the road; others simply peered out of their kitchen windows and waited with pursed lips.

Finally, the car door opened and a leggy blonde sprung out.

Kyra Aberdeen whipped off her aviator sunglasses and took in her new home.

"I own a freakin' *house*," she said, her voice full of wonder. She'd never bought a home before, let alone a house in need of a bulldozer more than a fresh coat of paint.

A tall Victorian with turrets, fish scales, and curling little accents sat slightly crookedly in the center of the small lot. Paint peeled off the shutters in clumps and fell to the ground with every strong ocean-scented breeze, like snow in June. Thin, scrappy trees grew along the base of the house, uprooting the foundation and making the poor house look like it had hairy legs. Overgrown grass and patchy, thorny weeds dominated the front garden, and fragrant confederate jasmine vines crawled across the collapsing picket fence line in a great wave of white blooms.

The house could only be defined as a total disaster, which suited Kyra fine because she happened to be an expert on being a disaster.

She'd come to Canaan Island to be healed by the ocean and salty air, the seagulls and Southern food. And no matter how bad it looked on the outside or how much her stomach twisted with the tiniest flare of buyer's remorse, she would not let herself regret purchasing her mother's childhood home.

She *needed* this place, and it needed her.

Of course, it wasn't like she had boatloads of money to sink into restoring an old home. She uploaded videos to YouTube for a living. Granted, they were pretty popular. Her tutorials on makeup and health tips had millions of views. Since she'd graduated college last year, her channel had grown to over three-and-a-half million subscribers. She could be funny, sexy, or easygoing at the drop of a hat. People proposed to her over the Internet, which wasn't weird at all. But she certainly didn't know how to use a jackhammer. And this house needed a jackhammer.

Thank God she'd had the foresight to hire a contractor.

As if on cue, a white work truck parked in front of her house, carefully aligning to the curb. Kyra turned and watched as a tall man with light-brown hair emerged, carrying an armload of rolled-up papers. His grin widened when he caught sight of her.

She pushed her unease down and called up her brightest, best smile, the one that flashed her perfect white teeth and practically oozed cheerful happiness, even if she didn't feel it. Especially if she didn't feel it. "You must be Mr. Cooper. I'm Kyra."

The man was all legs and arms, making him seem more like a gangly teenager than a business owner, but he stuck out his hand with confidence. "Nice to meet you, Kyra. Please call me Cade." His smile hooked in the corners, revealing the cutest set of dimples. "Welcome to Canaan. We may not be the most exciting island off the southern coast, but we sure are the prettiest!"

Kyra laughed, shaking his hand and noting the way he carefully enunciated every word he spoke, as if he had to think about how his tongue moved to form the words. "Thank you! Is that the town's motto?"

"It should be," he said with a good-natured eye roll.

Kyra felt the smoothness of his palm before she released his hand. "You're the contractor?" she asked.

Cade flushed a little, showing a chink in his confidence. "Actually, my brother is the contractor. I primarily meet with clients and go over plans."

"Oh, okay." To cover her surprise at his words, she looked back up at the house and sighed dramatically. "So how bad is it?"

"Well," he said, drawing out the word. "It was brave of you to purchase it sight-unseen, and it's going to need some work, but Cooper Bros. Contracting is the best on the island. Some say the best in all of Georgia." He shot her a grin, which Kyra returned. "How about I show you around and go over some ideas?"

"Sounds good!" She took a deep breath and stepped toward the gate. It was a rotted, warped thing, hanging with a surprising persistence from its rusted hinges. She had to kick it open.

The garden needed hours of pruning and hacking to look less like a magical, overgrown forest where trolls and fairies lived and more like proper curb appeal. The jasmine smelled lovely, if not a little overpowering, and Kyra fought back a sneeze. Some of the flowers managed to stake their bit of dirt, but most were drowned by weeds. Wisteria weaved around the broken porch rails.

"No one has lived here for over a decade. The previous owners bought it for a beach home, but never got around to using it. Divorce or something," Cade said, toeing the edge of a broken glass bottle. "The garden is a bit of a mess."

"I think that's an understatement, but I can tame it."

"Hold onto that optimism," he said with a warm laugh. "The structure of the house is actually pretty good. We'll need to examine the foundation thoroughly and replace some of the support beams. In houses this old, wooden beams were just set into the ground. Over time, the moisture erodes the wood and causes instability."

"But it's safe to live in, right? I want to stay here during the renovation." Kyra said she wanted to, but the truth was, she needed to. Most of her savings had gone into the purchase of this house, and, after setting aside some for renovations, she didn't have much left.

"Don't worry. When my brother and I completed our walkthrough, we both agreed the structure was safe." Cade looked at her like he pitied her. "Living in a house being renovated is torture with all the noise and dust, but if you want to, you won't be in danger."

Kyra nodded thoughtfully. "Where will you be starting?"

"Let me show you." Cade took her elbow before she stepped onto the rickety step. "Watch these porch stairs. They may be a little rotten."

They carefully made their way up to the house and onto the porch. Even though some floorboards were missing and vines ran like snakes across the porch, Kyra pictured herself here, swinging and sipping tea. She smiled even as her loose, teal tank top snagged on a thorn.

Standing in front of the faded, warped door, Cade pulled out a set of keys from his pocket. "Here's your copy. The other will go to my brother until the reno is finished." He set the cool metal in her open palm, and when she met his eyes, he was grinning. "You can do the honors."

Kyra slid the key into the lock and twisted. The door didn't budge. Cade had to shoulder it open before they stepped inside. "Home sweet home," she said under her breath as she looked around.

The dark and musty entry led to a set of stairs that swept up in front of her. To the left, an archway opened into the parlor with murky windows and sweeping cobwebs hanging from the ceiling. To the right was a dining room, and, through another door, a tiny kitchen hid away in the back. More rooms led off those, like a maze, to the back of the house. Peeling, faded wallpaper coated all the walls, and dated light fixtures hung lopsided from the ceiling, where large water stains added their own form of décor.

"That's bad, right?" Kyra asked, pointing to a particularly large stain.

"It's not good, but most of the things you see can be fixed. They're typical in an older home like this." He walked farther into the space, showing her through the dining room and into the kitchen. They traversed the entire first floor, weaving through tiny rooms filled with more dust and cobwebs as Cade explained the renovations.

"We'll make sure the foundation and beams are solid first, like I said earlier. That, along with general demolition, will take a week or so. Once the structure is sound, we can start really opening up these walls so there's more of an open concept from the kitchen into the dining room. All these back rooms will be converted into a large living room and office space for you. Our goal is to make the house livable and functional without taking away its old charm. My brother is very careful with the demolition, as I'm sure you'll notice," Cade said. They stopped at the kitchen counter, where he laid out his floor plans. He pointed to one drawing and walked Kyra through the technical aspects of load-bearing walls and where they'd need to add support beams in the ceiling.

Kyra tried to listen, but she kept glancing around the space and taking in the wide windows. Removing a few walls would flood the room with natural light. She already pictured her eclectic, beachy style in this place.

"And this is where we will put in a small powder room . . ."

Cade trailed off as she walked away from him mid-sentence. She spied a back door leading out of the kitchen. Prying it open, she stepped onto the back porch and took in her new backyard.

"Oh my goodness." The words caught thickly in her throat as happy, excited tears sprung to her eyes. If this place couldn't heal her, nothing would be able to.

Beyond the reach of her entangled, wild backyard dominated by two large magnolia trees, stretched the ocean at the edge of a narrow white sandy beach. The crashing waves of the Atlantic Ocean and salty air instantly soothed Kyra's frayed nerves. She took her phone out and snapped a few pictures for her social media sites. Cade was right; with its Spanish moss-laden trees and bright houses along her street, this place was the prettiest island off the coast of Georgia she'd ever seen. She imagined the town of Canaan would be just as picturesque.

"It does have great views," Cade offered from behind her.

She laughed. "I want to be out in the water so bad."

"I saw your boards. You'll fit right in here."

A familiar darkness descended in the pit of her stomach at his words of fitting in, but she brushed it off with another laugh. She came here to get rid of all that. "Do you surf?"

"No, but my brother does. I don't li-like . . ." Cade's voice stumbled slightly, and he stuttered the tiniest bit, ". . . the water much." A shadow passed over his eyes, but he brightened up as fast as Kyra had. "So what made you want to move out here?"

"You mean what in the world possessed me to buy a rundown, piece-of-crap house?" she asked with a crazy grin to put him back at ease.

"You could put it that way."

She thought about telling him the same lame story about loving old homes and wanting to be near the ocean that she'd told her realtor, but her therapist had encouraged her to be sincere with her friends. She didn't know him well yet, but she already liked Cade Cooper, and she wanted to start being more honest with people instead of keeping them at arm's length like she normally did.

"Actually, it was my mom's childhood home," she said carefully. From the corner of her eye, she saw Cade's surprised expression. "My grandparents are Florence and Garlan Aberdeen. They've lived on Canaan their entire life."

"Oh! Yeah, I know the Aberdeens. Florence is, um, interesting?" He coughed, clearly uncertain about how to be polite in the situation.

Kyra grimaced when she thought about her ice-queen grandmother. "She's pretty awful, I know."

Cade relaxed, raking his hand over the slight scruff along his jaw. "She's not the nicest lady I've ever dealt with." He laughed. "So your mom lived here? Funny, I never knew the Aberdeens had a daughter. I used to only see Thomas around town before he and his wife moved to California."

Kyra shifted uncomfortably, sweat slicking across her palms. "Thomas is my uncle. He and his wife raised me because my mom died when I was really little."

"Dang." He cringed. "Kyra, I'm sorry. I didn't mean to pry."

Pangs of sadness radiated through her chest, but she ignored them and forced herself to shrug casually. "No, it's okay. I never knew her or anything."

Fine lines formed between Cade's tanned brow, but he didn't question how she never knew her mother. He must think she was crazy, moving out here and buying her mother's home. Nerves twisted in her stomach, and she was just about to explain further when he spoke. "How about I finish going through the house with you? I am sure you want time to settle in and start unpacking."

Kyra let out a relieved breath and nodded, her smile more genuine this time.

They spent the next hour talking renovations and room layouts. After the walls came down and everything had been demolished that needed it, they would redo most of the plumbing and electrical so everything would be up to code. While they did that, all the windows, doors, and the slate roof would be replaced. Only then could they patch the walls and ceilings. Painting and reviving the ragged wood floors would come last.

A headache started to settle into her temples just from realizing the full extent of the cost. "And you're sure you can do all this under my budget?"

They stood upstairs in what would be her bedroom and temporary office during the renovations. A huge window seat filled part of the back wall. The sun streamed in, flooding across the original wood floors. From the back of the house, she had a perfect view of the ocean, and she imagined the sounds of the waves would keep the nightmares at bay.

Cade nodded. "Pending any unforeseen issues the home inspection missed, we'll stay on target with your budget."

"This can all be done in two months? With no delays, right?" Kyra pointed an accusing finger at him, but the crooked grin on her lips revealed her joke.

Chuckling, he held up his hands in surrender. "That's Hale's job. He's my brother. So you'll have to talk to him about that. But there's actually not that much renovation to do. Repairs will only take about a month, but Hale will spend some time adding in the custom furniture we talked about, like the built-in shelves and buffet."

"And he's coming here today?"

"He'll be by first thing on Monday morning to start work," Cade said. He adjusted his papers, readying to leave. "The crew will typically take Saturdays and Sundays off unless something requires the overtime, but Hale will make that call."

She liked the name Hale. It sounded sexy and dark, a good name for whispering late at night. As Cade continued to talk about the schedule, her attention slipped into a daydream of a sweaty, muscular man swinging a hammer with a tool belt low in his hips, his chest bare and sweating. Covered in dirt. Smiling at her as he unhooked the belt. Then his tattered jeans.

She jerked herself out of the daydream. Clearly, all those romance novels she read about alpha males were going to her head. And reading about sex was the closest she'd come to the act lately.

Cade stared at her, waiting for a response, but she didn't know what he'd said, so she changed the subject. She waved to the papers in his arms. "You've done amazing work with these plans. I don't know how you did it with just a few emails and phone calls between us, but it's like you took everything I wanted and made it so much more."

"Well, Hale draws up the plans," Cade explained, flushing slightly at her enthusiasm. "I just relay them to clients."

"I see," Kyra said cheerfully, "and you do a great job!" As she followed him out of the room and down the stairs, she cringed at her awkwardness, but she wondered what exactly Cade did if he didn't do construction or draw up the design plans. It sounded like he merely acted as a middleman between clients and his brother.

Like he heard her thoughts, Cade paused at the front door and said, "Hale is the best contractor on the island. He's going to turn this house into your home." His pride in his brother's work was obvious, but he paused and scuffed his leather boat shoes against a rough patch in the floor. "Just prepare yourself. He's a little different, and he likes to keep to himself. So if you have any questions, feel free to call my cell."

He handed her a business card, which Kyra slid in her back pocket. "I'll do that. Thanks for meeting me and showing me around."

She stood in the open door, watching as he navigated his way down the rickety porch steps. He stopped at the bottom. "No problem. Let me know if you need anything. Most of your neighbors are a little old, but Stevie Reynolds lives next door." He blushed, the redness making him incredibly adorable, and pointed in the general direction of the house next door. Kyra followed his gaze and saw a beautiful navy and white Victorian similar in style to hers. "She's your age and . . . fun." If it was possible, Cade flushed even more. "Anyway, if you want a tour of the island, I can show you around sometime when you're settled."

She beamed. "Sure! I'd love that."

Surprised by her enthusiasm, he took the tiniest bit longer to speak than normal. "Uh, great. I mean, that's great. Just give me a call whenever."

She watched him pull away from the curb with an easy smile— the kind she didn't have to contrive— and a peaceful heaviness in her limbs. If she met a couple more people as nice as Cade, she would be well on her way to making a life here on Canaan. And his brother sounded interesting.

Standing on porch, she took the opportunity to check out her neighbors' houses. The houses on Gardenia Street had all been restored to their former glory with fresh, bright paint and gardens teeming with bold blooms and tall trees that cast long shadows across the street. She sighed; her house was the eyesore of the community, which meant she really needed to start unpacking so she could get ready for the construction crew arriving Monday. Her eyes settled on her Jeep and trailer.

"You really need to learn how to park," she told herself. She'd been too excited to worry about pulling her Jeep off the curb, and a large construction dumpster blocked her narrow driveway between her house and her neighbor's.

Just then, her phone rang. Pulling it from her pocket, she recognized the name on the glowing screen. "Hey, Aunt Carol," she answered in a patient tone.

"Kyra! How are you? Did you make it down there okay? Your car didn't give you any trouble, did it?"

Her aunt spewed out the questions like any concerned parent, and technically, she was Kyra's mother, or, at least, the only mother Kyra had ever known. Her Aunt Carol and Uncle Tom had taken her in when she was a baby, just like she'd told Cade. But the rest of the truth was that her mom had been in prison when she had Kyra, and she'd never made it out to be a part of Kyra's life. On Kyra's first birthday, Lila Aberdeen had killed herself in her prison cell.

No one talked about her mother. She was the sore spot in the Aberdeen family, and Uncle Tom had hated his sister too much to ever show any kind of real love to Kyra.

"I made it fine," she said patiently. "The drive was easy. I just talked with the contractor about the house. It looks . . ." Squinting into the sun, she glanced up at her house and a protectiveness blossomed in her. "It's not that bad actually. The contractor had some really great plans."

"You watch those contractors, now. They'll take advantage of a young girl like you."

"He was actually really nice. I doubt he would do that," Kyra said, feeling the need to defend Cade just as much as her crumbling house.

"Just be careful down there by yourself." Aunt Carol's tone softened. "Are you sure you're okay? I can come down there and help you settle in."

Kyra nibbled on her fingernail. "I'm fine, I promise. I feel good about this."

"Have you talked to Dr. Standifer yet?"

"No," she sighed. She loved her Aunt Carol very much, but she tended to nag sometimes, and the long drive to the Georgia island had fried Kyra's nerves.

"You'll need to get in touch with a new therapist down there soon."

"I will."

"As soon as possible. You don't want to have to go on medication again."

Kyra cringed. She'd been on medication once before for her depression during her freshman year of college. Since then, she'd weaned off the daily meds under the supervision of her therapist, who believed she'd learned to cope with her issues in a healthy way. Unconsciously, she rubbed at the stack of bracelets on her left wrist. Technically, she was better, but her therapist didn't know about a few relapses that had happened since she'd been off the medication. "Yes, Aunt Carol."

Her aunt breathed out in relief, the sound rustling in the phone. "Okay. I won't take up any more of your time. Get settled in and rest."

"Thanks. Tell Uncle Tom I said, 'hello.'"

"I will. He misses you," Aunt Carol lied.

"I miss him too," she lied back. "I better go . . ."

"Right. Right. Call the therapist Dr. Standifer recommended tomorrow and lock your doors. I love you, Kyra."

"Love you too." She hung up and looked around at her new neighborhood. She wondered if her mother had played on the street as a little girl, riding her bike or chasing a young Uncle Tom around. She would've been happy when she lived here, before the darkness stole her away.

Kyra shivered and wrapped her arms around her middle to hold herself together. The familiar sadness, like a gaping dark chasm, tugged at her, but she steeled herself. She fought it off and forced a smile even though no one was around to convince she was a happy, carefree girl.

She told herself to walk down the porch stairs and start unloading boxes, but instead her feet carried her away, toward the back of the house and into the backyard. She picked her way through the overgrowth and out the back gate. Tugging off her flip-flops, she walked down the path to the beach.

Her toes hit the sand, and Kyra knew she was home.

2

Kyra couldn't resist the temptation.

She ran back to her Jeep and pulled off her assortment of surf boards. On her back porch, she stripped off her clothes, revealing the lavender bikini she wore underneath. Some days she wore underwear like a normal person, but they were few and far between.

She was a Californian at heart, after all.

She jogged to the water, toting her favorite board. Once she was hip-deep, she began to paddle, savoring the feeling of the water undulating beneath her. The waves were smaller than she was used to in California, but she loved every moment. Thirty minutes later, she forced herself to get out of the water.

After she'd put away her boards on her back porch and pulled her clothes back on, she regarded her Jeep and trailer. "It won't unload itself," she muttered. For the next couple hours, she hauled boxes up and down the stairs and into the back bedroom with the ocean view.

When she'd unloaded everything, she pulled out her cleaning supplies and started working her way around the musty bedroom. The bathroom had a beautiful old claw-foot bathtub and porcelain vanity sink with a medicine cabinet above it. She tested the water from the sink, relieved to see it had been turned on for her. As she worked, she kept a list of all the things she needed to pick up in town.

When the two rooms she'd be living in for the next two months were as clean as possible and she'd unpacked only what she needed day-to-day, she settled into the window seat with her sleek white Mac and turned on the wireless from her phone. She caught up on her social media sites, posting the pictures she'd taken throughout the day. She watched the latest video she'd finished editing one last time before she tried to upload it. After ten minutes of staring at her screen, the uploading status remained less than thirty-five percent. She blew a piece of hair out of her face. She was going to miss fiber-optic internet speeds, but she would make do. Leaving her computer plugged in and her phone beside it, Kyra stood and dusted off her hands. Her video could upload while she shopped.

Outside town, she dropped off the U-Haul and bought a mattress set at a large outlet mall, arranging to have it delivered on Monday. Back inside her Jeep and without the burden of the large trailer, Kyra took her time as she cruised into the town of Canaan with her windows rolled down and her Ray-Bans perched on the tip of her nose.

The actual town center consisted of one long stretch of brightly colored buildings advertising everything from art galleries to candle stores to bars. There weren't many cars on the road, but lots of people strolled down the sidewalks in their flip-flops and sunglasses. Live oaks laden with drooping Spanish moss lined the side of the road. To Kyra, the town seemed to fold into the island, like a tucked-away secret.

Aunt Carol had warned her that Canaan wasn't accepting of strangers, especially people with a past like hers. As in, no one would want the daughter of a broken woman wandering their neighborhoods. But Kyra couldn't imagine how she wouldn't fit in here; Canaan Island felt like it was made for her.

She parked her Jeep in front of the local grocery store. A large, opened garage door made up the front of the store and let in the fresh, ocean air. Bins of fruit and vegetables had been rolled out onto the sidewalk and emitted a sweet fragrance in the warm sun. Kyra grabbed a basket and started filling it up with food that wouldn't need to be prepared or refrigerated.

The sun had sunk lower in the sky when she checked out and put the groceries in her car. As she drove home, she admired the darkening sky, filling with reds and oranges. With her windows down, her hair twisted in the breeze and she hummed along to the radio. Already, the streets felt familiar, and she easily made her way back to her new house.

She dumped the groceries in the kitchen before she grabbed a plum and headed back outside. Standing on her front porch, she bit into the fruit, juice running down her chin, and regarded her disaster of a front garden. She finished her plum and tossed it into the overgrown weeds.

"I saw that."

Kyra jumped and pivoted. A woman walked through her front

gate carrying a bottle of wine and two glasses. Her pale legs stretched for miles beneath her linen shorts. Flaming-red hair hung in frizzled waves around her freckled face, and her green eyes glinted with mischief.

"Alert the litter police," Kyra said, laughing.

"I would, but I think it actually helped improve this dump. If a discarded plum can have such powers." The woman stopped at the base of Kyra's steps. "My name's Stevie Reynolds, and I hail from there." She pointed with a wine glass to the navy house next door.

"I'm Kyra Aberdeen. Nice to meet you."

"Yeah, yeah." Stevie waved off the chitchat. "I brought you wine. I figured I'd share a glass with my new neighbor, because I'm friendly and *not* crazy."

Kyra cocked her head. "I wouldn't think you're crazy."

"You might after all these old, stuffy women start telling lies about me." With a dramatic eye roll, she motioned to the other houses on the block. "When Cade told me a young woman was moving in next door, I knew I had to snatch you up before the neighborhood gossip tainted your opinion of me."

"Cade mentioned you too," Kyra said, remembering the obvious crush he had on Stevie, and she understood why now. Stevie was gorgeous and clearly quirky. "And, um, I don't drink."

Stevie threw up her hands in despair. "Great! The first young, pre-Medicare-aged person to move into the neighborhood doesn't drink."

Kyra couldn't resist laughing again. She liked Stevie already. "Are you drunk now?"

"I'm an artist. Being drunk inspires me."

Kyra looked around on her porch for a place to sit. "I would invite you inside, but I don't have any chairs yet."

Stevie grimaced in sympathy. "Follow me then." She looked down at her wine bottle and sighed. "I guess I can swap this out for some iced green tea."

Kyra followed her down the path out of her garden and onto the sidewalk. "On the bright side, you get to keep it for yourself," she said cheerily.

Stevie paused at her garden gate. "You're one of those 'on the bright side' kind of people, aren't you?"

"Is that bad?"

"I'm more doom-and-gloom myself. So if you catch me scowling at you a lot, you'll know why," she said as she pushed the gate open with her hip.

Grinning and shaking her head, Kyra followed Stevie onto her porch, waiting as she opened the door. Stevie opened the front door and motioned her through.

"Welcome to Château Stevie."

"Oh, wow," Kyra marveled. A modern chandelier hung from the vaulted ceilings and a bold coral paint coated the walls, which went perfectly with the soft gray color of the wooden floors. "Is this the original flooring?"

"Eh, who knows," Stevie said, dropping a quick glance at the floors. "Here's the kitchen. I'll grab some tea, and we can sit out back."

Kyra soaked in the modern kitchen with glass-faced cabinets and floating shelves. The back porch was just as charming as the rest of the house, because it had the best view. Stevie handed her a sweating glass of tea before they both sat down in the plush wicker seats. The ocean shimmered under the remnants of the sunset, and through a patch of tall seagrass, the waves crested against the beach. Kyra took a sip of her tea and sighed with contentment.

All her life, her Aunt Carol and Uncle Tom had acted like they hated Canaan Island. But how could they hate something so peaceful and beautiful? All along the beach, house lights turned on for the evening and illuminated the sand and ocean waves. It all felt so easy, so perfect, that Kyra didn't understand why anyone would want to leave this place.

"So what do you do?" Stevie asked, drawing Kyra's wandering attention.

"I upload health and beauty videos to YouTube and run a lifestyle blog." She shrugged. "It started as an assignment for college, but it kind of took off. A lot of people don't consider it a real job, but I make good money and I'm lucky to do what I enjoy for a living."

"Cheers to that," Stevie said, toasting Kyra. They clicked their tea glasses together.

"You mentioned you were an artist back at my house." Kyra settled back in her chair and enjoyed the breeze from the sea. "What kind of art do you make?"

"Photography. I do all that artsy-fartsy stuff for magazines and journals. Like you said, I'm lucky to do what I enjoy and not be stuck in some office all day." Stevie shivered like it was an awful thought. She propped her feet up on a clearly expensive wicker and glass-topped ottoman. "What brings you to Canaan Island?"

Turning her gaze toward the ocean, Kyra said as evenly as possibly, "My mom grew up in that house, and I have some family who lives on the island."

"Oh, really? Who?"

"The Aberdeens . . ." she ventured, already knowing Stevie's reaction.

Stevie spewed her tea. "Holy shit! Florence Aberdeen is such a bitch." She must have registered Kyra's shock, because she added, "Bless her heart."

Kyra may have been raised in California, but she knew from Aunt Carol, who was a Southern woman at heart, that everything became instantly nicer with that phrase added to the end of an insult. In this case, it wasn't needed. She knew firsthand how awful her grandmother was. It was a testament to her grandmother's reputation that the second person Kyra had met today wasn't a fan of the older woman. "Yeah, I know."

"I can sympathize with having bad relatives. My parents are Rory and Edith Reynolds."

Kyra couldn't help the little gasp of surprise that escaped her mouth. "The reality show stars?"

"More like the reality show train wrecks, but I appreciate your politeness," Stevie said with a long swallow from her drink.

Kyra didn't watch a lot of television, but she'd seen her share of the Reynolds across social media. They did anything for attention, and apparently had no dignity left to save. Without thinking about it, she instantly felt bad for Stevie. She couldn't imagine what it would be like to have parents like that. But then she didn't know what it felt like to have parents period.

Stevie didn't let the conversation dip into awkward silence. Instead, she changed the subject, which warmed Kyra to her even more. "Who's doing the construction work on your house? Please say Jesus cause that place needs a miracle."

"It really does," Kyra laughed. "I hired the Cooper brothers.

Have you heard of them?"

Luckily, Stevie didn't have tea in her mouth this time. She fanned her face with her hand. "Oh girl, you're in for a real treat."

"A treat?"

"The best kind of treat: *man candy*."

Kyra leaned forward in her seat. "Really?"

"Oh, yeah. Cade's brother is positively delicious."

Her earlier daydream threatened to make her blush again, so she said quickly, "I don't know, Cade is pretty cute." Remembering Cade's obvious crush on her neighbor, she shot a pointed stare at Stevie.

"For a total nerd. He's so not my type. Have you met Hale yet?"

"Not yet," Kyra started, feeling uncertain, "but Cade kind of warned me he was a little different. Do you know anything about that?"

"I'm not big for gossip. Shocking, I know, considering this street's favorite pastime is talking about me and my parents." Stevie casually waved her hand toward the other houses down the road, but Kyra didn't miss the flicker of true hurt in the young woman's eyes as she continued. "But Hale does good work. They're the best at what they do here on the island, but there's a reason Cade handles the people. Hale prefers to keep his distance. Before he moved back here to be with his brother and sick mother, I heard he got into some trouble back on the mainland. Now, he mostly stays to himself. He can be a bit of a bear, but he's not dangerous or anything."

"Sick mother?" Kyra asked, feeling sorry for Hale and Cade.

Stevie shrugged. "I don't know the details or anything, but I think she has cancer. Anyway, most of the people on the island keep their distance from him. Of course, I would be all over him if I could."

Kyra spent another half hour on Stevie's porch before they called it a night. Stevie would be out of town for a few days, but they made plans for supper at her house when she got back from her trip on Wednesday. She promised it would be take-out and not her own cooking.

Kyra walked back to her house with a smile on her face. She enjoyed the warm breeze off the ocean and the loose sand beneath her feet. Far out over the waves, the moon beamed down, casting its light alongside the glow from the nearby houses.

Back when she was younger, just the thought of Canaan Island used to terrify her. In her imagination, it became this dark place where her aunt and uncle had run from. The place where her evil grandmother reigned. Where her mother had lost herself.

But after meeting Stevie and Cade and seeing the beauty of this place, the island didn't seem so intimidating after all.

3

Blood rolled down Kyra's wrist, rising and dipping over the perfectly straight, raised scars like speed bumps, and trickled down her pinky. The flare of pain satiated her craving, awareness jolting through her blood from the sharp, ripping sting of the cool blade against her tanned skin. For that one moment, when the pain fully cleared her head of everything else, she felt at peace.

She woke with a start. Rubbing her pounding head, she blinked to clear her vision of the dream. Her eyes fell to the stack of bracelets on her wrist as the skin beneath her eye started twitching in time to the pulsing heartbeat in her head.

Only when the grogginess of a deep sleep had cleared from her mind did Kyra realize the pounding wasn't completely in her head. The smashing, wrecking sounds echoed throughout her house. Because of the dream and the phantom ache on the underside of her arm, it took her a long moment to remember today was Sunday, and the construction crew wasn't supposed to start until Monday.

Which meant someone had broken into her house.

She surged out of her folded-up position in the window seat, adrenaline jerking her away from the remnants of her dream, and grabbed her baseball bat before she started down the stairs at a breakneck run.

She skidded around the corner into the kitchen and came to a screeching stop. Hard rock blasted from a stereo on the counter. A man—a shirtless, very muscular, and tattooed man—wielded a large mallet to obliterate the cheap kitchen laminate floors with heavy, grunting swings that vibrated the floor beneath her feet. He reached down and ripped up a section nearly three feet wide, making the muscles in his inked shoulders stretch and strain.

Her mouth fell open at the sight of him. Her daydream yesterday had not done Hale Cooper justice. His tattoos and multiple piercings glinting in the morning sunlight surprisingly really did it for her. Like, really, really did it for her.

But sexy or not, he'd started work on her house this morning without bothering to knock and introduce himself. Or let her know he was simply going to let himself into her house. Just as he stopped swinging and looked up to see her standing in the doorway, Kyra realized she'd rushed downstairs wearing only panties and a baggy tank top with no bra. Before the wave of mortification hit, she reminded herself there were worse things she could be wearing. Like *nothing*.

Besides, he was the one who'd just let himself into her home with no warning.

Hale cocked a brow at her, and she noticed the dermal studs

above it. He had a looping scrawl of tattoos down his neck and across his chest. More ink lined both of his arms in an assorted mixture of words and images. He cleared his throat and turned down the radio.

"Morning," he said gruffly.

"You scared me," Kyra breathed out a shaky laugh. "I didn't expect anyone until Monday." She swung the bat up and over her shoulder without bothering to cover herself up. She was certain Hale had seen it all before, and maybe she was giving him a little show anyway.

Her overly cheerful laughter fell flat. He just stared at her a minute before he said, "I wanted to get a feel for things before the crew gets here tomorrow. Cade should have told you that."

She noticed he didn't bother to apologize. "Oh, okay." She smiled, sticking out her hand. "I'm Kyra. And you must be Hale."

He stared at her offered hand, but didn't bother to shake it. "Yeah." He raised his mallet and crashed it down into the floor again. The loud bang made Kyra jump and giggle nervously.

"Um," she fumbled, blushing with embarrassment as he ripped up another section of flooring. "It's really great to meet you. I look forward to your work on my house." She grimaced; she had no clue what she was saying. "Or whatever."

He sighed heavily as if she was annoying him. He raised his brows and made a point of looking her up and down. "Do you plan on just wearing your underwear to meet my crew tomorrow?"

"Oh, uh, you just surprised me is all. I normally wear clothes when I meet people for the first time."

"Sure."

He reached over and cranked the radio back up, effectively

dismissing her. Before he could raise his mallet for another swing, Kyra walked around him and gathered her groceries up in her arms.

"If your crew is anything like you, I guess I don't have much to worry about," she muttered under her breath.

She sensed Hale's narrowed eyes on her as she walked out of the kitchen, toting her bat and groceries. She probably looked like an idiot, but that bothered her even less than Hale Cooper seeing her in her underwear the first day she met him. She knew she shouldn't be too quick to judge since Cade had explained his brother was a little different, so she tried to keep her less-than-favorable first opinion of Hale from forming in her mind on her way back to her bedroom.

Not that she'd been around many guys in her underwear lately, but she would've expected Hale to be a little more *interested*.

She quickly changed upstairs. When she came back downstairs, she wore her favorite board shirt and bikini bottoms. Her long blonde hair hung loose and wavy around her shoulders. Without sparing a glance into the kitchen, she walked down the hall by the stairs and out the back door, letting it slam behind her.

She grabbed her board from the carefully organized rack and started for the water. The waves were stronger this morning, and she enjoyed herself. By the time she came in an hour later, her muscles wavered with just the right amount of exhaustion, and she was ready to face the day. She wrung out her hair and headed for her porch.

In her garden, she caught sight of a disheveled Stevie watching her from across the fence line. She clutched a large mug of coffee in her hands like it was a life preserver. Even from this distance, Kyra saw her roll her eyes.

"Overachiever!" she shouted and flipped Kyra off before she

went back inside.

Kyra waved, laughing. Feeling light as bird bones, she put her board up and headed inside. She was still chuckling when she saw Hale had stopped working to watch her, his eyes flicking between her and Stevie's house. Humming to herself, she smiled at him and headed upstairs for a bath since her little bathroom didn't have a real shower yet.

She spent her entire Sunday catching up on all the work she'd missed during her move. Sitting cross-legged in her window seat as the sun warmed her shoulders through the open window and the salty air from the ocean filled her nose, she edited footage for hours until her latest videos were perfect enough to upload the next week. She checked all her social media sites and posted some more pictures as she bobbed her head to the sounds of Twenty One Pilots playing through her headphones. Logging onto her blog, she responded to comments and scheduled a few posts for the week. The advertising on her website made up the main source of her income, along with brand-sponsored videos she uploaded to her YouTube channel.

By Monday morning, after another restless night sleeping in her window seat, the sounds of hammers and demolition had amplified tenfold, which meant Hale's crew had arrived and had wasted no time in tearing her house apart. Kyra sighed and dug back into her emails, which she could never keep up with.

Around lunchtime, her stomach began to gurgle with hunger pains. Sitting back and stretching, she thought about texting Cade. She hadn't had much time to explore the island yet, and it would be cool to have a native show her some of the non-touristy spots. Pulling out her phone and the business card he'd given her, she sent him a text.

Kyra: Hey Cade! It's Kyra Aberdeen. Would you have time to show me around the island some? Whenever you're free :)
Cade: Sure! Be there in 30.

Thirty minutes later, after dealing with her mattress being delivered and set up in her room, Kyra turned her computer off and headed downstairs in a pair of hot-pink shorts and a white baggy tank top she'd picked up at a surfing competition. She pulled her hair into a ponytail as she walked, tucking the loose strands of hair behind a stretchy teal headband.

Her house had become a warzone, with hazardous swinging hammers and shards of plaster flying through the air. Fifteen men stopped what they were doing, which mostly consisted of hardcore demolition, and looked up at her. "Hey!" She waved, smiling to ease the awkwardness. It didn't help. "I'm Kyra."

"Nice to meet you, Kyra," an older gentleman said. He came forward, setting aside his hammer, to shake her hand. "I'm Hale's foreman, Chevy."

She flicked her ponytail over her shoulder and pumped his hand. "Your name is Chevy?"

"It's a long story," he replied, looking sheepish.

Just then, Hale stalked in wearing a faded T-shirt and ripped jeans that hung low on his tapered hips from the weight of his tool belt. Saliva pooled in Kyra's mouth before she remembered to swallow.

He scowled. "What the hell is everyone doing? Get back to work!"

With that, the men jerked back into action and the cacophony started up again. Kyra cringed and hurried to the front door, sparing a quick glance over her shoulder. Hale had his back to her and was hammering a large hole in one of the walls.

Outside, a gusty sea breeze tugged at the hem of her shirt and cooled off her feverish face. She took a deep, cleansing breath and looked up just in time to see a herd of her neighbors all toting food containers make their way down her overgrown garden's path. Nerves fluttered in her stomach, just like they did whenever a large group of women surrounded her. The disgusted looks on the women's faces and their whispered tittering confirmed Kyra's fear that they were judging her.

"Morning!" Kyra said brightly—too brightly. Her voice cracked slightly. She pulled at the bottom of her shorts, realizing too late how short they were.

The women all looked up and plastered huge smiles on their faces. The leader, who wore a bright-yellow dress and orthopedic white shoes, spoke first. "You must be Kyra Aberdeen! My name is Betsy Harrison. I live just there." She pointed over her pudgy shoulder to a traditional Victorian across the street. She looked back at Kyra and smoothed her tightly curled hair down.

"It's nice to meet you, Mrs. Harrison! You have a beautiful house. I apologize for all the construction." Kyra giggled nervously. "Renovations and all that, you know."

"We understand, dear." Another woman stepped forward wearing a billowing sundress that made her hips look ten times larger than they actually were. "I'm Marla Walker. My house is on the other side of Stevie Reynolds."

Mrs. Harrison wrinkled her nose. "That girl is trouble. You

would do good to steer clear of her. We have to complain to the police at least once a week about her loud, devil-worshipping music. Of course, with parents like hers, it's no wonder the girl never learned any proper manners."

Kyra nodded, feeling like an ass for not defending Stevie. She didn't know what else to say, so she asked the most obvious question, even though she already knew the answer. "Who are her parents?"

"Some reality show stars out in California," Mrs. Walker said, waving her hand in front of her nose as if she'd smelled something foul. "And you know how those Californians are."

"That's unfortunate," Kyra murmured, not revealing she'd lived in California all her life. She felt about a foot tall in front of these women, and shrinking by the second. Inwardly, she cringed at being such a pushover.

"Very much so, the poor thing." Mrs. Harrison's kind words did nothing for the mean tone she spoke them in. "Anyway! We wanted to come by and welcome you to the neighborhood. I made you my special chicken casserole. Marla here made you some of her orange-filled éclairs."

Mrs. Walker and Mrs. Harrison stepped forward and deposited their respective Tupperware containers into Kyra's outstretched arms. "Oh, thanks!" Kyra exclaimed, shifting under the hot weight of the food.

"Now, Kyra," Mrs. Harrison said. She stepped forward and put her arm around Kyra's shoulders. Together, they and the other women of the neighborhood surveyed her prickly, thorny garden. "Our local garden club chapter will be by next week to take pictures of our gardens. For years now, we've had to crop out this particular," she paused and sniffed, "*area*. Mrs. Walker and I believe this eyesore is the very reason we haven't won the state's first place prize in all these years."

Mrs. Walker added in her honey-dipped voice, "Sweetie, it would just mean the world to us if you could get this mess cleaned up soon."

"Oh, sure." Kyra blushed. The heat from the containers scalded her arms, but she gritted her teeth and tried to move them to lesser fried flesh spots. "I'll do that as soon as possible."

"Perhaps today, dear?" Mrs. Harrison suggested.

"Today?" She caught the looks of the women, and quickly changed her answer. "I mean, sure! I can do that today."

"Wonderful! Now about the outside of the house. We wanted to run a few neutral colors by you. See, we don't want your house to clash with ours."

"Oh, um, well." She looked down the road, desperately hoping Cade would pull up.

"Morning, ladies!"

Kyra jumped, rattling the food in the containers. Hale swooped down the steps and barged into the middle of the group. Mrs. Harrison released her viselike grip on Kyra's shoulder and quickly stepped away from him, like he was the devil himself. As if he knew her discomfort, he took the containers from Kyra, who quickly hid the red burns behind her back.

"Hello, Mr. Cooper. We were just welcoming Kyra to the neighborhood," Mrs. Harrison said primly. She sniffed and smoothed her hair again. Even from her distance, Kyra smelled the load of hairspray the woman had coated her brittle hair with.

"Is that what you were doing? Cause it kinda looked like a

railroadin' to me."

"Excuse us?" Mrs. Walker's mouth gaped open. He went on as if he hadn't heard her. "Kyra can't do much in her garden until we get the foundation fixed. Guess your first prize in the Petunia Patrol will have to wait another year."

Mrs. Harrison sniffed. "Mr. Cooper, I've never in all my life—"

Just then, Cade pulled into the drive, and from the worried look on his face as he jumped out, he already knew what was going on.

"Morning, Mrs. Harrison! Looking good, Mrs. Walker!" he called as he rushed through the garden's open gate. "Hale," he said, nodding to his brother as he came up to the group. "Hey, Kyra. About ready?"

"Uh," Kyra started, wavering, her eyes bouncing between the growing crowd in her yard.

"Funny seeing you here." Hale's words weren't harsh, just a familiar dryness between brothers.

"Not all that funny," Cade said patiently. "Just taking Kyra for a tour of the island. Oh, Mrs. Harrison! Did you make some of that delicious chicken casserole?"

Cade redirected the ladies' attention to him as he fawned over their cooking abilities. They'd completely forgotten about Hale after a moment. Kyra turned to him and whispered, "Can you let your crew know they can eat that for lunch? It'll go bad without a refrigerator."

He shrugged. "Whatever you say."

She watched him walk back into the house. She couldn't decide if he'd rescued her or ruined her reputation with her neighbors. When she looked back at Cade, the ladies were all leaving and his shoulders were slumped with relief.

"Mrs. Harrison has terrified me since I was a child," he said once they were out of earshot. "And I'm pretty sure Mrs. Walker used to be a man. Anyway, are you ready for your tour?"

Kyra cringed, her eyes snagging on her unruly garden's weeds and overgrown vines. It really did look bad. "Maybe I should stay and work out here . . ."

"Don't let them bother you." He bumped her shoulder with his. "All they care about is their stupid garden club. Besides, Hale's crew will just tear it all up anyway when they start out here."

"Yeah," she said, biting her lip. "I just don't want them to hate me, you know?"

"They won't hate you. They just might act like it if your house doesn't match theirs perfectly, but who cares?"

Kyra shot him a smile that she hoped wasn't as shaky as it felt. *She* cared. She cared a lot. But she took a deep breath and shook her anxiety off. Surely, her neighbors would understand. "You're right. Let's go."

They started toward his white work truck with a Cooper Bros. Construction logo on the side. Inside, the leather seats were clean and the air smelled like the Mango Tango air freshener dangling from the rear-view mirror. "I have to say, Cade Cooper," Kyra said as she pulled herself into the tall truck, "this is the cleanest construction truck I've ever seen."

He grinned as he slammed his door shut. The truck's engine cranked over with a vibrating rumble. "I hate messes. You should see Hale's." He shuddered. "It smells like molded socks and month-old coffee."

"Speaking of your brother," Kyra ventured, thankful he'd been the one to bring up Hale, "I don't think I've made a good impression on him."

He shot her a worried glance. "He hasn't yelled at you or anything?"

"Uh, no. Does he yell a lot?"

He grimaced, like maybe he was recalling a few instances. "He's not much of a people person."

"I can tell," she said.

Kyra looked at the other houses with perfect gardens as they drove down the street. Weeping willows and blooming magnolia trees were dotted along the freshly paved road. Mrs. Walker was just entering her house, and Kyra didn't miss the nasty look Mrs. Harrison gave the car as they went by. Clearly, Kyra's new house had been the bane of Gardenia Street's perfect existence.

"Don't let the stuff with the neighbors bother you," Cade said quickly. He turned off Kyra's street and made his way toward town. The stretch of road was mostly empty, aside from clusters of trees and the occasional glance of the ocean. "I know it looked like Hale was being an ass, pardon my language, but he was sticking up for you. He *hates* bullies."

She noticed the uneasy way he chewed on his lip. "Was he bullied when he was younger?" she asked, instantly feeling sorry for Hale.

"Something like that . . ." Cade didn't seem to want to talk about it, so she didn't press the point. "People around here judge him really harshly. They see the piercings and the tattoos and they just assume he's a bad person, but that's really not the case at all." Cade glanced over at her nervously, as if he wanted to convince her about his brother's character. "He's a good guy, and he hates seeing anyone get picked on."

"Then why doesn't he stand up for himself if everyone thinks so poorly of him?"

He shrugged. "I've asked him the same thing. But he doesn't care. He's going to be who he is without any apologies. People don't like that. They want an apology for everything you say and do in this town."

"I think it's brave," Kyra said. "That he would just be himself and not worry what other people think."

"Hale is the bravest man you will ever meet then," Cade said with a snort. "Sometimes I wish he would care a little more. It would help me out a lot."

She smiled. "Maybe some of that will rub off on me. I care too much about what other people think. Those women would've had me weeding in a few minutes if Hale hadn't come out."

"You and me both," Cade chuckled. "But just give him a chance. He doesn't have many friends, and I can tell you're an understanding person. He needs more people like you in his life."

"Of course." Feeling guilty for her earlier mean thoughts about Hale, Kyra vowed to do better next time. "Thanks for showing me around today. I'm excited to see more of the town."

"No problem!" Cade rolled down the windows and turned the radio to an oldies station. She relaxed into the smooth leather and enjoyed the ride as Cade put on his blinker and turned onto the main street in Canaan. "Don't let those ladies fool you, Canaan is actually a great place to live. The tourists keep it young and fresh, and you can't beat living on an island."

They drove around, and by lunch, Cade had made her completely forget about the neighborhood ladies and her disastrous garden. He told her story after story of him and Hale growing up on the island and all the trouble they got into, like when Hale had convinced him to sneak and eat all the cookies their mom had baked for church one morning and Cade got sick and puked during the service like the girl from *The Exorcist*. As they talked and laughed, Kyra started to feel like she not only knew the Cooper brothers better, but that she knew the island better too. The cheery town with its downtown square and church bells ringing on the hour started to feel like home, and not once did she feel the slinking pull of sadness.

All her smiles were real and genuine, and that was the best feeling of all.

4

Kyra woke Tuesday morning feeling pretty good. She called her Aunt Carol first thing to assure her everything was fine, and her aunt took the opportunity to hassle her more about calling a therapist. Logically, she knew she should, because any little thing could trigger her and send her recovery into regression, but the thought of sitting and discussing her feelings made her fidget with her bracelets again.

She imagined happy people didn't have to deal with things like therapists and coping mechanisms. So she pretended to be happy, and some days, like today, she actually felt it.

And Canaan Island was already working some magic on her.

She walked out of the bathroom, and her eyes instantly settled on the surf through her bedroom window. It looked spectacular and inviting as it broke against the sand. Too inviting.

"You should be working, Kyra," she murmured to herself, but it was no good. She quickly changed into her bikini and jogged down the stairs. Already hard at work, the crew's hammering filled the house and the basement, where they worked to fix the rotted beams.

"Hey, Chevy!" she called as she stepped into the construction zone.

"Morning, Miss Kyra." Hale's foreman scratched the top of his head when she breezed by, his eyes noticeably averted, which made her grin.

All around her, the sound of hammers stopped, which made her heart thrum with satisfaction. She knew how she looked because men and women had stared at her all her life. It used to bother her, but she'd stopped letting herself feel self-conscious about it years ago and started using it to her advantage. All the stares and friendliness made her feel like people liked her, like she belonged. Feeling the warmth of their eyes on her skin became a source of happiness for Kyra, even if it was the fleeting, effervescent kind that sometimes left her a little hollow if she thought too long about how they didn't see her with sweaty hair or when she'd just woken up in the morning. They didn't see all the active hours she spent during her day to keep her body in shape. They thought she was beautiful when she looked her best, and she found that the men who smiled at her in her shortest shorts didn't cast a stare her way without her hair fixed up and makeup applied.

Maybe if they'd still stared when she was just her natural self, she might have looked back more often.

Until then she'd found it easier and safer to focus on other things. She busied herself with ensuring she'd be able to make a life for herself without depending on anyone else, especially anyone from her family. She'd paid her way through college with no debt, she had an amazing job, and she'd bought her first house. She found happiness was so much easier to maintain when she kept a distance from others, because others had such a power to destroy.

If she was a twenty-four-year-old virgin because she couldn't trust anyone else with her tenuous happiness, so be it.

"Hey!"

Kyra jumped, her hand fumbling the surfboard she'd pulled from the rack. She glanced over her shoulder right as Hale stormed out of the back door, rusty springs squealing in complaint.

"Hey?" she said, but she had a slight inkling he wasn't being friendly and saying good morning. Over her shoulder, a seagull squawked.

"You can't just parade around in front of my men wearing those skanky scraps of material," he said, his green eyes snapping with anger. She hadn't remembered his eyes being so green before. Actually, she realized, this was the first time she noticed his eye color.

Kyra forced herself to keep calm because she didn't want to snap at Hale. After her conversation with Cade yesterday, she wanted to be more understanding of him and cut him some slack.

"I'm sorry," she said, but she had to force the apology just like she had to force herself to smile, "but I doubt they minded much."

He clenched his jaw. "I don't give a damn how much they minded. It's a distraction."

"For you or them?" She couldn't help her small snort of laughter, but his anger popped like a lash in the air, and she stepped back without meaning to. "Look, I'll wear a cover-up next time. Will that work?"

"Wear *something* is all I'm asking."

Kyra's patience wore thin. She wanted nothing more than to give Hale a piece of her mind, but she forced herself to think of Cade and what he'd asked of her. Keeping her smile plastered in place, she laughed like Hale had been joking. His scowl deepened, like everything she did only pissed him off further.

"Sure thing!" she said brightly, picking her board back up. As she turned to walk away, she saw him roll his eyes at her before he went back inside the house. Even all the way down at the beach where the lapping waves tickled at the tips of her toes, she heard him yelling at his guys.

She hated it when people didn't like her. It felt like a failure, like she wasn't good enough to meet their standards. The tears pricked against the back of her eyes, but she refused. It took all she had, but she pried her lips into a big smile and told herself the sand under her feet and the ocean in front of her made her happy, and that was all she needed right now.

Certainly not Hale Cooper's appreciation of her body.

With a sigh, she forced herself to forget him and focused only on the soothing water and paddling out past the shore break, but the short hour in the water didn't do much good. As soon as she walked into her kitchen after waxing and putting her board away, the tension returned, her thoughts on Hale's pissy attitude.

Apparently everyone had gone to lunch, so she took the opportunity to sneak back to her bedroom and close the door. She hid in there for the rest of the day, only emerging after Hale and his crew were gone.

Kyra hid in her room most of Wednesday too. She'd caught up on all her work and had started getting ahead on the next week's when she grew angry. She admitted to herself that Hale intimidated her, but that didn't mean she had to hide out in her bedroom for the next couple months until the renovations were over. This was her house.

She was strong enough to face him.

When her stomach rumbled with hunger, she'd worked up the courage to leave her bedroom. When she went downstairs, she didn't bother to look around for Hale. In three days, the crew had replaced most of the faulty, rotted beams and started to get things ready for the plumber and electrician.

A door slammed somewhere on the first level, causing Kyra to jump. Forgetting her previous anger, she decided she would find some lunch in town.

After unloading her bike from the back of the Jeep, she took off down the street. She passed a lot of kids playing street hockey or zipping around on rollerblades, all enjoying their summer break. The mile or so before she reached town went by quickly, and she wheeled onto Main Street faster than she'd thought. She stopped at an organic deli and ordered a veggie sandwich, which she ate outside at a small table. Propping her feet up on the chair beside her, she enjoyed the laid-back hustle and bustle of the small island's town life with people on bikes whizzing by and music from nearby stores spilling out onto the street. She took a big bite of her lunch and munched as she thought. Her eyes landed on a bakery called Maggie's Sweets and inspiration struck.

She hadn't got off on the right foot with Hale, but his crew was another story. They would be in her house for two months, so she might as well be friendly. She could take them some cookies and lemonade to win them over to her side, convince them to like her.

She pictured Hale's scowl, and she liked her idea even better.

She finished her sandwich and crossed the street's sun-warmed pavement, aiming for the bakery. The door let out a sweet chiming noise when she opened it, and the scent of lemon and what could only be the smell of honey buns blasted her in the face as she stepped inside. A younger, curvier lady, presumably the Maggie in Maggie's Sweets, looked up from the back of the shop. She smiled at Kyra and swiped a hand over her brow, spreading flour above her eye.

"Hey there!" she called from the back. "I'm Maggie. Let me know if I can help you with anything."

"Nice to meet you, Maggie." Kyra waved. "Your shop smells amazing!"

Maggie laughed, the sound as bright and cheery as the bells above her shop's door. "It's those new lemon cookies I put out. They're divine."

Kyra spotted the cookies in question. A dollop of lemon icing pressed in the middle of the round, plump cookie, and her mouth watered just looking at them. She picked up a couple boxes and grabbed two jugs of fresh-squeezed lemonade from the cooler section. Tossing a package of plastic cups onto the pile, she smiled with satisfaction.

"That was fast!" Maggie called as she bounced up to the cash register.

"I wanted some treats for the crew at my house." Kyra pushed the pile toward the old-fashioned register so Maggie could start ringing them up.

"You just moved here?"

Kyra leaned against the counter display, her gaze dancing along the homemade donuts and brightly colored macaroons. "I bought the vacant house out on Gardenia Street."

"I've always said that house would be beautiful once it was renovated. Good bones and all that."

"I think so too." She pulled her wallet out of her shorts' back pocket and paid for her purchases.

"You're awfully young to be buying a house," Maggie said, her wide mouth hooking up into a dimple. She couldn't be much older than twenty-seven herself. "You must be a smart girl."

Her words made Kyra beam. "Thank you. I hope it's going to be a good investment and not just a money pit."

"All old houses are money pits, but they're worth it," she said with a wink, her dimples flashing on her heart-shaped face. She was stunning, Kyra realized.

"I hope so. I better get these cookies to the guys. I'll be back soon, I'm sure."

"Thanks for stopping by! Enjoy this beautiful day."

Kyra waved and turned to leave as the door chimed again to announce a new customer. She adjusted her grip on the brown bag and looked up, already smiling. But her smile faltered.

The older lady with a tight gray bun and pursed lips didn't even look her way as she entered the store in a flurry of cracking perfume and tailored slacks. But Kyra didn't need to see the woman's face to know. She would recognize that haughty look and disdainful chin lift from anywhere. As the woman drilled off a catering order, Maggie rushed around to get a pen and notebook.

Kyra stood stunned for a moment, her mouth gaping open at the sheer rudeness. As if she could feel her staring, the lady turned and glowered at her until recognition registered.

"Kyra?" the woman asked, shocked. She was a beautiful lady, and when her face wasn't twisted into an expression of scorn, her wrinkles smoothed out and revealed regal features that could've been associated with a classic Hollywood actress.

"Grandmother," Kyra said.

Florence Aberdeen's brilliant blue eyes snapped at the endearment she'd never appreciated, even though she hadn't been around much for Kyra to use it. Twenty-four years to be exact, aside from the occasional holiday gathering to keep up appearances, but even then, Florence had hardly glanced at her granddaughter.

"How . . ." She couldn't seem to find the words that should come so natural to a grandmother and granddaughter. The bond binding familiar was just a gossamer strand floating in the air between them, loose and fragile in its brokenness.

Kyra swallowed back the swell of pain rising up her throat; Aunt Carol had tried to warn her about how her grandmother would react to the news of Kyra on the island. So maybe it was naïve of her to hope for anything different. But her heart broke nonetheless.

Kyra squared her shoulders and smiled widely at Florence. "I'm great! Thanks for asking. I hope you're well, *Grandmother*."

The soft skin above her grandmother's lip lifted slightly and her nose twitched with disgust, like she'd stepped in dog poo or something equally gross. "But what are you doing here?"

Straight to the point, Kyra thought. No niceties for the granddaughter Florence had never wanted. "Haven't you heard? I bought the white Victorian on Gardenia. I believe it was once your house, right?"

Florence's face paled, and Kyra almost felt guilty, because the old woman appeared a breath away from a heart attack. But her guilt was short-lived when she reminded herself that after she was born in prison, Florence and her husband, Garlan, had refused to take her in, leaving only her aunt and uncle to raise her. She'd been lucky, though. Her life with Aunt Carol and Uncle Tom had been as good a childhood as any, but she would never forgive Florence for disowning her mother and doing the same to her.

How could family turn their backs on each other? On a baby?

"Why?" Florence asked, her voice stifled with shock. "Why would you buy that house?"

Her grandmother's shock was so absolute, so wrecking, that Kyra felt like she might be sick at any moment. She turned to go and shoved the door open, sending the chimes squealing, and headed out into the fresh air. She jogged to her bike and plopped her purchases into the basket. She pedaled faster than necessary, but feeling the exertion in her muscles and the breeze in her hair helped calm her. Once she was out of town, she slowed and let herself take a deep breath.

She knew Florence hated her daughter, but Kyra couldn't understand how her grandmother could blame Kyra for something she had no control over. Lila Aberdeen had been busted for felony possession of drugs with the intent to sell twenty-five years ago. She'd been pregnant at the time, which no one knew. Nine months later, Kyra was born in prison.

"Come on, Kyra," she muttered to herself.

But she couldn't shake the bad thoughts. The tell-tale signs of anxiety crept up through her chest and clutched at her throat, making it nearly impossible to breathe. The skin beneath her bracelets started to itch, and she had to force herself not to fidget with them.

To escape the feelings, as if they were a dog chasing her, she stood up on her pedals and pushed the bike even faster. The street was empty, so she closed her eyes and let her head fall back, the breeze playing through her hair. This place was her home now, and she would belong here.

She *had* to belong here because she belonged nowhere else.

She opened her eyes just in time to see a large black truck backing out of the alley next to her house. For a split second, she registered the driver through his tinted passenger window.

She slammed down on her bike's brakes, making the mechanism squeal like a baby pig, but it was too late.

She catapulted over the handlebars and hit the asphalt.

5

Kyra vaguely heard a car door open and then hurried, heavy steps. A shadow stretched over her, blocking the sun. "Are you fucking crazy?"

She groaned; the impact from colliding with the pavement knocked the breath from her lungs. Everything hurt: her knees, her palms, her bucking, panicked lungs. But she knew that voice. It took a special hatefulness to be mean to the person you almost turned into a greasy spot on the road.

Cracking an eye at Hale, she confirmed his grumpy expression and moaned some more, mostly because she felt sorry for herself. "What the hell are you thinking, riding that fast down this street? Were you even watching where you were going?"

"My eyes," Kyra sucked in a breath, "were closed."

"Oh, that's even better!"

Her breath slowly returned, and she opened her eyes, blinking into the sun beaming around Hale's tall silhouette. After struggling to sit up without his help, she examined her legs. Both knees were torn to bloody shreds, as were her elbows and palms. She fingered her chin, which was unscathed. Once she confirmed she hadn't broken anything and that she actually wasn't floating toward a bright white light, she discovered she was angry.

Very, very angry.

She was *done* being nice to Hale Cooper. He didn't deserve it if he couldn't even be nice to the person he almost killed. Thoughts of making Cade happy slipped to the far reaches of her mind, and she channeled all her inner hatefulness and glared at Hale.

"I'm fine," she said, pleased when she sounded just as nasty as he did. "So thanks for asking, asshole."

His eyes flashed with the most meager sign of sympathy Kyra had ever seen, and, as if it burned his soul to do so, he stuck out his hand, offering to help her up. She smacked it away before she stood up on her own, grimacing as the scraped skin stretched across her battered knee.

"I'm *fucking* fine." Her voice rose; she never cursed. Furious tears from out of nowhere threatened to spill. She hated the fact that she rarely cried when she felt sad, only when she was fuming, raging mad. "I don't need your *fucking* help. And the next time you *fucking* swear at me and call me crazy, I'll punch your *fucking* nose."

Just then she caught sight of the crumpled boxes of cookies. The lemonade had busted and spilled across the road. So much for making Hale's crew like her. She groaned and picked up one of the boxes that had fallen from her bike's basket.

"Hey, look, I'm sorry. You just scared me is all," Hale said to her back.

Kyra looked up and turned around slowly, her eyes turning to slits. "You were scared?" she asked, leveling her gaze on him. "You were scared?" She started yelling. "*You were scared?*" As she shouted the words, she practically itched with the neighbors' eyes on her skin. She flung the crushed box of ruined cookies at him.

Satisfyingly enough, he was so surprised that he didn't even deflect the box. It hit him square in the chest, spilling cookie crumbles all down his shirt. Sputtering, he looked at her, anger resuming its normal place on his face.

"Oh, sorry," Kyra snipped. "You surprised me."

She picked up her bike and tried shouldering past him, but he caught her arm and held her in place beside him. Her eyes raked up to his, ready to yell some more, until she saw the intensity in his stare, the way his gaze roamed over her panting lips.

"Are you really okay?"

Her spine tingled from his proximity, which she told herself was crazy. He'd almost run her over. Now was not the time to get all lusty. "I'm fine."

She jerked her arm away and set off, her eyes catching movement on Stevie's porch. The redhead leaned against the railing while she sipped a tumbler of suspiciously dark liquid. Kyra suddenly remembered today was Wednesday, which meant dinner tonight with Stevie. The thought brightened her mood considerably.

"You go, girl!" Stevie called, raising her glass to Kyra.

Hale got back in his truck, squealing the tires on the road before he zoomed away. Kyra waved to her neighbor. "Thanks for the support, Stevie."

"That was awesome. Best thing that's happened all month." She thought for a moment. "I take that back. It's the best thing since old Mr. Henderson mowed his yard naked after he took a Valium instead of his arthritis medicine."

Kyra groaned. "Do you think everyone saw?"

"Oh, hell yeah. Expect a notice of improper cookie tossing to be posted on your door in the morning." She waved her arm at the houses across the street, sloshing the liquid over the rim. "Nothing gets past these bitches!"

Kyra laughed. "Are we still on for tonight?"

"Definitely. I want to hear all about Hale Cooper's hospitality." Hobbling from her injuries, Kyra pushed her bike toward the front porch, flipping Stevie off as she went. "I saw that!" Stevie called.

Kyra spent the rest of the afternoon editing videos. She took pride in her work, and she wanted everything she posted to be perfect, but her banged-up knees and elbows made sitting in her window seat extremely painful. Even typing hurt her torn palms. After catching up on her emails, she stood up and stretched, feeling her previous anger plummeting into a sensation of despair. The sounds of the crew filled the house since everyone had returned from lunch, and the bashing and banging was all too much.

She couldn't think. She couldn't handle one more minute of noise. Tears sprung into her eyes and suddenly she just wanted to lock herself in her bathroom and open her medicine cabinet, where she kept the shiny, cool blade secreted away in the back. She scratched the skin beneath her bracelets and whimpered.

The anxiety built up in her chest and closed off her throat, but before she descended into a full-on meltdown, she took a deep breath. Then another. And another. She couldn't force herself to work like this, but she could just put on some headphones, listen to some good music, and lay down for a while.

Even after she'd put some ointment on her knees and elbows, they still complained as she climbed under her duvet. She sighed heavily. Hale Cooper wasn't just different; he was a douchebag. As much as she liked Cade, she refused to waste any more time being nice to his brother.

She put on her headphones and cranked up her music.

A while later, a knock sounded on her bedroom door, surprising her. Not knowing who to expect, she opened it and found Hale slouching on the other side. She let out a disappointed breath as she tugged out her ear buds.

"What do you want?" she asked.

He sighed, raking his hand over his closely cropped brown hair. The motion made the muscles in his arms bulge. His shirt lifted, exposing a stretch of skin above his jeans and treating her to a full view of his delicious tapered, chiseled stomach. She hadn't noticed until now how perfect his body was. He lowered his arm and coughed. She looked up, her cheeks flushing.

"I'm sorry for earlier today."

His apology came out so forced and reluctant Kyra had to laugh, which only made his jaw clench. "You mean when you almost killed me?"

He crossed his arms over his chest. "Yeah."

Hale might have been bullied when he was younger, but Kyra didn't know how much more understanding she could be. "I accept your terrible apology, but watch where you're going next time."

"Next time keep your eyes open," Hale snapped back. "Who the hell rides a bike with their eyes closed?"

She saw red. "Who the hell cusses out the person they almost ran over? Did you ever think an 'are you okay' or maybe 'can I help you' would've been a lot nicer than calling me freaking crazy?"

"I didn't mean you were crazy. What you did was crazy," he said, glowering.

"You're right. I shouldn't have had my eyes closed, but that's no excuse to act the way you did." Her grip tightened on the doorknob. "You know, you're proving all these people right."

She tried to slam the door closed, but he stuck his boot out. "What does that mean?" he growled.

"All these people who think you're an asshole." She made a face. "You give them good reason to."

His nostrils flared in quiet rage. Before he responded, she tried to close the door, but he stopped her once more. "Oh, really? And what about you? Parading around with that cheesy-ass smile plastered to your face? You're so fake I'm embarrassed for you."

She recoiled like he'd slapped her. "I'm fake?" She barely managed to get the words out. A cheesy-ass smile? Fake? Of all the things she was, she'd never considered fake. Her anger shriveled up in her chest to protect what little warmth she still felt in her heart.

She was fake?

Hale must have registered her devastation a moment before he comprehended how shattering his words had been. "Hey. Wait a second. I just mean—"

"Get out," she whispered. Her hand tightened around the doorknob, ready to slam it in his face.

"Kyra, hang on a damn minute. I—"

Her voice lowered to a shaking, trembling whisper as she asked, "Have you ever thought maybe it's better to pretend to be happy and maybe believe it sometimes than act like the biggest dick in the world and make people uncomfortable in their own homes?"

It was his turn to cringe at her words. "I—"

"Get. Out." Like she could channel all her heartbreak into one moment, Kyra slammed her door so hard he stumbled backward to keep it from hitting his face.

She twisted the lock and leaned her forehead against the wood.

She hated confrontations; she'd rather just try and get along with people. Sure, that meant she pretended to like some people more than she did, but didn't everybody? And maybe her smile was a little disingenuous sometimes, but that was for her, so *she* would feel like a happy, normal person everyone if she wasn't. It didn't make her fake. It made her human, but his comment still cut her at the knees.

Her battered knees and elbows made the pain in her heart real and unavoidable. Leaning against the door, she sensed a breakdown barreling toward her. Her chest tightened, her throat contracted. If she thought about the painful heat in her palms for a second longer, she would lose it.

And if she really, really let herself think about it, she knew what she wanted. The skin hidden beneath her bracelets sang for it. Only a few steps separated her from the blade.

But she would've done that a few years ago, when she was weaker. She was stronger now, and people like Hale or her grandmother didn't have a power over her. She could choose to overcome it as easily as she could choose to fall apart. At least, that's what her therapist in California had said, and for the first time, Kyra understood what she'd meant. She felt just enough anger from her argument with Hale to decide to not give him that power over her.

Turning away from the door, away from her breakdown, she went back to her laptop and started working. She fired off emails and responded to comments and edited until her mind turned numb. She forced herself to work without a break until Hale and his crew had left for the day. Only then did she open her bedroom door and go downstairs.

She found a note taped to the bottom banister.

Kyra,

I'm sorry for being such a dick. I didn't mean to call you fake. I really am sorry for almost killing you today. I'll do better tomorrow.

- Hale

P.S. We cut the water off before we left. Plumbing check tomorrow.

Kyra stared at the note for a moment, unblinking, because her eyes watered furiously. She hated herself for wanting to cry, for feeling thankful he'd apologized. She should've crumpled up the pathetic little note and tossed it away, but she clutched it in her hand like it was a baby bird.

She walked aimlessly through her house for a while, feeling like she was stuck in a warzone. The plumbing and electrical wires were all exposed for inspections. Huge drop cloths covered the floors. Ripped-apart walls and extra lumber stacked in the kitchen made the room feel like a bare scab.

Kyra took the note with her as she went back upstairs. She carefully weighed it down with a pretty starfish beside her laptop.

Since she couldn't shower, she squirted herself with body spray. She tried to fix her hair before she dressed for dinner, but it was a hopeless mess. Giving up, she wrapped it up in a messy topknot, and she didn't even bother with makeup before she made her way over to Stevie's.

Kyra knocked on the front door. After a short moment, Stevie answered, already holding a glass of wine. "You look like I feel."

Kyra couldn't talk about it yet; the tears still itched at the back of her throat, even though she had no clue what she felt like crying over. Instead, she asked, "How was your trip?"

Stevie wrinkled her nose. "People annoy me, and I was surrounded by them."

Unable to resist, Kyra laughed, loosening the tearful itch at the back of her throat, and followed Stevie inside. She led them to the back porch again, where a chilled pitcher of green tea and a fresh glass awaited Kyra. An assortment of takeout menus laid across the table.

"The old birds across the street have already called about your fit out in the road today." Stevie took a sip of her wine, staring at Kyra with raised brows over the rim of her glass.

"My fit?"

"You did throw cookies at the man."

"Ugh." She rubbed her temples. She'd almost forgotten about throwing cookies. "This has been an awful day."

"Almost getting creamed by a truck will do that." When she didn't respond, Stevie said, "Uh-oh. What else?"

"I ran into my grandmother today at Maggie's Sweets. That didn't go too well. And then I had another fight with Hale when he tried to apologize."

"Oh!" Stevie leaned forward in her seat. "Did he throw you down on the bed and kiss you until you apologized for almost making him kill you?"

"Not even close. He called me fake."

Stevie pursed her lips, the amusement fading from her eyes. "Now that pisses me off."

"I guess he's kind of right," Kyra said, frowning. His words had crushed her for a reason. "But he apologized. He left me this note." She pulled the note from her pocket and handed it to Stevie, who quickly read it.

"Hmm . . ."

"What does that mean?" she asked, frowning.

"It means I don't remember him leaving a note for poor Mrs. Campbell when he told her he didn't have a magic trick for ridding her carpets of cat piss, but that she could try a litter box."

Kyra's mouth dropped open. "He said that?"

"Oh, yeah. She was red in the face for months afterwards."

"Are you trying to tell me he likes me? Because I have quite a bit of evidence to the contrary."

"Maybe. Maybe not." Stevie shrugged. "Nearly committing vehicular homicide might've rattled some good manners into him."

"It didn't rattle hard enough," Kyra said under her breath.

"Enough about Hale Cooper. Men are stupid. Let's order burgers."

"Well," she said, drawing out the word, "Here's the thing. I'm a vegetarian."

"Bless you."

"No, I'm *vegetarian*," she repeated, grinning. "How about a veggie pizza?"

Stevie was quiet for a long moment, barbeque menu in hand as she studied Kyra carefully. "As in you don't eat meat. Only vegetables and shit?"

"Only vegetables and stuff," Kyra confirmed.

"Dear God."

6

The next morning, Kyra had to drag herself out of bed. If she let herself dwell too long on the sinking feeling in her stomach, this would be one of *those* days. A day where she could stay in bed for hours, sleeping or just staring at the wall. Her limbs sunk heavily into the mattress, her thoughts unclear through the murky fog of her brain.

She almost started crying when she forced herself to get up, to put on her running gear.

After ripping her hair into a brutally tight ponytail, she hurried out the door, scared that if she stayed any longer inside, she wouldn't leave. Taking off down the beach in her bare feet, she set a grueling pace right from the start with her legs churning over the sand. Her hair bounced against her back as the rising sun began to warm her skin.

She ran for an hour to punish herself. Only when her knees wobbled and her muscles quivered did she allow herself to slow down. By the time she got back to the house, she was sweating like crazy but she felt better, felt *alive*.

Hale Cooper stood on her back porch, watching her walk up the garden's path. He had a thermos in his hand and a grumpy look on his face. "You run too?"

She climbed the porch steps and cocked her head at him. "You don't?"

"Mixed martial arts," he said. He stuck the paper thermos out at her. "Here."

She took the cup, her eyebrow arching, feeling skeptical of his intentions. "What's this?"

"I thought you might like some coffee this morning. I had no idea what you like, so I got you what I normally get."

She took a sip, her eyes widening as the coffee hit her tongue. "Holy cow! Where did you get this?"

One side of his mouth quirked into a grin. It was the closest to a smile she'd ever gotten from him, and she couldn't help but feel a surge of satisfaction, like she'd won some game against him. "The coffee shop in town has the best coffee. It's, uh, organic or whatever."

She took another sip, savoring the aroma. "I really appreciate this, Hale."

He shoved his hands in his pockets and scanned down the length of her body, landing on the scabby remains of her accident yesterday. She felt exposed in her spandex shorts and tank top with him looking at her. Never before had a man made her feel so vulnerable under his gaze.

She kind of liked it. And, to top it off, she didn't even look pretty.

He brought his eyes back up, and Kyra sensed him linger at her exceptionally short shorts. Seeming to shake himself out of whatever he was thinking, he forced his eyes back up to hers. He cupped the back of his neck with his hand. "Look, I really do feel bad about yesterday. I know I can be kind of . . ."

"An a-hole?" she volunteered.

His brows rose, which did tantalizing things to his dermal piercing. "Sure. All I'm saying is that I really am sorry. Maybe we can start over or something."

A surge of happiness fractured in her stomach. "I'd like that."

"Okay. Fine." Hale shuffled his feet. It felt good to make him nervous for once. "Anyway, your water will be back on tomorrow."

She smacked her forehead. "Oh, man. I totally forgot. And I'm all stinky and gross." She lifted up the bottom of her shirt and sniffed it, exposing a wide swath of her flat, tanned stomach.

She looked back at Hale in time to see his eyes widen at her. He shook his head, this time smiling completely. It was a beautiful, shy kind of smile that completely changed his hard face. It softened his piercings and tattoos, instantly warming him up, and she found herself leaning toward him.

"You're not that gross," he said before he turned and left, which made her laugh. She watched him go back inside her house, thinking this was the kind of Hale she could like.

And it didn't hurt that she'd caught him checking her out.

Since she didn't have to bother with a bath this morning, she turned back and went to the beach. She settled in the sand to watch the waves as she drank her delicious coffee. All in all, her bad morning had turned into something good and warm.

When she'd finished her cup, she rose and went back inside. The construction sounds had already risen to a deafening level. From somewhere in the front of the house, she heard the strains of Hale's angry rock music. She waved at Chevy and the crew as she headed for the stairs, and they all waved back, following Chevy's lead and calling out greetings, which made her smile again.

Back inside her room, she changed her clothes and stared at her hair in the mirror. Hale had been kind; she was gross. Between surfing yesterday and running this morning, she looked awful, but it gave her a great idea for a video on styling dirty hair.

She set up her video equipment. It took her longer than normal because she had to find the right lighting and adjust her lamps, but she finally settled down in front of her camera and started recording.

It took her most of the morning. It wouldn't be a perfect video, because the construction noise made for awful background music, but her subscribers would understand. Besides, she thought the video had turned out to be pretty funny. Most of her channel consisted of videos where she looked perfect and effortless with flawless editing. To upload something where she didn't look her best unsettled her, but in a way that made her heart pound with excitement.

It felt freeing.

After she'd answered more emails and caught up on her social media sites, it was well past noon and the construction sounds had disappeared. Kyra grabbed a banana from her stash of groceries and headed out of her room to stretch her legs.

Her footsteps rang across the wooden floors, echoing in the

silence. Tool belts hung from saw horses or sat in a neat pile on the floor, like the men who'd worn them had evaporated into thin air. Only now did Kyra realize just how big the house actually was, and how lonely it would be for one person. To distract herself, she kept walking the rooms, forcing herself to count all the pretty charms of the house. She weaved her way through the upstairs bedrooms, none of which would need as much work as downstairs. When she reached the room in the front of the house, she paused. A huge bay window, like the one in her bedroom, looked out onto the street. It was painted in a warm yellow—bright and happy. The anxiety in her chest loosened.

She settled on the window seat and chewed her banana. For once, she was the nosy neighbor watching from her windows. She snickered at the thought of the old women on the street catching her throwing cookies at Hale. Few cars drove up and down the street, most people at work or inside their homes to avoid the heat. A mailman strolled down the sidewalk to deliver mail from his carrying sack. A few houses over from Kyra's and across the street, Mrs. Harrison pruned her shrubs, which reminded her she needed to start work on her own garden.

"Maybe today," she murmured to herself.

She was about to leave when Hale's black Dodge pulled up in front of her house. Kyra watched as he climbed out, letting herself appreciate his good looks and taking her time to soak him in. No matter what he said about running, he took care of his body. His tattoos were carefully done, most in black and gray. Kyra would never appreciate his awful attitude toward her in the beginning, but she started to think Cade might have been right about his brother just being harder to understand than most. They'd gotten off to a rough start this week, but he'd made the effort today.

As he walked up to her house, his eyes lifted to the window she sat behind and locked on her. Caught in the act of checking him out, Kyra jerked back, heat spreading across the back of her neck and a tingling deep in her belly. Downstairs, she heard the front door open.

Kyra rose from the seat, taking her banana peel with her. As she stood, the cushion she'd been sitting on rattled. Turning, she pulled up the cushion, which she discovered was actually a lid.

Surprised, she adjusted her grip and sank down onto her knees to look inside. To her delight, old photo albums and books filled the small, musty space. She began sorting through them after she propped open the lid. The books were dusty and she sneezed a lot, but she eventually had the contents spread out onto the floor.

She sat cross-legged on the floor and reached for the first photo book. She opened the creaking, stiff binding and stared at the first picture, her breath catching in her throat. It was her grandmother and mother, standing together in front of this very house.

Her mother was a little girl, fresh faced and smiling, with one of her front teeth missing. Even Florence looked happy, her face much younger and sweeter, without the contemptuous look she had now. Below the picture, in careful script, read "Florence & Lila 1968."

Kyra knew nothing about her mother, Lila. Even her aunt and uncle hadn't told her much about her, but she knew her mother had a privileged youth. She and Thomas grew up in big houses and private schools. Thomas had been a typical older brother: aloof but protective. When rumors started circulating that his little sister dabbled in drugs and boys, he'd ignored them, thinking it was just a phase for Lila, but she didn't get much better. Eventually, because of the drugs, Thomas and his parents turned their backs on Lila, disowning her and cutting off her trust fund. Things had gone too far, they'd said. It was tough love.

Their tough love drove Lila further away. Thomas told Kyra they'd rarely spoken to Lila after high school. Sometimes she would call, asking for money or just to yell at them when she was high. Though she liked her weed, they knew she was falling into harder drugs. And then she'd been arrested.

Struggling to breathe, Kyra realized it was possible all these books contained the life of her mother, or at least tidbits into her past. Trying not to feel too hopeful, she turned the page in the photo book, revealing a picture of a baby splashing in a sink. She instantly knew it was her mother, because the pain in her heart spiked sharp and unexpected. She slapped the book closed.

"Hey."

Kyra gasped. Hale stood in the door, looking uncomfortable without his usual scowl.

"You surprised me," she said, pressing her hand to her heart. She gently set the book down and stood.

"What's all this?"

She looked down at the books and back at the window seat where they'd come from. She opened her mouth to tell him, but she didn't know what to say. "I don't really know," she managed.

"Okay," he said evenly. "I need you to start picking out some stuff for the house. I brought samples."

Kyra pressed her lips up into a smile. "Oh, great!" She tried for excitement, but even she heard it fall flat. She picked her way over the books. As she tried to pass through the door, Hale's hand settled on her arm. Her skin twitched at his touch, her heart dipping. She looked up at him, wide-eyed.

"You really okay? No faking," he said, and she glimpsed the compassion in his green eyes. He could smile and be kind; she'd found that out today. He could apologize when he was wrong and bring her coffee. And, apparently, he could see past her bullshit.

Choosing not to fake it, she said, "No, I'm not. But if I look at some pretty colors, I'll feel better."

He studied her for a long moment, his eyes warm across her skin. She trembled beneath his gaze. Feeling her reaction, his body stiffened, his eyes darkening, but he removed his arm. "Let's get you some pretty colors then."

They spent the next couple hours going over counter choices and fixtures. She picked out wall colors and then changed her mind. She decided on new ones then doubted herself, but her excitement built as she finally began to imagine her new home.

Hale stayed patient with her, walking her through her options and telling her the pros and cons of quartz countertops versus granite, but Kyra liked soapstone. He sighed and leaned around her to gather up new soapstone options.

The press of his body sent a feverish set of chills through her; she enjoyed the feel of him sitting next to her. His rough voice right beside her ear made her throat close. Her body came alive, quiet shivers cascading down her spine just from being close to him.

She really hoped he couldn't tell.

"Oh, that one!" she exclaimed over a beautiful mint-green color. "I want that for the outside of the house."

"No," he said, his voice flat.

"Why?" she asked, surprised. "What's wrong with it?"

"It looks cheesy." He raised his eyebrows at her, like she was crazy for even picking it.

"It does not!" Kyra laughed. "It's really cute!"

"It's disgustingly ugly. And it's bad for business."

"Do we need to go over who hired who?" she asked, smiling sweetly. Somehow, he'd made her feel better, and he'd made her laugh. "I want that color."

"Fine." Hale scrubbed his eyes with the heels of his hands, but she whooped with joy, unbothered by his reluctance. She jumped up and danced a little.

"I'm going to have the prettiest house on the street!" She fist-pumped.

Hale watched her without speaking, and for the first time in her life, she thought someone was seeing past her long legs and blonde hair, and seeing *her*. And he seemed to like what he saw.

Kyra stopped, every cell in her body hushing under his gaze. She couldn't help the smile creeping across her face as they watched each other unabashed.

This wasn't faking it.

Not even close.

7

"Oh, my gosh."

Kyra stared at her reflection in the bathroom mirror. Two days' worth of sweat, sea water, and dirt layered her hair. Where she'd slept the night before, one side was flat, while the other stuck up like an electrocuted rooster.

She couldn't make a video like this. She couldn't even look at herself. Scrunching her nose up, she quickly turned away and pulled on a ball cap.

Downstairs, the construction had come to a halt as the electricians Cade had contracted worked inside the walls, pulling out wires and checking them. The plumbers had come yesterday like Hale had said. He'd met with them to look for any issues on getting the pipes up to code after he'd helped her pick out some options for the house. She hadn't heard the outcome of the plumbing evaluation, but the crew was working hard to get the house up to code so they could pass all their inspections.

Hale was easy to find. She heard his voice in the back and followed the flutter in her stomach. She tugged the brim of her cap lower as she made her way over to where he was directing an electrician.

She cleared her throat when the conversation was over. "Good morning."

Hale turned, his eyes looking her up and down. "Morning."

"Uh, do you know when the water will be turned back on?" she asked, refusing to be flustered under his gaze. She smelled like a sweaty cow; she couldn't be checking out guys right now, even if they were possibly, maybe, potentially on friendly terms now.

"Feeling gross?" The corner of his mouth twitched at his question, like he could read her mind or something equally terrifying.

"You have no idea. When is it happening?"

"Lunchtime. Plumbers will be done by then," Hale said. Someone called his name from the front of the house. "Gotta run."

The electrician Hale had just been talking to regarded Kyra in her ball cap. "Hey. Wanna go out some—"

"No."

She took off for the back door and scurried across her back porch. She rushed around to Stevie's house and knocked on the front door. No one answered. She spent the next five minutes banging on every door and window within reach. Even though Stevie was clearly home—her car sat parked out by the curb—Kyra remained standing in Stevie's bushes, feeling like a dirty weirdo.

She made her way back to her house and up the stairs. The

electrician gave her a mean look as she passed, but she ignored him. She needed to feel gross in her own room with the door closed. She just had to make it until lunchtime.

Before she set down to work, she lit a few candles and coated herself with body spray. Finally, she was able to focus on work.

Before she started on anything else, she checked the comment section on her last video about styling dirty hair, which had finally uploaded during the night, thanks to the slower internet connection out here on the island. Kyra laughed at a few of the funnier comments, a smile ghosting across her face, until she came to one particularly nasty one.

The user who merely called themselves "anonymous" called her ugly and nasty. A greasy loser. They asked if she ever got laid looking like that and if men could even get it up around her disgusting, fat face.

She read it over and over. Each time, she told herself it was normal; she often got comments like this. But never on a video where she actually did look dirty. And greasy. And ugly. Kyra tried to swallow, but her mouth was too dry. Frantically, she watched the video in question back through. At the end, she really did feel like an ugly loser.

Quickly, she went into the settings and deleted the video. Just like that, it vanished, taking with it the mean comment.

Slowly, she closed her laptop. With tears in her eyes, she climbed back into bed. She counted down the minutes until lunchtime rolled around and she could take a shower and be herself again. She vowed to never make another video like that again, to always be perfect and flawlessly edited. Then, if someone left a nasty comment, she could hide behind the armor of her pretty video.

Lunchtime finally rolled around, and Kyra sprung from her bed. She tested the water in her bathroom sink, relieved to see a gush of spewing, sputtering water exploding from the pipes. The only problem was her bathroom only had a bath, and she desperately needed a shower. A long, steaming-hot shower. She grabbed her toiletries and some new clothes before she hurried to the downstairs bathroom.

Only then did she remember why this bathroom wasn't in useable condition yet.

"You've got to be kidding me."

Kyra dropped her toiletries onto the ripped-up tile floors of the bathroom and groaned. She felt like having a temper tantrum as she took in the flapping plastic sheet covering the gaping hole where a window had been. She remembered now that Hale had to take it out and get a tempered replacement glass, but that didn't help her now. She *needed* a shower.

She tested the water in the shower. It spewed forth in hot, pressured glory. She chewed on her lip and looked at the plastic sheet again. It had been a large window, meaning the hole it left behind was extra . . . gaping. She leaned into the shower and looked through the plastic. It faced the side alley of the house that connected to her back garden and the beach.

She knew the crew normally parked in that particular alley to keep from blocking the street and walked around to the front of the house. But they'd gone to lunch, which meant most of the trucks were gone, and she just needed a quick shower. A very quick, hot, steamy shower.

"That's it."

She stripped as fast as she could and hopped in the shower,

moaning out loud as the hot water pounded onto her skin. She lathered up her hair and scrubbed her body with fierce intensity. Balancing on one leg then the other, she shaved quickly, nicking her skin a few times.

By the time she rinsed out her conditioner, she felt a little more human. She leaned her head into the spray, arching her back and enjoying the feel of the scalding water working its magic over her. She smiled in complete and utter sensual pleasure. Showering was *divine*.

"What are you looking at?"

Kyra jumped at the sound of Hale's voice. She peeked through the shower curtain and checked the bathroom door, which she'd left cracked. No one had come inside the house because she would've heard the front door open. With horror building in the pit of her stomach, she slowly turned her head to the plastic-covered window hole beside her.

Please, no, she prayed.

Hale's entire crew stood outside staring with open mouths at her. They seemed as surprised as she did, although some of them looked as if they were enjoying the show. Only sweet, older Chevy averted his eyes, his cheeks flaming red. Hale strolled over and looked up at the window to see what all the fuss is about.

"Is something wrong . . . Oh." His voice trailed off as he began to snicker, and within seconds, he and most of his crew bent over double, laughing at her.

Snapping out of her temporary shock, she screamed and dropped below the view of the window, covering herself with her arms and hands. She tumbled out of the shower and sprawled onto the floor in a wet, slippery mess. Grabbing a towel and jerking it around her, she army-crawled out of the bathroom.

She was in a dead sprint up the stairs when the door opened and Hale came in. "Are you decent?" he called, laughing.

She screamed in frustration and slammed her door.

"Oh, my gosh. Oh, my gosh. Oh, my gosh." She sank to the floor, her body shaking in embarrassment. How was she ever going to go downstairs again? Parading around in a bikini was one thing. Being seen naked and *laughed at?* An entirely different situation.

Hale had laughed first, which had Kyra simmering in shivering anger. If her mortification hadn't been so off-the-charts, she would've stomped down the stairs and yelled at him. Instead, she dressed in her pajamas and crawled into bed.

She was done with today. *Done.*

A knock sounded on her door, making her gasp. "Kyra? You in there?"

She covered her head and hid under her covers, but her phone beeped and gave her away. "Come on. I heard your phone. I know you're in there," Hale called through the door. "Can I come in?"

"Go away!" she shouted, the sound muffled from under her covers.

He sighed. The door groaned, and Kyra wondered if he was propped against it. She pictured his hard, muscular body pressed against the wood and realized she really needed an intervention.

"Look, I'm really sorry about earlier."

"You laughed at me!" she shouted back.

He stifled another laugh. She reared up in bed and threw her pillow at the door. It hit its target with a satisfying thud. "I'm sorry about that too," he said, muffling another laugh.

"You're laughing now!" But she couldn't hold back her own

snort of laughter. The urge to see Hale when he laughed itched up her spine. She wondered if he was smiling right then, right on the other side of her door. She hated the thought of missing it.

"No, I'm not. You just caught us by surprise is all," he said.

"Whatever, Hale. You could've been gallant and told your crew to look away or something. Since you're so worried about them being *distracted* and all."

"Ah, come on. Chevy's ticker ain't so good, I was just protecting him when I told you not to parade around in your bikini."

There it was; she heard it in his voice. He was smiling. Silently, she stood up from her bed and tip-toed across the room. "And seeing me stark naked is fine?" She pressed her ear to her door.

"I mean, I didn't say every distraction was bad."

She ripped the door open and jumped to the side.

Hale tripped inside, nearly falling flat on his face as Kyra laughed. He recovered and turned a squinty-eyed stare toward her. "That wasn't very nice."

She smiled. "But it made me feel better."

He glanced around at her video equipment. Slowly, his brows rose. "What's all this?"

"I make YouTube videos."

Kyra waited for the skepticism, but instead, he said, "Cade said you were a blogger."

"I do that too."

He nodded, clearly impressed. "I'll leave you to it then. I just wanted to say sorry."

"I appreciate that," she said as the blush crept back to her cheeks.

Hale noticed as he went by, but he didn't tease her. He went down the stairs, his heavy boots thunking on the wood. Kyra watched him go for a moment before closing her door and grabbing her phone.

She had a text from Stevie.

Stevie: We're going out tonight. Don't even think about saying no. Ho.

Kyra: Fine. I have a funny/awful story to tell you.

Stevie: Those are my faves.

A few more hours passed before she rose from the floor and stretched her back, thinking how badly she really needed to get a desk. Stevie had texted again and told her to meet her at her house in an hour. While she used to go out all the time, drinking and hanging out with her friends, it wasn't something she allowed often of herself these days. But for Stevie, Kyra heaved a sigh to fortify herself before she started getting ready.

She settled on a fluttery shirt and white, ripped jeans. Her hair had dried in her natural beachy waves after the shower debacle, so she let it be. She took more time with her makeup because she needed some armor, and she craved to look pretty. No way would anybody be laughing at her tonight. The smoky eyeshadow set off the bright blue of her irises. She swiped on some lip gloss and grabbed her favorite wedges before she left the house.

Stevie waited on her front porch, wearing cute jeans and a peplum top with high heels. "You look hot!" she called as she skipped to Kyra with a huge grin plastered on her face and her fire-engine red curls bouncing against her shoulders.

"I'll drive?" Kyra volunteered, rolling her eyes good-naturedly.

Stevie's breath smelled of wine.

Once they were in the car and heading toward downtown Canaan, Stevie asked, "So what's the story?"

"Oh, man," Kyra groaned. "It was awful. My water has been turned off the last few days and I really needed a shower. Like, really bad. I tried knocking on your door to ask you." She cut a sharp, joking stare toward Stevie.

"Hangover. What can I say? An earthquake could happen and I wouldn't hear it."

Kyra faltered in her story, her thoughts snagging on the fact Stevie had drank last night as well. But it wasn't her business, and lots of people had wine every night. She laughed uncertainly. "Right. Well, I waited until lunch when the water came back on and took a shower downstairs. The only problem was this big hole in the wall . . ."

Open mouthed, Stevie turned fully in the seat to stare at her. "I know where this is going!"

"Hale's entire crew saw me naked." Kyra put on her blinker and made a turn.

"But the big question is if Hale himself saw you naked."

"He did."

"Hell yeah!" Stevie whooped. "That's awesome!"

"How is that awesome?"

"I bet he's picturing your naked, wet body right now."

"I seriously hope not," Kyra groaned.

"Liar, liar, pants on fire," Stevie sang.

As they talked some more while Kyra drove, she realized Stevie was a lot drunker than she'd initially thought, but she still managed to direct them to a bar on the corner of the main street in town, which was lit up with lights in the trees like it was Christmas.

The bar, like most businesses on this street, had an open front. Sliding glass doors led into a little courtyard and outside bar area. Music pulsed out onto the street as Kyra parked a few blocks down. All along the sidewalk, people emerged from a couple different watering holes to smoke and flirt with each other. Large groups of friends clotted the walkway, chittering and laughing among themselves. Stevie and Kyra weaved their way through until they stepped into the bar. Dim lights lit the warm space, and televisions played different sports on mute. The bar itself took up most of the space in the middle of the room with people crowded around it, their loud voices mingling with the televisions and live country band set up in the corner.

Kyra lifted her chin and followed Stevie through the crowd. She was surprised to see how packed it was, but Stevie knew where she was going. She steered them over to the bar, sliding along the back wall and finding two empty barstools.

"How did you see these?" Kyra shouted into Stevie's ear.

She pointed to a guy with long hair and chiseled arms behind the bar. "Troy saves me seats when I come in." She waved when Troy blew her kiss. He made his way over.

"The usual?" he asked. She gave him a thumbs-up. "And what about you?" he asked Kyra.

"Water, please."

Stevie groaned, but Troy nodded, moving away to take more orders and mix Stevie's drink. Kyra looked around the room, taking in all the bodies at the bar and the ones dancing to the band. Troy brought their drinks, handing Stevie a Long Island iced tea.

"You better watch her," he said to Kyra with a tilt of his chin toward Stevie.

Kyra's brows rose. "Why's that?"

"She gets handsy when she drinks LITs." His knowing smirk at Stevie suggested he knew just how handsy she got from first-hand experience.

"I'll keep an eye out."

Stevie leaned toward her and fake-whispered, "He likes to play hard-to-get at first, but I always win in the end."

Troy's glinting smirk traveled to his eyes. "I let you win," he said before moving away to wait on other drinkers.

"Who's he?" Kyra shouted, leaning close to Stevie.

She waggled her brows at Kyra and said, "We hang out some—if you know what I mean. Isn't he hot?"

Kyra looked back over her shoulder at Troy. He caught her staring and winked. "Cade's cuter!"

"He's no Hale, huh?" Stevie poked her in the ribs.

"Whatever," she said, laughing. "I don't know what you're talking about."

"Well, he's standing right over there."

Kyra started, following Stevie's pointed finger. She spotted Hale in the crowd just as he saw her and Stevie. He stood against the end of the bar with Cade and a group of guys from his construction crew who Kyra recognized. His green eyes cut through the dim bar and scalded her; she knew he was picturing her naked by the way his eyes danced with amusement. The piercing above his brow danced, his lips twisting into a smirk.

"Oh, yeah," Stevie called. "He wants you."

"He does not!"

Stevie went on for a little longer, pointing out different people to Kyra. Troy brought over two more Long Islands. They flirted shamelessly, but Stevie was having fun, and Kyra found herself relaxing.

A hand settled on the back of her chair, causing her to stiffen. Hot beer breath leaned down into her hair. "Hey, sexy."

Kyra looked over her shoulder. A guy about her age with gelled hair and an Affliction shirt was undressing her with his eyes. "Hey," Kyra said flatly.

"Wanna dance?" The guy's eyes roamed all over her body. He pressed into her, nearly knocking her off her chair, and she fought back a sneeze from his over-powering cologne.

"No, thanks. I'm not a big dancer," she responded, looking away.

The guy's hand crept onto her back. "Oh come on, baby. Let me feel that hot body."

She glanced back, her bitch face in place. "The only thing you'll be feeling tonight is yourself through a sock."

The guy recoiled. He opened his mouth to say something, but he quickly closed it and turned away, but not before Kyra caught the flash of fear in his eyes as he left. She looked over her other shoulder.

"Hale," she said, her breath catching in her throat at the shock of seeing him so close.

"Hey, Kyra."

Her name sounded rough in his mouth, and she instantly knew he would kiss like he talked: raspy and with enough heat to set her hair on fire. He had his arm around her chair before anyone else could come up and talk to her. She knew by the way he propped his leg on the bottom of her stool and leaned against the bar that he was staking out his territory. It was basic bar real estate, and she was enjoying it for the first time in a very long while.

"Thanks for running that guy off," Kyra said over the blare of the band.

Hale leaned closer, his skin a mere breath from hers. The heat of his body slicked against her like a warm blanket. Her stomach fluttered upward, twisting and spinning. "What was that?" he asked, not hearing her.

"I said thanks for running that guy off. He was creepy," she spoke into his ear.

He turned his head and looked back into her eyes. "Every guy in here was thinking about coming over. He was just the first to work up the courage."

"Yeah, right." She rolled her eyes.

"Do you forgive me for today?" he asked.

"You didn't sound that sorry," she shouted. Stevie was talking to Troy, leaning over the bar and pressing her boobs into the wood.

Hale said something, but Kyra didn't hear. "What?" she called.

He leaned even closer, his chest pressing into her. His arm wrapped around her back and pulled her closer as he lowered his head. For a crazy, shivering moment, she thought he might kiss her. Instead, he leaned into her ear and said, "I wasn't sorry."

Her eyes widened. "Hale!" she accused, but she laughed. "That's awful!"

His mouth pulled sideways in a crooked, knowing grin. "I would've preferred if my whole crew hadn't seen. We'll have to spend all day Monday fixing the mistakes they made this afternoon because you were all they could think about."

She blushed. "Yeah, right."

"Hey, Hale!" Stevie shouted, leaning around Kyra. "What's up?"

"Not much. Good to see ya, Stevie," Hale said with a polite nod of his head. It was odd coming from a man who looked like him, but it warmed Kyra's heart. His hand grazed her arm, skimming the skin gently. She shivered.

"I hear you're a Peeping Tom," Stevie said.

Kyra turned and gaped at her friend, but Hale laughed. "Kyra shouldn't go around flashing everybody. That's what she gets."

Stevie died laughing as Kyra smacked Hale's chest, but it only made her palm sting. His chest was rock hard. He looked down at her, his eyes dark in the bar as his hand made another tickling trail down her arm. A shaky breath escaped her mouth.

"Want to dance?" Hale asked, leaning close to her ear again. She imagined what it would feel like to have his fingers caressing the sensitive spot below her ear. The only coherent gesture she managed was a nod.

He took her hand and helped her down from her stool. "I'm going to go dance with Hale," she shouted at Stevie, who waved them off.

He led her down the back wall to the dance floor. Kyra squeezed past the bar's patrons, thankful Hale seemed to cut a path before him. She saw the stares of a few men as she passed, but she ignored them. Her eyes were focused on the wide, flexing muscles of Hale's back.

Once on the floor, he turned and pulled her into him. There wasn't much room for dancing, not that she minded. She ran her hand up his chest as she wrapped her other arm around his neck. His hands were on her hips, holding her to him as they moved to the music, his fingers finding the bare expanse of her back where her shirt had raised.

Her hand skimmed from his chest to the muscular swell of his shoulder and back. She smiled, watching him watch her. His head bowed toward her, cocooning her in his embrace. She felt completely hidden with him, like he was blocking her from everyone's stares, which meant he had seen the other guys checking her out, and he didn't like it. The thought made Kyra happy.

Hale bent and said something warm and hot into her ear, but she couldn't hear him over the band. She pressed in tighter, her hand going up to his neck to pull him down close to her mouth. For a crazy second, she considered turning her head and kissing him, but she lost her nerve. "What?" she asked, speaking into his ear.

He leaned back, a slow, easy smile spreading across his face. "I said—"

But then his eyes caught something over her shoulder. She noticed the stiffening of his muscles beneath her hands, and his body stilled against hers. A hooded anger slipped into his eyes as he focused on whatever was happening behind her.

"What is it?" Kyra shouted over the band, but he didn't respond.

He released her and slid past, his body slicing through the other dancers easily. The fury radiated off of him like steaming pavement on a hot day. She followed his line of vision and saw Cade talking to a burly guy with a large beer gut.

The guy was clearly in Cade's face about something. Cade tried to hold his ground, but his eyes were wide. He didn't see Hale barreling toward him, and neither did the guy, Kyra figured, because he wouldn't be laughing at Cade if he'd seen Hale coming.

He clearly didn't see the fist, either. Hale took the guy down with one swing. Then it turned into a brawl, with Hale's crew jumping in to take down beer-gut guy's friends. Bouncers rushed over and tried to break up the fight while women screamed and guys howled their approval. The band stopped mid-song, knowing they couldn't compete with a bar fight. The sound of fists hitting flesh could be heard like an echo between the cheering and hooting.

Not knowing what else to do in the jostling madness, Kyra made her way back to Stevie, who was watching the fight with bland interest while she sipped on her Long Island. "What did you do?" she shouted into Kyra's ear when she finally took her spot next to Stevie again. All around, people jostled about to get a better view of the fight.

"I didn't do anything!"

"That's not nearly as exciting as I hoped," Stevie huffed out in disappointment.

The bouncers separated the fight, and escorted everyone out. Hale didn't look back at Kyra and Stevie as he left in the grips of a burly security guy. Cade hurriedly settled their tab with Troy. As he turned to leave, he saw Kyra and Stevie across the bar. He waved and mouthed "sorry" before he rushed out after Hale.

"He'll probably be in jail for the weekend."

Kyra looked up at Troy, who'd just spoken. "They're going to put him in jail?" she shouted above the rowdy crowd.

"They always put Hale Cooper in jail," Troy said with a shake of his head. "Even if he didn't throw the first punch."

"Or even if he didn't throw any punch at all," Stevie added. "The prim and proper of Canaan Island like to see the likes of him in jail. It lets them sleep better at night."

"Why won't he make bail tonight?"

Troy shrugged. "Small towns. Judges don't work on weekends."

"That's ridiculous!"

He nodded in agreement and slid Stevie another drink. Kyra pulled out her phone and texted Cade.

Kyra: Is everything okay?

Half an hour later, he responded, and Kyra's stomach sank.

Cade: We're fine. He'll have to wait until Monday to see the judge. Sorry, K. We'll start back on your house on Tuesday.

Kyra: Screw the house. Let me know if I can do anything for you and Hale.

As she waited for him to text back, she fiddled with her bracelets, but when she didn't hear from him after an hour, her shoulders slumped. She felt too sick with worry to stay in the crowded, hazy bar a moment longer.

She turned to Stevie. "I don't feel so good. Are you ready to leave?"

"Leave?" She sounded shocked at the thought. "You go ahead. I'll catch a ride with Troy when his shift's over."

"Are you sure?" Frowning, Kyra darted a glance toward the bartender.

"Yeah! Go on. I'm fine, and Troy will make sure I'm more than fine in a few hours."

"Gross, Stevie," she said, laughing when her friend waggled her eyebrows at her. But it seemed Stevie would be safe here alone. "Okay," she agreed, "but do you want to go antique shopping with me tomorrow?"

"Yeah!" Stevie nodded enthusiastically. "I've always wanted to be the type of person who does shit like that."

"Tomorrow then," Kyra said. She hugged Stevie before she left a tip for Troy and left. As she slid her way through the crowd, like a fish fighting upstream, her fake smile faded.

8

Kyra normally took Saturdays off from work to unwind, but today she'd woken up early to work in her front garden ripping out weeds and pruning ruthlessly. She hacked and pulled and tugged. She fell onto her butt with a muffled oath. Almost feverishly, she swiped her brow, spreading dirt across her face, and dug back in.

She was relieving tension, and hacking tended to relieve tension.

"Good morning, Kyra."

She jerked and peered up through the overgrown bush she was currently trying to tear in half. Spotting the ample hips of Mrs. Walker, she stood.

"Morning, Mrs. Walker. How are you today?"

"Just stretching my legs," Mrs. Walker said with a sniff. She tucked an imaginary piece of loose hair behind her ear.

"It's a good day for it," Kyra said, trying to sound nice.

"Right. I just wanted to come by and see if you'd heard about the . . . *incident* with Hale Cooper."

"Incident?" she asked through gritted teeth.

"Oh, yes. I figured you would want to know since he's your contractor and all." Mrs. Walker looked around as if she didn't want anyone else to hear her bit of gossip. Kyra resisted the urge to roll her eyes. "But he was arrested last night. For getting into a fight. At a *bar*!"

Anger clenched like a balled-up fist in her gut, and for the first time in her life, she didn't care what this woman thought about her. She just wanted to say what she felt, what she believed. And she didn't give a damn about the consequences. "Yeah, I know," she snapped, feeling a titling sense of giddiness at her cavalier words. "I was *there*."

Mrs. Walker couldn't recover in time to keep the horror from her face. "Nice girls don't go to bars, Kyra. At the very least, you should expect your contractor to be respectable. Nonetheless, I hope you're aware alcoholism runs in the blood. I would think with your mother's . . . situation, you would want to avoid all that."

Mrs. Walker looked about two seconds away from shaking her finger in Kyra's face. Before she could, Kyra cut her off. "I've learned that the most respectable people are normally the biggest assholes. As for my grandmother, I don't give a shit what she thinks."

Mrs. Walker's mouth flapped opened and closed like a fly trap. "I'm going to be relaying this conversation to your grandmother!"

"Fantastic! Be sure to tell her I say 'hello.'"

She watched Mrs. Walker turn seven different shades of red before turning and stalking off. Taking her spot in the overgrown flower bed, Kyra realized she felt better than she had all morning. Maybe she needed to be rude more often. With a grunt, she went back to work.

She worked until lunchtime, when the sun became stifling and sweat ran down her back. She stowed away her tools and pushed the wheelbarrow full of torn weeds to the back of the house where she'd set up her composting bin. When everything was put away and as tidy as possible, she went inside and took a lightning-fast shower in her exposed bathroom.

She hung up a towel over the window, but it did little to comfort her unease. She was in and out in under three minutes—a new record for her. She snickered, thinking she could make a video on snappy showers.

She pulled on her uniform of shorts and a tank before she ran a brush through her wet hair. She always gave herself a break on Saturdays, meaning no makeup and no hairstyling. She twisted her long blonde locks up into a high bun and left the house, feeling better than she had all day.

When she went over to Stevie's house, Troy was the one who answered the door.

"Oh," Kyra said, fumbling the word. "Ah, is Stevie here?"

Troy looked ruffled and tired with red-rimmed eyes. He sidled past Kyra on the front porch. "Just waking up," he said, his voice scratchy, before heading down the steps toward his car, which Kyra had missed on her way over.

Not knowing what else to do, she went inside and pulled the door closed behind her. "Stevie?" she called out, wandering into the kitchen.

Behind her, on the stairs, Stevie hobbled down wearing a pair of sunglasses and a hood pulled up over her head. Kyra looked up at her friend and laughed. "Is this what you're wearing to go antiquing?"

Stevie groaned, still clutching the stair's banister until she came down to stand next to Kyra. "That's today?" her voice cracked, and Kyra was treated to a ferocious fog of bad breath, which she waved away with a crinkled nose.

"We just talked about this yesterday," Kyra reminded her.

"Ugh. I forgot about it in all the excitement. Let me change then."

"And brush your teeth!" Kyra called after her.

After a shower of both body and mouth, lots of coffee, and a pep talk, Stevie trailed behind Kyra as they entered a building salvage warehouse. She still wore her sunglasses, even in the dim building. "How are you even functioning right now?"

"I drank water instead of Long Islands by the gallons, and I left before midnight."

"And who had more fun?"

Kyra snorted, her attention on the ceiling. She gaped up at all the amazing old light fixtures above her head. A particular chandelier with tons of draping crystals caught her eye. "Yeah, you really look like you had a lot of fun last night."

"Oh, I did. I'm just paying for it today. Nothing comes for free," Stevie muttered. Her voice was far away and drew Kyra's attention.

"Stevie," she started, unsure of how to proceed. "What was it like growing up with your parents?"

Stevie dropped the tassel of the lamp she was playing with. "What do you mean?"

Kyra fiddled with the stack of bracelets on her arm. "I mean, you talk about them sometimes, and you sound pretty bitter."

She couldn't see to know for sure, but it looked like Stevie rolled her eyes behind her massive glasses. "'Bitter' is an understatement. They're idiots."

"Because of the reality shows?"

Stevie meandered down the aisle ahead of Kyra. "Yeah. They sell their souls to make another spinoff. It's gross, and they go broke trying to produce these things because no one else cares about them anymore. It's pathetic, really. They're so desperate to be relevant they'll do anything for the spotlight."

"Anything?"

"Pretty much. My entire childhood consisted of one big reality show. I couldn't even cry over a skinned knee without some producer in my face telling me not to look directly at the camera, but I was just a little kid looking for someone to make my ouchie better. For my fourteenth birthday, my parents sent me to fat camp and made a spin-off of it. That spin-off was quickly followed by another when I went to recovery farm out in Colorado for my eating disorder."

"Stevie . . ."

She ignored Kyra. "Since then, I've learned to stay out of their damage path."

Kyra let the subject drop for now because she didn't want to push too far. She moved on to a row of mirrors, her fingers trailing over the dusty frames. She couldn't begin to image what kind of pain Stevie must feel to always come second to her parents' fame. Maybe that was why she and Stevie got along so well; they had a lot of things in common, and they both lived a life of hurt.

"What's up with you and Hale?" Stevie asked, animated now

that they weren't talking about her.

"Nothing much at all," Kyra grumbled. She looked at the price tag of one mirror. She grimaced and moved on.

"That was a pretty hot dance y'all had, even if it was cut short." Stevie found a bin of old cabinet knobs. "Oh! Kyra, these are cute!" She held up a pair of sea glass knobs.

"They are! What else is in there?" They sorted through the knobs, finding and matching an assortment of bright colors for the kitchen. Kyra put them in her basket.

"He's been friendlier lately at the house, but that was the first time he actually acted like he wanted to be around me. Of course, that was before he just went off and got into a fight," Kyra said, returning to their previous conversation. "Do you know the guy Hale punched?"

"He's a local guy, probably went to school with Cade and Hale, but I don't know their past or anything."

"I just wish I knew what set him off. Be honest with me, Stevie. Am I crazy for being interested in him? I mean, I literally thought he hated me earlier this week." She thought for a second. "Actually, he still might, I don't know."

Stevie frowned at her question. "No way. You're not crazy. Maybe a masochist or something 'cause guys like Hale are just heartache waiting to happen."

"He always seems so frustrated with me, like I'm not his type or something."

Stevie sighed, working her fingers through the tangles in her long auburn hair. "I don't know what to tell you. Any normal guy would be all over you."

"That's the thing," Kyra said, shaking her head, "Hale isn't just any normal guy. I can tell he's different."

"There's your problem. Stick with what you know." Stevie wagged her finger at Kyra like she was an errant child.

"That's kind of another problem," she said carefully. "I'm a virgin."

Stevie took a moment to process her words, but when she did, her mouth dropped open. "Are you fucking kidding me?" Stevie practically shouted. Kyra shushed her. "You don't drink, and you're a virgin?"

This was exactly the reaction Kyra was expecting. It's why she never told anyone. "I'm not a goody two-shoes. I've, like, done *stuff*. And I used to drink a lot in high school. It didn't get me anything but trouble. So I quit." Her voice trailed off as she went, but she reminded herself she was going to be different and open up with her friends. "My mom died in prison because she was a drug addict. My drinking was starting to feel a little uncontrollable, so I stopped. And I haven't done it since."

Stevie's mouth closed, and she took a moment to recover. Kyra knew she'd dumped a lot on her at once, so she waited, her hand running across old cabinets. "And you don't want to be like her?"

"That's why I'm like this," Kyra gestured to herself, pinning a cheesy, fake smile on her face. "Because I'm terrified she was a scared, depressed woman who used guys and drugs to feel happy. I don't want to be anything like her."

"Shit, Kyra. I'm sorry to hear that. And I'm a bitch for all those remarks I made about you not drinking."

"Don't feel bad. I don't tell a lot of people that."

Stevie took off her sunglasses. Her eyes were red with black circles underneath, but she looked at Kyra with sincerity. "Look, if you're a virgin, I'd tell you to back away from Hale. I mean, it's okay to have a crush, but give it some time and space, you know? Don't rush into anything with him."

"What do you mean?"

Stevie chewed on her lip. "Just that guys like Hale aren't very understanding, you know? They're not sensitive enough. They need girls they can't . . . mess up. People like us? We need the Cade Coopers of the world. Not the Hales."

Kyra wondered if her mother had found a Hale. If maybe a guy had been the one to point her toward a life full of drugs and eventually prison. Quietly, she said, "I get it."

"Just be careful is all I'm trying to say. Those kinds of guys can ruin you." The way Stevie pursed her lips and turned away to pull her glasses back on had Kyra wondering if she'd had her own run-in with a guy like Hale.

"I will. Thanks for the advice." Forcing herself to pull up a smile like everything was fine, Kyra slung her arm around Stevie as they headed down the next row of salvaged goods.

"Just remember that the next time Hale Cooper shakes his tight ass in front of you."

Kyra spent her Sunday soaking in her upstairs bathtub and enjoying the sun. She read a book, listened to Kings of Leon, and went to dinner with Stevie. By the end of the day, she'd started to feel human again, and she hadn't thought much about Hale or the fight.

But she was now. She drifted to the front bedroom, hovering at the door and staring down at the piles of albums. There was her mother's entire life, laid out before her. It was a lot to take in and a lot to handle. Her therapist probably would've told her something prolific about facing her past and accepting where she'd come from, but Kyra didn't even know what kind of past she needed to face. How could she face something she didn't even know?

Finally, she went inside the room and sat down in front of the album she'd closed earlier in the week. She picked it up and brushed off some dust before she opened the book, pausing at the picture of Lila and Florence in front of her house. She avoided looking at her grandmother, her focus solely on Lila.

She flipped to the next page, studying her mother's baby picture. She turned another page to see a laughing Garlan standing beside a young Lila in a ballet outfit. She was leggy with big teeth, laughing and twirling with her hands above her head.

Carefree. Happy. Loving life.

She slapped the book shut, her eyes stinging with tears. She didn't understand what had happened to her mother or how her seemingly perfect life had turned so sour. Kyra would always be on the outside looking in, and she was destined to never fully know her mother's struggles. All the people who had known about Lila's life refused to even acknowledge her, as if she'd never existed—as if her life was worthless.

Throughout her childhood, Aunt Carol had refused to talk much about Lila, because it often made Uncle Tom angry. Kyra had been completely isolated from her mother, and when she mourned not knowing her, she'd mourned alone. She'd never felt lonelier than when she missed her mom.

Looking at all the books around her, she counted at least twenty. It would take her a long time to go through them if she could look at only one picture at a time. That would never work.

"Maybe it's like ripping off a Band-Aid," she mused. She picked up the book and flipped to a new page. It was her mom at a dance recital, wearing the same outfit.

Kyra took a deep breath and flipped the pages, letting herself see the pictures without feeling them. All the pictures were of her mother at a young age, growing up, finding herself.

Or losing herself. However, she wanted to see it.

Feeling hollow and aching, she set the book behind her on the window seat and rose from to floor to call it a night. One album a day wasn't so bad. She could handle that.

Ignoring the film of tears blurring her vision, she walked back to her room. As she passed the bathroom, her gaze landed on the medicine cabinet. She knew what she'd hidden inside, what was waiting for her if she needed it bad enough. Unconsciously, she picked at the stack of bracelets on her wrist, her finger finding the raised scars hidden beneath.

Her cell phone rang, saving her from making a bad decision. When she walked over to where it sat charging, she saw the call was from Aunt Carol.

"Hello?"

"Kyra!"

She knew from her aunt's tone she was in trouble. It took a moment before she remembered her talk with Mrs. Walker yesterday. Rolling her eyes, Kyra said, "I take it you talked to Florence."

"Yes, I did, and I raised you better than to cuss out old ladies."

"I didn't cuss her out." She sat down on her bed, putting her head in her hand. "I just cursed while talking to her. That's different."

"Florence is very upset, and so is your Uncle Thomas. I told you when you moved down there you needed to avoid your grandmother. She's not a person you want to be enemies with."

No, if it were up to Aunt Carol, Kyra would never talk to Florence ever again. Her family just wanted to hide her away, in California, and never have to speak about her mother ever again. They wanted to bury Kyra like they buried Lila. But that wasn't going to work anymore. Kyra needed to know. And Canaan would be her home, whether Florence liked it or not.

She wished she could ask Aunt Carol about the photos, about her mom, but Kyra didn't want to fight anymore.

She huffed out a breath. "I really don't care what she thinks of me."

"Kyra! She's your grandmother!"

"She gave up that right when she disowned my mom and me."

"Now, Kyra . . ."

"Look, Aunt Carol. I don't really want to talk about this tonight. I'm exhausted."

After she said her goodbyes, she hung up the phone. Her eyes shifted back to the medicine cabinet, but she forced herself to look away. She didn't need that tonight. She was okay.

She was okay.

9

Monday morning rolled around, and Kyra woke. She sat up in bed, pushing her sleep mask onto her forehead and mussing her hair. The quietness throughout the house still disorientated her, even after a weekend of silence. She looked around her room and felt truly alone for the first time since she'd moved to the island.

Forcing herself to get out of bed and out of her slump, she went about her morning, keeping to her typical schedule. She threw in a longer workout than was necessary, but she had a lot of anxiety to burn off. She couldn't help it; she was still worried about Hale.

A knock sounded on her door before lunch. She picked her way down the stairs and crossed over the expanse of tools and dropcloths. She wasn't surprised when she opened the door and saw Cade.

"Hey," she said, her voice quiet. She stepped back and invited him in, shielding her eyes from the bright sun. He looked miserable. Dark circles stained the skin under his eyes, which were red and irritated. Even his hands shook slightly as he raked them through his hair.

"Hi," he sighed and looked around the house like he was lost.

"How are you doing?"

"I'm okay. He'll be let out on bail in a few hours. I wanted to come by here before I picked him up."

Kyra pulled Cade into a hug. He looked so confused and hurt, and the pauses before his words were more prolonged than normal. "He's going to be okay. Lots of people go to jail in their lives."

Cade shook his head when he stepped back. "Not Hale. He's had some tr-trouble . . ." He stumbled over the word. ". . . in his past. This kind of thing finds him."

Kyra frowned. She wanted to ask him what had happened in Hale's past, but she didn't want to pry. "He does have an image in this town," she said instead.

Cade ran his hand over his face. "He's not a bad guy, but everyone here judges him anyway. And it's my fault. He moved back here for me, when I started the business. I knew he would. That's why I started it. I wanted something he could focus on and be good at. I thought . . . I thought if he was here with me and Mom, we could keep him safe." Cade's eyes rose to Kyra's, his gaze pleading. "I know Friday night made him look like a bad guy, but he's really not like that. I understand if you don't want us working on your house."

"No! Cade, no. Not at all. I understand," Kyra said hurriedly.

He breathed out a long, trembling breath. When he met her eyes again, he smiled softly. "I can't tell you how much I appreciate that."

"It never crossed my mind, Cade. I promise. But why did he react like that? I've never seen him so angry." Not that Kyra had known him for long, even though she'd seen him angry plenty of times before. But Friday night at the bar had been an entirely new level of angry.

He took a long moment to prepare his words, and she waited, letting him sort through them before he spoke. "When we were kids, I was bullied a lot. I had a pretty bad stutter, and the other kids called me names and knocked me around a bit. We were just in middle school, but Hale became really protective. He ran all the mean kids off with just a glare, but sometimes he hit them. He got into so much trouble. I think it all started back then, and it's followed him around ever since. Last night when that guy from our high school got in my face and made fun of the way I talk, it just set Hale off. He lost it."

"That sounds awful, Cade. I'm so sorry you went through that." She'd thought from previous conversations with Cade that Hale had been the one to be bullied, but now she understood. Hale's behavior made a little more sense.

"I'm sorrier for Hale."

"Can I get you anything to drink? I have warm bottles of water." Her laugh was weak, but she tried.

"No." His eyes flitted around the room again. "But thank you. I just wanted to drop by and tell you work would resume tomorrow. And . . . and I wanted to apologize for Hale. I hope he didn't scare you."

"Oh, gosh no!" she said quickly. "You don't have to apologize for him, Cade. And he certainly didn't scare me. If I'd known what was happening, I probably would've punched that guy too."

Cade's smile was faint. "I appreciate that."

She realized too late she might've insulted him by saying she would've stood up for him too, as if he couldn't have done it himself. To cover her blunder, she said, "What if we all hang out tonight? I can cook dinner and we can relax over at Stevie's? I'm sure she wouldn't mind, and maybe Hale would enjoy it?"

Cade's shoulders sagged in relief. "That would be great. I've been worried about how to distract him. He'll be in an awful mood if I take him straight to his house."

"Okay!" Kyra clapped her hands together. "I'll get everything arranged. Just come over to Stevie's when you're ready."

"I really appreciate this, and I am sure Hale will too, even if he doesn't say anything."

Cade must be exhausted from having to apologize and smooth things over for his brother. She wished he didn't feel the need to do that with her. Maybe if they all became better friends everything would be more comfortable.

"Of course he will," Kyra said. "This will be fun."

She used her best chipper voice, and Cade rewarded her with a relaxed laugh. "If you say so. I better get going. I'll take him home so he can shower and change, and then we'll be over."

"Sounds great!"

He opened the door and started off her porch. He waved over his shoulder as he picked his way through her scraggly garden, which still needed work. She'd have to put that task off another day. When he'd pulled out of the driveway, she closed the door and hurried upstairs to call Stevie, who hopefully wouldn't be mad Kyra had just invited people over to her house without asking.

Kyra crossed her fingers and pressed send.

"Humph." Stevie answered the phone on the last ring. From the clatter, it sounded like she either dropped the phone or rolled out of bed. "Yeah?"

"What just happened?"

"Er . . ." The phone shuffled around making awful scratching noises in Kyra's ear. "Do you really wanna know?"

"Not really. So, guess what?"

"What?" Stevie didn't sound interested.

"Hale and Cade Cooper are coming over to your house tonight. We're going to hang out."

Stevie groaned. "Dude."

"I thought you'd be okay with it!"

"I'm not even out of bed yet," Stevie said as if that was an answer.

"It's after noon . . ."

"Exactly! Who wakes up before noon?"

Kyra adjusted her grip on the phone and walked to her closet, flicking through her shirts until she found one she wanted to wear tonight. "Come on, Stevie. Please? My house is a mess."

"Is this just a ploy to hang out with Hale?" Stevie asked, her voice suspicious.

"No! Cade and I just think it would be good for him to get out of the house tonight."

"Oh, right. Well, in that case." Stevie snorted with laughter.

"Cade is a good guy. Maybe you two would hit it off," Kyra offered. From Stevie's end of the line came a muffled voice. A man's voice. "Oh, are you not alone?"

"Uh, Troy's here."

"Again?" Kyra shook her head; her question sounded too judgmental, even to her own ears. "I mean, did you go to the bar again last night?" But that sounded just as bad.

"It was Saturday night!"

"Is every night a party?" Kyra asked, aiming for light-hearted this time. She tacked on a laugh, but it rang hollow.

"Obviously."

She heard Stevie's music crank up all the way from her house, which meant Stevie was going to get in trouble with the old ladies of the street. Her shower screeched to life, and the phone got shuffled around some more. "Fine. I'm going to get ready. You're in charge of the food. I'll provide the booze."

"You need to turn that down. Mrs. Harrison is going to call the cops on you."

"Let her try."

The phone went dead in Kyra's ear, but the conversation had gone better than she'd expected. She hurried up and dressed, picking a shirt that was slightly sheer with some high-waisted shorts. She grabbed her purse and rushed out the door.

She stopped first at the grocery store with the garage door front that stood open to the salty breeze. Inside, a reggae station played softly. Squeezing vegetables and sniffing fruit, Kyra made her way through the produce section, placing an assortment of goods in her basket. Humming to herself, she checked off the last item on her list and turned to head back to the front of the store. She looked up and gasped.

"Florence," she said.

Her grandmother stood before her, looking stern and cruel. Kyra had a flashback to the photo albums in her front bedroom, to the laughing woman who stood beside her mom with their arms wrapped around each other and smiling. They'd once had the same eyes, both summer-sky blue, but now Florence's were shrouded in ice and venom as she glared at her granddaughter.

"Don't you dare." Florence raised a trembling hand and pointed at Kyra. Her eyes darted around to make sure no one was around. "Don't you dare speak to me like you know me."

Kyra stiffened. "You made certain I would never know you when you sent my aunt and uncle away to raise me in California."

"I don't know why you bought that house or why you're here." Florence jabbed her finger in Kyra's face. "I guess to torture me by spreading your filth around town. Maybe you want some money? Would you leave if I paid you?"

Shock flooded Kyra's system, and the words to form a coherent argument were lost. She wished more than ever she could be the type of person who could come up with something witty and sharp in the moment. "I don't want your money," she managed to sputter out.

"Then what is it you want?" Two bright-red spots bloomed atop Florence's cheeks.

The desperation in her voice shocked Kyra. Her grandmother genuinely wanted her as far away as possible. "Did it ever occur to you that I might need to be here? That I might want to live in the place where my mother grew up?"

"This place has nothing to offer you. Neither does that house!"

"Is that why you left behind all those albums? Because you were tossing out your memories of her like trash?"

Florence's face paled. Kyra had struck a nerve. Perhaps her grandmother thought she'd destroyed every trace of Lila. But she'd missed some, and now Kyra had them. Had a piece of her mother, finally. It wasn't much, but a small blossom of power pulsed through her blood and she forged on.

"For the first time in my life, I'm actually figuring out what type of person my mother was and it's no thanks to you! You've bred such hatred for her within your own family that I can't get a word out of Uncle Tom about who his own sister was!"

Florence snapped. "I don't want you here!" she screamed, her voice cracking. The other shoppers had stopped perusing the food bins to openly stare at them. "Nobody wants you here. Why won't you just leave? I *hate* being reminded of her."

Tears sprung up in Kyra's eyes. "You've made it quite clear you've never wanted me."

"And you think Lila would have? If she hadn't been in prison, she would've taken care of her 'situation.' You can bet on that."

Kyra startled. Her grandmother's words stunned her. Never before had she been so vicious, so cruel. This was the woman Aunt Carol had warned Kyra about. "I hate you," she hissed. "I hope you die."

Florence gasped, her hand fluttering to her heart. "You're filthy, white trash, just like your mother!"

"I'd rather be like her than you!"

Kyra couldn't risk another second of standing in front of that awful woman without crying, and she refused to let Florence see her cry. She hurried away without a backward glance, shaking slightly as she rushed to the closest checkout counter, her fingers tugging at her bracelets like they were choke collars stifling her breathing. Her darting glances confirmed some people were still watching her.

Across the store, Florence abandoned her cart and hurried

toward the sliding glass doors. Kyra saw her grandmother swiping beneath her eyes, like she was crying as well.

"Do you know her, honey?" the clerk asked, glancing toward Florence's retreating back.

"No." Kyra flicked at the tears on her cheeks. She *hated* Florence. She didn't care one bit if the old woman was crying. She deserved to cry for what she said about her own daughter, but Kyra's heart still hurt a little too much.

"Don't feel bad, honey," the clerk said as she started ringing up Kyra's groceries. "Everyone hates her. Always have."

Kyra jolted at the clerk's words because, even in her anger, she knew they didn't quite ring true. She'd seen the pictures of Florence when Lila was younger, in the photo albums in her house. Florence had been happy, had been a part of this town once. She hadn't always fostered hate in the people of Canaan.

If she allowed herself to explain Florence's behavior, she knew it had everything to do with Lila and losing her. Nothing else could explain how the woman had gone from the smiling, happy mother in the photos to the heartless, ice-queen in front of Kyra. But tragedy wasn't an excuse to be cruel, and she refused to feel any sympathy toward the woman.

She handed over her debit card, feeling like she might be sick. When she'd paid and grabbed her bags, she hurried out of the store and to her car. For the first time since she'd arrived in Canaan, she didn't drive slow enough to enjoy the view. Driving quickly and with a singular purpose, she arrived back to Stevie's in five minutes.

"What happened?" she asked as soon as she opened the door and saw Kyra's face.

"I just ran into my grandmother. Again."

"Ah, the infamous Florence Aberdeen. It's truly amazing how terrible she is. You know when I first moved here, she mailed me a restraining order that mandated if I have a film crew here, we couldn't go within fifty yards of her." Stevie shook her head, following Kyra into the kitchen. She sat the groceries on the counter and huffed out a breath. "I mean, this island is barely bigger than fifty yards. Anyway, what did she say to you?"

"Oh, not much. Just that she didn't want me on the island or in my house. She asked how much it'd take for me to leave."

"She was going to pay you to move away?" Stevie asked, shocked. She opened a bottle of wine and poured herself a glass.

"Apparently she hates me that much."

"The good news is she's pretty old, so at least she won't be around much longer," she said with a shrug.

A snort of hysterical laughter bubbled between Kyra's lips. "That's awful." She raked her hand through her hair. "But you know what's worse? I don't want her to hate me. I literally dream about her calling me up and inviting me over. I want to be a part of the family."

Stevie sighed as she pulled out the rice from the grocery bag. "I get it. I really do, but the sooner you realize you don't need her love, the better you'll be. Maybe one day, she'll come around. Until then, you just have to be happy with you."

Kyra wished she could tell Stevie that was the exact crux of the situation: her tenuous happiness with herself. "My aunt warned me about Florence, but I didn't listen. For some reason, I thought if she just saw me here, fixing up their old house, she would understand why I had to come. You know?"

"I know, sweetie." Startling her, Stevie pulled her into a tight hug.

As they talked and started dinner, Kyra reevaluated the thought of calling the therapist. Running into her grandmother appeared to be inevitable, and clearly Kyra wasn't equipped to handle those situations well since she'd practically told an elderly woman to go die.

When the guys knocked on the door an hour later, Stevie led them into the kitchen where Kyra stood at the stove, frying the rice.

"Thanks for having us over, Stevie," Cade said, being careful with his words. He'd put some gel in his hair and wore a collared Polo shirt. "Your house is lovely."

Kyra snorted with laughter, causing Stevie to shoot her a dirty look. Her house looked anything but lovely; it was messy and disorganized. Art supplies littered the kitchen counters, and a huge drying glob of clay sat directly in the middle of Stevie's kitchen table from where she tried her hand at sculpting. From the looks of the drying lump, she would be sticking to photography.

"Yeah, sure. Whatever." She grabbed some beers from the fridge and handed them to the guys.

Kyra watched Hale from the corner of her eye. He hovered at the edge of the room by the windows, staring outside with a far-away gaze. His shoulders never relaxed, his jaw clenching and unclenching rapidly. She sensed his sharp edges, his short fuse. She'd thought they'd made progress Friday night at the bar, but he barely acknowledged her now.

When dinner was ready, the group gathered on Stevie's back deck. Plates and citronella candles lined a canary-yellow painted picnic table. The ocean waves did their dance against the sand, and across the water came the distant rumble of thunder. The air was almost chilly, and Kyra regretted her sheer shirt as she set the bowl of rice onto the table.

"Here."

She looked up at the sound of Hale's voice next to her. He stood so close she felt the proximity of his body in the form of pinpricks across her skin. Her stomach dipped with nerves.

"What?" she asked, fumbling like a schoolgirl with a crush. She looked down at his hand; he was offering her his jacket. "Oh, thanks. I'm fine."

"I saw you shiver," he said, pushing the jacket into her arms.

His tone wasn't outwardly mean, but it wasn't anything like the warmth he'd shown her at the bar. "Hey," she said quietly so the others wouldn't hear. "I'm not those guys you beat up in the bar so don't take your anger out on me. Why are you being like this?"

He stared down at her, his expression dark. She smelled the storm in the air and felt the change in air pressure. "This is who I am," he said as more thunder rolled across the ocean, and she knew he meant it.

"We better eat before we get rained on," Stevie said as she carried out more wine. She had two other bottles tucked under her arms.

Kyra glanced back at Hale, but he was already taking a seat beside Cade. Stevie plopped down the wine and promptly started opening one. As she finagled the cork, she asked, "So, Hale. How was jail? Drop any soap?"

Kyra cringed, and, across the table, Cade froze.

Stevie looked up from the bottle and blinked, confused by the silence. Before Kyra could interject, Hale said dryly, "Only for the pretty boys. By the way, One Nut Nick says 'hello.'"

Stevie's eyes widened. "One nut . . ." she mused, like she was dredging through many memories. Suddenly, her face lit up. "Holy shit tits! One Nut Nick! Damn. I haven't seen him in a long time. He used to do this thing where he . . . well, that's probably not dinner conversation, but it was like he was over compensating for the one nut thing. Not that I ever complained. I'm an equal opportunity gal."

"My gosh, Stevie." Kyra shook her head at her friend.

She just shrugged and poured herself some wine. She didn't offer anyone else a glass. "What can I say? He was a fun one."

Cade cleared his throat. "Uh, Kyra," he said. Kyra beamed at him, grateful someone was changing the subject. "How are you liking the renovations so far?"

Her eyes flicked to Hale. "They were fine once I got used to them."

"Loud and annoying, huh?" Cade grimaced in sympathy.

"Very loud and *very* annoying."

"Hey," Stevie chirped, pointing her fork at the stir fry bowl. "Pass me some of that rabbit food shit."

As the sun set, they ate and talked. Stevie turned on the lantern lights twined around her pergola and Kyra lit the citronella candles she'd brought. Thankfully, with Stevie, there were no awkward silences. As the evening wore on and she drank more and more, she seemed to open up, to come alive. She blossomed when she was drunk, becoming funnier and more vivacious as the night wore on.

Kyra laughed until her stomach hurt, and Cade didn't stutter once. She even caught Hale cracking a smile every now and then, thought he mostly stayed silent.

When it was time for the guys to leave, Cade thanked Stevie and

Kyra as Hale walked to the truck without a word. Raindrops splashed against the porch's roof slowly and deliberately. Kyra's eyes didn't leave him until he was inside the truck.

"Thanks for doing this. We enjoyed it," Cade said.

"Are you sure?" she asked, her eyes flickering back to the road. "I couldn't tell if he had a good time or not."

"He did. He just doesn't show it very well."

"Or at all," Kyra muttered as Cade left. Stevie elbowed her in the ribs.

"You're so obvious."

"What?"

"You like Hale Cooper." Stevie's wine sloshed against the glass's rim as she swayed.

"Yeah," Kyra said, rolling her eyes. She reached over to steady her friend. "And all of his personalities."

10

Kyra sat in front of her camera's tripod and mirror; a face covered in a clumpy, stinky layer of brown gunk stared back at her. A tight topknot sat high on top of her head, and she was talking to her camera in an overly perky voice with a plastered-on smile.

"This moor mud mask is *so* great to open up your pores and clean out all the gross junk that gets lodged in there, like makeup and dirt. It also helps brighten your skin and reduces redness. It's *so* great. Just really . . . great." She forced herself not to cringe at her words. In all honesty, the mask sucked and it smelled horrible, but the company who made the mask had sponsored the video, which meant they'd paid her to say she liked the product. She tilted her face this way and that to show all the angles. "Let it sit for ten minutes. I know it looks *so* gross, but trust me, you won't care once you see the results!"

She checked the clock on her laptop. She had a few more minutes until she could wash off the mask before it dried completely. She'd been waiting for a quiet moment to record this video, because the moor mud mask was extremely time sensitive and she wanted to do a time lapse during the wait before she took it off. She sighed and blew a loose tendril of hair out of her face before it got stuck to the mask.

Suddenly, she heard the front door slam from downstairs. It rattled the window in Kyra's room. Looking out her door, she saw the top of Hale's head pass by downstairs from between the banisters.

She couldn't shout down at him to keep it quiet. It would ruin her time lapse. And she couldn't get up and leave. She quickly checked the clock again. As much as she hated having to lie to her subscribers sometimes, these sponsored videos made up a huge chunk of her income. She couldn't mess this video up. Biting her lip and smiling at her camera, she tried not to think too much about how badly her bedroom stunk. There was only a minute left before she could wipe the mud off. She looked at the blinking red light on her camera and held her breath, crossing her fingers that Hale wouldn't do anything too loud downstairs.

Today was not her lucky day. From the back of the house came the blaring sounds of his stereo. She gasped and covered her ears. It was louder than ever before. She felt the vibration of the music from the floor beneath her. People on the other side of town could likely hear this music.

Not knowing what else to do, she leaned outside of the camera's view and shouted, "Hale! Turn it down!"

Nothing happened. The clock said it was time to take the mask off, but if she didn't get that music off, her video would be ruined entirely. She would rather risk messing up her time lapse than ruining the entire thing. Decision made, she raced out her door.

Hale was in the dining room, shirtless and sweating, as he destroyed a wall with a heavy sledge hammer. He swung again and plaster flew in bits from the gaping hole he'd made. Through her rage, she sincerely hoped they'd agreed to actually tear down the wall and Hale wasn't just taking out his anger on her house.

She stomped into the room and unplugged the stereo. The silence echoed as loudly as the music had. Hale whirled around, his expression murderous. He flung the sledge hammer to the ground.

"What the hell?" he shouted.

His pale-green eyes sparked wild with rage. Every muscle on his bare chest stood out in rigid salute. Even like this, Kyra had to admit he looked hot with his black and gray tattoos streaked with sweat and dirt, but he didn't hold a candle to her anger.

"You ruined my video!"

Hale noticed her mask just then. At the same moment, she remembered it too. She must look like an idiot, but the thought only pissed her off more.

"Do you know how hard this was to make?" She gestured crazily at her mask.

"Looks like you rubbed your face in cow shit," he said with a sneer. He crossed his arms over his chest.

"It's not. It's very expensive mud, actually. The company paid me to make this video!"

"So make another."

Her mouth fell open in shock. She sputtered, "Make another? Do you listen to anything I say? This video was sponsored, and the company only sent me enough for one mask!"

"It's on your face. What's the big deal?"

"The big deal? Can't you tell?" She gestured wildly to her face.

"It's not readily apparent."

"It's dry!" Kyra shouted, throwing her hands up in frustration. "I was supposed to take it off while it was still wet!"

"You're right. That makes complete sense." He bent and picked up his sledge hammer. "Probably should have taken it off instead of coming down here and yelling at me."

He went to plug in his stereo again, but Kyra blocked his way. "Are you serious?"

Hale looked around like she was talking to someone else. "Makes sense, doesn't it?"

"Ugh! What is your problem?"

"What's *your* problem?"

"I don't have a problem! *You* have the problem. I thought we were being nice to each other now. What happened? Do you hate me that much?"

A line formed between his eyebrows. He drew back slightly. "I don't hate you."

"Then why do you act like it?"

"Do I?" He seemed genuinely confused. "I'm just in a bad mood, okay? So back off."

"I'm *so* sorry you're in a bad mood," she said sarcastically. "Trust me when I say I really *hate* that for you, but my videos are important to me."

"My music is important to me."

"So keep it turned down!"

"I like it loud."

It was all too much. Hale Cooper was the most infuriating and stubborn man she'd ever met. Kyra howled in frustration.

"It ruins my videos!"

"I hate that for you," he said, his expression looking way too cocky for her taste. He was making fun of her; he thought she was a joke. Then he actually laughed at her, and she saw red.

She wanted, no, she *needed* to bring him down a peg or two. She wanted to knock him on his ass for once.

While he was still laughing, she launched herself up his tall frame. She was athletic and just tall enough to make it work. Her body hit his, and he staggered back into the wall he had been bent on destroying moments before, sending bits of plaster raining down on them. He struggled to catch her in his shock, but she latched her legs around his hips. She raked her hands behind his head and jerked his face to her.

Her lips crushed against his, but even before they connected, her anger shifted to something more, something wilder and warmer inside her body. When he opened his mouth and she flicked her tongue inside, all the heat in her body flooded between her legs. He tasted like coffee, which made the kiss literally delicious.

She'd completely forgotten the reason for her anger. Forgotten everything but Hale and his kiss.

His hands tightened on her waist, and he kissed her back after he'd recovered from his shock. She sucked in a breath at his attack against her mouth, but she'd barely recovered when he took control of the kiss and deepened it.

He was a fantastic kisser, even if it was rough, just like she'd imagined. He bruised her lips between his and thrust his tongue deep in her mouth. She'd kissed plenty of boys back before she learned kissing boys made her feel like she was losing herself, but none of those kisses had been like this; never before had she been so happy to be lost in someone else.

She couldn't keep up, with the kiss or her spiraling heartbeat, so she gave into him.

When he'd claimed every part of her mouth, he pulled back. His eyes gleamed with the hard lust she felt pressing into her. He panted as his chest heaved against her.

But Kyra couldn't hold back the laugh. It bubbled out of her mouth until she threw back her head and howled with it. Hale's grip tightened, and when she looked back at him, his expression turned thunderous.

"You laughing at me?" he growled.

Kyra managed a nod as tears streamed down her face. When he sat her down, she bent over double and pointed at him as she laughed.

"*What the hell?*"

"Your face!" Kyra gasped, clutching her side.

Hale's face was covered with thick, crumbling chunks of the mud mask. He reached up and confirmed it. His fingers pulled away with a dark brown, cakey sludge. "This shit stinks!"

"I know!" Kyra howled. "It really does!"

"You don't look much better," Hale said as he tried to wipe off the mask. He looked so indignant that she lost it again. He watched with a glower, but apparently it was too much for him too. The tiniest form of a smile spread across his lips and brightened his eyes.

It was so unbelievable that Kyra's laughter died off. She stared at him in awe as he smiled at her, his shoulders vibrating with his own slight laughter. He was the most amazing thing she'd ever seen. His smile, this smile, was so perfect. Everything she'd felt that night at the bar came flooding back.

He finally noticed she wasn't laughing anymore. His smile fell away and his eyes darkened once again. "What are you staring at?"

"You," she breathed.

"Why?"

Kyra shook her head at him. He let everyone assume the worst of him with their judgments, but if he would just try a little harder and let people see who he really was, they would see how amazing he could be. She felt like one of the privileged few to have broken through his rough exterior, and she betted he didn't give away those smiles often.

She would treasure every one.

She grinned. "Because you're a beautiful person, Hale Cooper. And for some ungodly reason, you let everyone in this town think you're an asshole, but now I know different."

He didn't seem to know what to say. Finally, he opened his mouth to speak right when a thumping knock came from the front door. She held up her other hand.

"Hold that thought."

She pulled out of his grip and jogged over to the front door. She threw it open with a smile that quickly fell away.

"Hello, Kyra."

"Florence," she managed.

Her grandmother stood in all her nasty glory on the sagging front porch. Her graying hair was in a perfect, prim bun. Even her shirt was buttoned to the topmost button, which suffocated Kyra just to look at.

"What in Heaven's name is on your face?" Florence asked, her lip curling up in disgust.

"Oh." Kyra wiped some of the mud from her face. "It's a mud mask. Why are you here?"

Florence sniffed and peered around Kyra into the house. She instantly spotted Hale standing at the stairs. "I've come to offer you this money to leave."

Her grandmother stuck out an envelope stuffed with cash, waving it at Kyra when she didn't take it immediately. It had to be a decent amount of money; the envelope bulged with the thickness of a brick. But Kyra crossed her arms over her chest and said, "I'm not going anywhere."

Florence laughed, the sound fit to come from an evil sea-witch. "I've been very generous. It's more than you deserve."

After the confrontation yesterday with her, Kyra's nerves felt fried. She didn't know if she was going to start crying or screaming at her grandmother. "I'm not leaving. This is my home now."

"You don't belong here," she hissed, leaning in close to Kyra's face. Her perfume was musty and too floral, and Kyra resisted the urge to sneeze into her face.

"Excuse me," Hale said from behind Kyra. She stepped aside as he walked to the door. "But it seems slightly rude to tell someone she doesn't belong in the house she just bought."

Florence looked Hale up and down, taking in his tattoos and piercings. Her judgment was perfectly clear on her face. Then she noticed the mud, and her dangerous gaze flicked back to Kyra. "I should've known you'd be just like your mother. She was a slut too."

Hale took a step forward, but Kyra put up her arm and braced it against the door frame to block him. "How could you say that about your own daughter?" she asked, completely shocked and repulsed by Florence.

"It's the truth." She wrinkled her nose at Kyra and Hale. "You're both trash, and you *will* be leaving." She jabbed a pointed, sharp-nailed finger into Kyra's chest as she spoke, emphasizing each word. Kyra cringed but didn't step back, though the skin over her sternum smarted. When Hale went tense behind her, she placed her hand on his chest to keep him back, which made her grandmother laugh again. "What are you going to do? Hit an old woman?"

"If she deserves it," Hale growled.

Florence's smug look fell away. She stepped back, looking truly afraid of him now. She hurried down the steps still clutching her thick envelope, but called back to Kyra, "One way or another, you will be leaving this place!"

With those words, Florence slid into her swanky white Cadillac sedan that idled at the curb and roared away, leaving Kyra standing in her open doorway, rubbing at the bruised skin on her chest. She didn't know why she'd expected anything different from her grandmother. Never once had the woman shown any interest in her. Not one birthday or Christmas card. Not even a toy doll.

She slammed the door a little harder than necessary before she turned to Hale. "You wouldn't really have hit her would you?"

Hale's voice was flat. "No."

"Good, because if I'm ever moved to violence, I want to be the one to slap some sense into her."

Her words must have surprised him. He let out a snort of laughter, and she won another rare, almost-there smile. "I'll keep that in mind. Did she hurt you?"

She tried not to be flustered by his eyes on her chest, but after yet another encounter with her grandmother, she couldn't keep her voice from trembling as she answered, "I'm fine. It doesn't hurt." She forced herself to lower her hand. "Much."

"Right," he said, clearly not believing her. "So that thing was your grandmother?" he asked. "Someone hide the puppies because she'd give Cruella de Vil a run for her money."

"You grew up in Canaan, but you still didn't realize that Florence Aberdeen was my grandmother?"

"I make it a point not to get to know these people."

"Clearly."

"Kyra . . ." Hale started, his tone changing to a more serious one. She knew he wanted to talk about the kiss, to possibly chalk it off as a heat-of-the-moment thing. She saw the uncertainty shifting in his eyes. But she couldn't take hearing that right now, not on top of everything else.

She needed to clear her head first, and all she could think about was getting to the water. She imagined the cool, salty kiss of the ocean on her flushed skin. If she didn't go outside right now, she couldn't trust herself to not open the medicine cabinet and pull out the blade.

The desperation—a tug between wanting the pain and wanting to run from it—was so thick in her throat that Kyra knew she had to call the therapist as soon as she returned from the water. She vowed to do it. Canaan Island might be able to heal her, but it would take a professional to help Kyra get over her grandmother.

"I'm going out," she said quickly.

Before Hale opened his mouth to argue, she'd already started bounding up the stairs to her room to change. She ripped her shirt over her head before she even slammed the door shut in her bedroom. Her clothes fell like stones to the floor as she hurried to find a clean bathing suit and wash the rest of the disgusting mud mask off her face. When she came back down the stairs a couple minutes later, Hale had washed the mud off his face as well and returned to the bottom of the stairs. He wasn't done with their conversation, but she didn't pause long enough for him to bring it up again.

"Surfing?"

Kyra flashed a smile as she darted around him and jogged toward the back of the house. Hale ambled behind her. "Yep," she called. "Want to come?"

She shoved the screen door open and let it slam behind her. Her favorite board sat tucked away on the rack, freshly waxed and waiting for her. Without another thought but getting to the water, she grabbed it and hurried down the back steps.

"I'll pass. Have fun."

Kyra flipped her hair over her shoulder and looked back. Hale stood inside the screen door, which made his features darker as he brooded.

"Always," she said, forcing her smile to be bright and breezy as the beach around her, even as her heart wrenched inside her chest and she wanted nothing more than to bury herself in her bed and cry until all thoughts of her vicious grandmother were gone.

When she turned back to the water, her smile fell away. She walked through the garden and out the gate. Her mind eased at the quick flash of heat when she stepped onto the sand, and the pounding of the waves overpowered the ringing in her ears. Her heartbeat slowed as she took another deep breath full of moist, salty air. The tension coiled tightly inside her chest released. And that was even before her body slid into the water.

She waded farther out until the surf started getting choppy. Her board slipped beneath her like a rough, calloused hand skimming down her body. She filled her lungs with air and pressed down just as a slight wave built above her. Then she was under, and it was miraculous.

The power surged around her. She opened her eyes and blinked, seeing the point of the board in front of her and the press of the water around her, cocooning and holding her. It felt safe as houses under the ocean as the waves crashed above her. She kept still on her board as it found its way back to the surface, and when they emerged, Kyra slung her hair back and shook the water from her face.

This was love, she thought. This was the safest kind of love possible.

She could die out here, she knew. The ocean could take her under and not bring her back up. It was a wicked woman, a beautiful kiss of death. Kyra paddled behind the break of the surf and sat up, bobbing along with the now peaceful waves. Even with its great capacity to kill, the ocean could be the biggest sigh of relief. And she liked that: the wavering, blurring line between calm and storm.

The swell was down today. It wouldn't be fun surfing, but Kyra didn't need that right now. She just needed to sit out here and feel infinite. She needed to feel like the ocean was taking out the darkness and clearing away the bad things pressing in around her, loosening more of the coils wrapped up inside of her.

She stayed out there for a while, sitting or riding waves whenever she felt like it. She paddled a lot against the current. Fatigue caused her arms to tremble, but even that felt familiar and safe. The brine in her nose smelled like home. Her hair was half dry and half wet, and even its mess seemed right.

Only when she could breathe and not feel pain did she let a wave bring her in. When she stood up, holding her board beneath her arm, and waded in, her smile came easy and free. The tension that tried to crush her had disappeared, and she felt buoyed, bobbing along the surface just as she had on the water.

She was fixed, and she didn't need the blade in the medicine cabinet to accomplish the peace she felt now.

Maybe she'd been wrong earlier. Maybe this island could really fix anything, even her grandmother. After a couple hours in the ocean, it was like the argument had never happened. Like she'd been perfectly happy all day. Feeling like this, she felt foolish for thinking she needed to return to therapy.

She was fine.

She set her board on the porch and went inside the house, expecting Hale to be working, but he'd gone and his absence turned the house into a hollow shell. As she walked back up to her room, she wondered why she'd kissed him.

Her primary intention to shut him up had quickly shifted when she realized she wanted to *keep* kissing him. She'd never done anything that felt so good, and if she was being honest, kissing him had felt right too.

She went into her bathroom and peeled off her suit. The water screeched to life in the ancient claw-foot tub. While it filled, Kyra stared at herself in the mirror.

She leaned closer, narrowing her eyes as if she could see past her reflection to the woman within. She thought she did that with Hale. She saw a man whose honesty looked brutal and strange to others. He told the story of his life on his arms for all to see: his wounds and triumphs, all forever cast in ink. Kyra hid her secrets deep beneath shimmering blue eyes, a toned body, and a bright smile.

She wondered what it would be like to bear a secret on her skin, to pass a stranger on the street and let him see a mark on her body that told a story of her. She swallowed, her eyes widening. Suddenly, all she wanted was to give away a secret.

She hopped in the bath and washed off, bypassing all her normal products and just let the water cleanse her again. By the time she'd gotten dressed, her heart hammered against her ribs. Before she chickened out, she pounded down the stairs and out the front door.

She glanced at Stevie's house only briefly before she headed to her Jeep. She wanted to do this alone.

She wanted to see if she *could* do this alone.

11

"Let me get this straight. You got a tattoo *without* me?"

Stevie held a glass of wine in one hand and a spatula slathered in icing in the other. "Yeah, but I didn't leave you out on purpose or anything."

"Oh, good. That makes me feel better." Stevie huffed and turned back to the doughy glob of cupcakes in front of her. "Something about this doesn't look right," she mused.

"Did you cook them?"

"Of course I cooked them," she said, rolling her eyes. Suddenly, she set down her wine glass and turned back to Kyra. Her eyes had gone serious and, almost as if she'd turned it off, the sheen of alcohol had disappeared too. "Why did you get that?"

"What do you mean?"

"You know exactly what I mean. That tattoo makes it seem like you have problems, but you're a girl who acts like she doesn't have a care in the world except for getting Hale Cooper to kiss her."

"We can mark that one off the list because I kissed him yesterday." She offered a smile, but Stevie wasn't falling for it.

"Why that tattoo, Kyra? What's wrong?"

Something in her voice, whether it was her sincere concern or just her tenacity to know the truth, made Kyra's eyes prickle. Not enough to form tears, but she still had to fight down the urge. She flipped over her right wrist and looked at the tattoo she'd gotten yesterday evening.

A small, thin anchor adorned the pale hollow of her wrist. Beneath it, the words 'I will not sink' were inked in a fine, swirling script.

"I have problems too," she said, meeting Stevie's eyes.

"You're not your mother," her friend whispered.

"Sometimes," she said, biting her lip, "I think I have all her worst traits and none of the good. If I had the good, maybe Florence would love me."

Stevie cringed. "That's like me thinking if I do one more reality show, sell my life's memories one more time, that my parents will love me for me and not the dollar sign I represent. It's useless, Kyra."

"How do you deal with it?"

She lifted a long finger toward the wine glass on the counter. "The only way I know how."

"I know a way too," Kyra said, the skin beneath her bracelets itching. On one wrist, she'd permanently reminded herself to not sink beneath the weight of her problems, but on the other, she bore the proof of being a sunken ship already.

Stevie scrutinized her face as if she could pick apart her truths. She studied for so long Kyra thought maybe she really was. Finally, Stevie blinked, and the seriousness vanished. She went back to her counter and picked up her wine, making Kyra think the conversation was over—until Stevie spoke again.

"You hide your problems well. Too well." Stevie looked up. "Do you think I hide mine well?"

"No," Kyra answered honestly. They bore their pain in very different ways.

"Me, neither. I guess I can thank my parents for that," Stevie said with a dark laugh. "No more lies though, okay? Let's just be us with our problems unhidden when we're together. It's too much work to fake it all the time, and I'm not into manual labor."

Kyra's smile was real this time. It was shy and small and very hopeful. For a second, she thought now would be a good time to talk to Stevie about her drinking, which Kyra had started to suspect was a bigger issue than Stevie let on. They were being open and honest, and so very, very close to speaking about the darkness within them, but the moment passed, and Stevie cranked up the music after she'd tossed the cupcakes in the trash.

"We can just eat the icing," she announced. She hopped up on the counter and dipped her spatula into the frothy glob. "So, you kissed Hale Cooper."

Kyra took a spoon from the countertop and dunked it into the bowl. "Yeah."

"Don't just 'yeah' me. Give it to me good."

The icing tasted a little too sweet, but Kyra took another nibble anyway and licked her lips. "We kissed yesterday. And it was . . ." She didn't really know what it was; she needed to figure that out herself. "It was honest, I guess."

Stevie plunked her spatula back into the bowl, sending a glob of icing over the rim. "You're not going to tell me kissing him was just 'honest.' If you tell me that's all it was, I'll burn down your house."

Kyra figured a girl like Stevie probably knew how to go about burning down a house, so she didn't press her luck. "He came alone to work on the house and started playing his music too loud, but I was trying to make a sponsored video. I had a time-sensitive mud mask on and the sound of his radio was ruining my time lapse. It did ruin it," she added with a sigh. "I was pissed. I went downstairs and started yelling at him, but he ignored me. I wanted to get his attention." She shrugged.

Stevie mimicked her shrug and made a face. "*I wanted to get his attention*," she repeated in an awful rendition of Kyra's voice. "*So I kissed him*."

Kyra shook her head at her friend and laughed. She took another bite of frosting. "I got his attention for sure. And that's what I meant by being honest. I thought about kissing him because I knew it would shut him up. And I did it. I just . . . *did it*. And that felt almost better than the kiss." Stevie raised her eyebrows at her words. "I mean the feeling made the kiss even better. I never do things like that. I'm not that type of girl. If it means putting myself in a position where I could be rejected, I don't do it. But after that kiss . . . I kind of want to do it again."

"Oh, girl, you're so screwed." Stevie grimaced in sympathy and picked her spatula back up. "So I'm going to start with the most obvious question: Is he a good kisser?"

Kyra bit her lip and nodded. "It was probably the best kiss I've ever had. I had my legs around his waist—"

"What?" Stevie screeched, throwing her hands in the air and flinging icing everywhere. "That's so *not* just a kiss! You pounced on the poor guy! You're a freaking animal!"

"I did," Kyra agreed, smiling rather dreamily. "I jumped onto him, and he caught me. I could feel the muscles in his arms go all tight to hold me. And then I kissed him, but that didn't last long."

"He stopped it?" Stevie asked, slightly breathless.

"No. He starting kissing me back, and it was like . . ."

"Like what?" she yelled.

"Like he needed to taste every part of my mouth. Like maybe he'd wanted to kiss me too, but I was the one who did it first. It kind of felt like he wanted every inch of me, but all he had was my mouth. So he took it. All I could do was just hold on." Kyra shrugged when she was finished.

Stevie was wide-eyed with her mouth parted slightly. She blinked as if waking up from a dream. Then she shivered. "I'm good to go for another few months." She squeezed her legs together and made a face. "Oh, yeah. That'll do."

Kyra's laugh bubbled up from deep in her chest. It was the most authentic kind, the kind she couldn't control. It overtook her until she doubled over with the force of it. When she looked up, she saw Stevie laughing the same kind of laugh.

"That's good to know," Kyra said when she could speak again. She wiped at the tears beneath her eyes.

When she'd recovered too, Stevie asked, "I don't mean to be the buzzkill here, but what are you going to do about him? Because making out is pretty much the exact opposite of steering clear of him."

"I don't know. We were talking about it, but then my

grandmother came by."

"Oh, good grief. No wonder you went and got inked. I guess we're lucky it doesn't say, '*screw you all,*' or something."

"Not quite."

"You've got to deal with your crazy-ass grandma."

That killed Kyra's good mood. She stared into the bowl of frosting. "I have no idea what to do about Florence. She's awful."

Stevie crinkled her nose like she'd smelled something sour. "Yeah, she's a real piece of shit. And I hate being disrespectful toward old people . . ." She paused, considering her words. "Just kidding. I hate old people. I hope she kicks the bucket soon."

"Stevie!" Kyra sputtered, choking on the big bite of frosting she'd just taken. "That's terrible!"

Stevie shrugged, clearly unconcerned. "Eh."

Their silence stretched out comfortably. Together they cleaned up Stevie's baking disaster, discovering she hadn't even turned on the oven, hence the unbaked cupcakes. That ensued another round of bellyaching laughter. Kyra was glad she'd met Stevie, who was possibly the only person on the island who would accept her and all her darkness. Emotions weighed on her, which didn't make her crazy; it just made things tough.

After she said goodbye to Stevie, she felt happy enough that she figured today was as good as any. She crossed over to her house and locked up before piling into her Jeep. She couldn't avoid it forever. Sitting behind the wheel with the engine off, she evaluated herself.

Her afternoon with Stevie had left her feeling strong. Happy. Peaceful. She could do this. The Jeep's engine turned over, and she pulled onto the street.

She found the cemetery easily because she'd passed it on her way onto the island the first day. On that day, she'd forced her eyes straight ahead, not trusting herself to look out the window as she'd driven past. But today she parked in front of the gates that read "Canaan's Cemetery."

She'd never been afraid of cemeteries. Actually, she'd always admired their beauty; they had a profound quietness about them. Something about the stillness drew Kyra—and that was the very reason she rarely let herself go to one. Happy people didn't hang out in cemeteries.

She passed through the gates and walked down the cracked pavement of the narrow road situated beneath a multitude of towering trees, which were likely hundreds of years old with their reaching branches weaving above her head. Spanish moss dangled from almost every branch and cast wavering, veil-like shadows across the ground. The smell of flowers and pollen tickled deep inside her nose, but the trees created a coolness that soothed the itch in her throat.

She threaded her way to the center of the cemetery, marveling at the crumbling statues as she passed. All the graves sat above ground, which made her feel as if she was truly walking amongst the dead and not just above them.

The breeze ruffled through the loose strands of hair at the back of her neck, and a clammy sweat slickened across her skin, even with the shade. She swallowed to wet her drying mouth.

In the center of the cemetery was the Aberdeen crypt. It was elaborate and Victorian, with an antique hanging lock on the front stone door. Not like she wanted to go in anyway. She already knew her mother wouldn't be buried inside with the other family members. Fury clenched her heart at the thought. Even in death,

Florence had insisted on estranging her daughter. To deny someone ever-lasting peace seemed like the ultimate form of disrespect. After all her mother had gone through, she deserved to at least be buried with her family, to find the love she'd missed during her short life.

Kyra walked around the crypt to the side where a wrought-iron fence with heaps of green vines entangled around the bars enclosed a small statue garden. The vegetation grew so dense and untamed, she couldn't see inside, but the heavy gate was unlocked, so she heaved it open and entered.

A lone granite grave presided in the center of the garden.

Her feet carried her forward of their own accord. Inside the garden, the temperature dropped ten degrees from the tall fencing casting a perpetual shady darkness into the garden. Tall statues of angels stood at each corner of the garden, their faces tortured in everlasting sadness. A path wove to a side door of the crypt, while another path led to the front gate. Kyra doubted the paths were ever used, but it was typical in small, Southern communities like Canaan to bury suicides at a crossroads, which was formed by the paths.

Kyra settled her hand on the icy top of the grave.

She's in here, Kyra thought. Right beneath her hand.

She pulled her hand away. Her eyes settled on the engraving on top of the lid, which was just an elaborate, scrolling L. No dates. No name.

The breeze rustled through the trees above her, spreading chill bumps down her arms and causing tears to inexplicably prick at the back of her eyes. She felt *something*, and the sensation tightened her heart and twisted her stomach. Looking around as if a spirit might materialize from the depths of the vines, she held her breath, a shiver working down her spine like a cold finger on her skin. She stood still as long as she could, but the feeling became too powerful. Unable to stand it any longer, she hurried outside the garden and back onto the little road that wove back to her Jeep.

She didn't look back as she rushed away, wrapping her arms around her middle to warm herself. She wasn't scared; she just couldn't handle standing in her mother's lonely garden anymore. It felt purposefully solemn and forlorn, with its sad statues of weeping angels and crossing paths. The grass was kept tidy, but there were no flowers. Everywhere else had tons of bright, blooming perennials, as if trying to keep the cemetery purposefully cheerful. But her mother's garden had been cold and dark, with only crying stone for comfort.

It was the first time she'd ever visited her mother's grave. She'd been too young to attend her burial. She hadn't come in college because she'd been sorting through too many of her own issues. Now that she was here, she wished she could've stayed longer, but she knew the length of time at a grave didn't make one a good daughter.

On her way to her Jeep, Kyra spotted a young woman bent over a flower bed teeming with vibrant rose bushes. As she passed, the woman looked up and locked eyes with Kyra.

Her hair, swept into a braid over her shoulder, was startlingly pale, almost silver beneath her wide-brimmed gardening hat. She wore a vintage yellow halter-top dress, like something out of the forties, even though soil stained the knees where she knelt. But it was her eyes that shocked Kyra the most. She'd never seen anything like them. They were so light blue, they almost looked like ice.

Kyra shivered and hurried on. Had she just seen a ghost? What else could explain the old clothes and eerie eyes?

She hopped into her Jeep and cranked up the heat until the chill in her bones disappeared. Her eyes kept scanning the cemetery's entrance, but she didn't catch another sight of the strange, light-eyed woman. Grappling through her purse, she found her phone and punched in the number to the new therapist on Canaan.

She finally made an appointment for next Wednesday.

After hanging up the phone, she felt ready to drive. She started the car, feeling its throaty rumble beneath her as she looked out the windshield. The cemetery looked like a hidden oasis through the gates. It didn't quite fit with the bright town of Canaan beyond it.

Kyra forced herself to look away to back out of her parking spot. She'd be back, she promised herself. And she would never forgive Florence for burying her only daughter in the saddest spot of the cemetery.

12

Kyra opened her house's door to find a slew of workers installing her new, energy-efficient, hurricane-resistant windows and sliding glass doors while the plumbing and electrical was brought up to code. All of the men waved and called hellos to her as she passed through. She smiled and chatted with Chevy for a moment, but her eyes instantly found Hale. He nailed a piece of framing for a new window and looked back at her. Their eyes met, and she offered a small smile. His expression immediately turned stormy, like he was thinking about their kiss yesterday.

She looked away and hurried up the stairs. Instead of turning toward her room, she went into the front bedroom, where the albums of her mother remained spread out across the floor. Without pausing, she took her position in the window seat with the photo book she'd already started.

The pictures were likely typical to anyone else. Kyra noticed all the usual as she slowly flipped through—soccer games and swim parties. Halloween costumes and smiling over birthday cakes. It was all there: a whole life. It looked so happy. Florence smiled at her daughter, her love readily apparent. Garlan likely took most of the pictures, a proud father. Uncle Thomas was in many, smiling and teasing his little sister.

Kyra closed the book and leaned her head back, thinking about how many mistakes it must take to ruin that kind of love. She thought a family's love was unbreakable, especially a mother's love. Aunt Carol had tried hard to replicate it, but it had never fit quite right inside the hole in Kyra's heart.

There seemed to be no love in Florence now. Her eyes were cold and bitter. Her mouth twisted into a condescending sneer when she looked at her granddaughter, making Kyra wonder if Florence saw Lila when she stared at her. It'd certainly seemed that way in the grocery store, but Kyra had been right about Florence. She hadn't always been this way, even though the people of Canaan seemed to only remember her as a cold-hearted bitch. The pictures in Kyra's lap told another story.

A story before the love between a mother and a daughter had broken.

If she allowed herself to be honest, Kyra knew living through that kind of breaking and fracturing within a family would turn anyone into an ice queen. Maybe Florence had only showed tough love to her daughter for so long that she'd forgotten any other way. Or maybe she'd purposefully cut her daughter out of the family, like digging out rot in a tree, to remove the bad for the health of the good. The thoughts spiraled through Kyra's mind until her head lolled against the wall and she fell asleep.

When she woke, the sky had darkened outside and her back was as stiff as the wall she'd slept against. Blurrily, she set the album aside and picked her way through the trail of books. She eased the door closed behind her, as if there were spirits inside the room she didn't want to wake.

Maybe there were.

Only then did Kyra hear the low thrum of music from downstairs. Frowning, she wondered if Hale had left his stereo on. With a sigh, she headed down the stairs and to the back of the house. She found the source of the music in the back bathroom where she'd exposed herself not so long ago. Hale worked inside, tiling the back wall of the shower around the brand-new tempered window that had finally closed in the gaping hole.

"I didn't realize you would be working so late," she said. He didn't act surprised or even look back at her when she spoke.

"Needed to get this done." He carefully layered the back of the tile with a thick paste and placed it on top of tiny plastic spacers. Only when it was secure did he look back at her. Instantly, he frowned. "What's wrong?"

"Um . . ." Her eyes darted around the room, searching for a mirror to see the flaw he'd found in her face, the one that showed her sadness. "Nothing?"

"You look like you've been crying." He said the words like they were an accusation before bending over and picking up another tile, slapping more stuff on the back.

"Oh, I'm fine." *Liar.* "Just took a nap upstairs."

He placed the tile and added some more spacers on top of it. Then he picked up another one. "Do you know what kind of tile this is?" He held it up for her to see.

"Subway tile?" she offered, confused at the turn of the conversation.

"It is. But this is new subway tile." He turned slightly in the shower and tapped on a tile already on the wall. "This is old tile. When we demoed this room, we were careful to leave the original work. I'm only replacing what I have to or what was already broken."

She remembered Cade telling her something about keeping the original tile work in the bathrooms. They'd even worked carefully to keep the original floors throughout the house. She'd agreed it was the best thing to do to keep the original charm of the house.

"Okay," she said, hesitantly.

"It's harder work, and it takes longer, which is why I'm still in your bathroom this late. But it's good work. It's worth it."

"Why?" she asked quietly. She wasn't stupid; she knew where this was going.

"Because it's original, Kyra. It's a pain in my ass to order replica tiles to match the originals perfectly. It sucks to feather in these new tiles in a way that isn't obvious they're new. You don't ever want to take away from the original work. These tiles have been here for generations. Never destroy what's real or authentic in a house."

"I get it," she said.

He bent close and studied the angle of a tile, tapping the corner with his finger to adjust it infinitesimally. Finally, he said, "No, you don't."

"No, I do. You're calling me fake again." She forced the words out through her gritted teeth. "But you shouldn't judge me. You don't know anything about me."

He set down the tile he'd just picked up and stepped out of the shower he'd been working in. He approached her with a hooded look in his eyes, making Kyra wonder if he was going to yell at her or kiss her. When he was a foot away, he stopped, and she had to resist the urge to step back. The richness of his sweat enveloped her, clouding her mind.

"Cade told me about your mom and why you bought this house."

She blinked in surprise. She hadn't expected that, and she couldn't help but feel a flare of annoyance with Cade. "Oh."

He opened his mouth to speak when he caught sight of her tattoo. Kyra tried to pull away, but he easily caught her arm in his grip. Carefully, he lifted her wrist and studied her fresh ink. It was still raised and sore, and his warm breath across it made the tips of her fingers tingle. Finally, he let her wrist go.

"Don't be mad at him," he went on, his eyes searching her face. "I asked him to tell me. I wanted to understand you better, and it worked. At least you're not some stupid girl with a fake smile. I would've hated to be into a girl like that."

"Into a girl like that?"

"Yeah, Kyra. You're a beautiful girl. Any guy would be interested." Hale shook his head, his eyes falling to the tiles stacked at their feet. "But that's not the point. You have these moments, and they're normally when you're really pissed at me and start cussing like a biker, where I see the real Kyra. That's the girl I'm interested in. Not the faker."

She didn't really know what to say. The words, fake or mean, didn't come to her. She stared at Hale and wanted to cry.

"Here. I'll start." He sighed and rolled out the muscles in his shoulders, like he needed to warm up for the words. "My mom's cancer has spread to her blood. She doesn't have much longer to live," he said quietly.

She sucked in a breath. "I'm sorry—"

"I'm terrified of losing her. Every time my phone rings, my heart feels like it's about to explode in my chest because I *know* it's the hospital calling about her. I live in fear every day." His words were quiet as he reached an arm around her waist to draw her closer. "Now, your turn. Be honest with me. Let me in."

"I'm not honest with a lot of people." There was a hitch in her voice she tried to cough out. Honesty hurt. It forced her to feel the sharp edges inside her and made her crave a certain pain that made her wrists itch. There was a form of safety in hiding behind her smile and fake feelings. It saved her.

"What's really wrong, Kyra?"

Something in his voice kept her rooted in place, because he really wanted to know. She stood before him, her rage and sadness coursing through her, and she'd never felt so naked in her life.

"I went to my mother's grave today for the first time."

Hale's eyes were unblinking as he studied her; the silent moment lasted so long she shifted uncomfortably. Finally, she had to look away from him, her eyes going back to the floor and her shoulders slumping. She needed to sleep, to fall away, or to find the blade in her medicine cabinet. She went to leave when he caught her chin in his gentle grip. His hands were rough against her skin as he turned her face toward him.

"You miss her?"

"Can you miss someone you never knew?"

"Probably worse than someone you did." He leaned in until his mouth was inches from hers. Their chests touched, and Kyra's nipples hardened at the contact of his muscles. "Thank you for telling me."

His mouth lowered to hers, and she gave in to him. Her knees sagged beneath her, but he held her tight against his chest with one hand. His other twined through the hair at the back of her neck and pressed her closer against him.

The kiss was softer than their first one, more intimate. He seemed to pull the sorrow from her like he was wiping her clean. She opened herself to him and let him kiss her and hold her and console her. The thick stubble along his chin and jaw rasped against her skin, but his lips were smooth and coaxing. She relaxed into his hold and echoed the stroke of his tongue with hers.

They kissed until every inch of her sparked electric and a trembling started in her bones. The flutter in her stomach sank low until she squeezed her legs together to relieve the ache building there. Only then did Hale pull away. Her lips stayed parted as she let out a small whoosh of air.

Kyra pushed her hair out of her face with a shaky hand. Her smile at Hale was tentative at best. His hand left the back of her neck and traced a tingling path down the length of her collarbone.

He released her and stepped away to go back to his tile work. Before he could reach for one, she bent and picked up a tile for him.

"Can you show me how to do this?" she asked, gesturing toward the wall he was repairing.

Hale smiled. Not his sarcastic one or the mean one when he knew he'd caught her in a lie. It was his true smile, and Kyra couldn't stop herself from grinning back.

"Sure," he said. "But it's your bathroom if you mess it up."

13

Thursday evening, Kyra and Stevie invited the guys over to Stevie's house for dinner again. They sat beneath her pergola, with strands of twinkling lights wrapped above their heads and the ocean at their backs. A table full of salad and spaghetti spread out before them, including lots of wine and candles.

"So instead of uploading the video I meant to," Kyra was saying, "I accidently used one with almost the exact same file name. It was just some camera test where I happened to be singing a Lady Gaga song at the top of my lungs. It was hours later before I realized what I'd done. By then, it was too funny to take down. So I left it up." Kyra finished with a shrug.

Hale and Cade both laughed. "I can't believe you left that up," Stevie said. "Didn't people make fun of you?"

"Yeah," Kyra said after she swallowed a bit of her salad. "But that happens with a lot of my videos. It doesn't bother me."

Of course, that was a lie. It bothered her a lot, and the vicious ridicule from that particular video had been the worst. After watching the video go viral in the worst way, she'd been forced to go back on her medication. Even worse than the drugs, she had to smile and laugh and pretend like that video was hilarious because, in a way, it had made her career. That one video had the most views out of all the others on her channel and got her the most subscribers. But no one else at the table seemed to catch her dishonesty.

"Why did you start making videos?" Hale asked from where he sat beside her. Every now and then, when he reached for the salt or the wine bottle on the table, he would lean over and his shoulder would brush against hers. It felt as though she'd closed her hand around a thread of electric fencing.

"Yeah, what made you want to submit yourself to ridicule?" Cade chimed in from across the table next to Stevie.

"Blah, blah, blah. Hand me the salt," Stevie commanded. Cade immediately reached for it before anyone else could.

"I started in college," Kyra said. "We had to make a YouTube channel in one of my marketing classes and upload some videos. I really enjoyed it, so I kept it up after the class was over. Slowly, more and more people started watching them at my school. Then it grew wider and eventually it just took off." Because she'd made a fool of herself and people loved watching it. She kept that part to herself.

"I bet it was your singing talent that really hooked them," Stevie said around a mouthful of dangling noodles. Cade laughed like she'd just said the funniest thing in the world. Kyra forced herself to keep from cringing.

"So why do you keep doing it?" Hale asked quietly, once Cade and Stevie had launched into a fierce debate about free-range chicken meat.

Kyra offered him a shy smile, which he returned. They'd spent a couple hours last night finishing the tile work in her bathroom, and then she'd helped him grout it this morning while his crew worked on her house's new drywall. The crew had spent all day slapping drywall mud onto her walls, which meant the plumbing and electrical was finally up to code. Some of the men walked on weird-looking stilts to reach the ceiling. When they'd finished grouting the tile, he'd gone to help his men, and she'd returned upstairs to work.

It had been a great day for her, and she'd wanted more time with him, so once again, she'd forced Stevie to invite everyone over. Stevie had pretended to bluster about how annoying Cade was, but Kyra knew she was excited about having everyone over again.

"Sometimes it's tough, because there are a lot of mean people out there. It'll get me down from time to time and make me doubt why I'm doing it. The money I make from blogging and advertising isn't that great. But then I'll get a message from some young girl saying that because of my videos, she had the confidence to try something new. That's all I need," she said, getting as close to the truth as she could.

"I think that's pretty cool," Hale said. His eyes lingered on hers for a long beat, stretching the silence at the table until she had to look away.

"It's certainly not destroying walls and playing in mud all day, but it's something," she said.

"It's called grout," he corrected.

"I know. I still have it stuck under my nails." She raised her hand to show him where her nail beds were stained dark.

He took her hand and pulled it back under the table. "You're fine," he said, but he didn't let go of her for a long minute.

She looked up just in time to see Stevie grinning at her from across the table, which caused her to flush even more. Quickly, she looked up at Cade and asked the first question that popped into her head. "So why did you two start restoring old houses?"

Hale snorted, but Cade answered, "We only get to restore a few old homes. Most of what we do is new construction. Restoration work is more of a passion than a fruitful income—especially when Hale is involved."

Cade's pointed look didn't miss his target. Hale threw up his hands in defense. "Hey. I like to do things right."

"At the expense of the company," Cade said, ribbing his brother.

It surprised Kyra how different Hale was when he was with his brother. When she'd first met Cade, she'd assumed he took care of his brother, and maybe he did in his own way. But Hale took care of Cade too. He acted like the fist around Cade that battered into anything in their path. He took the brunt of the impact for his little brother, and it showed. Cade was the bright, youthful one of the two. Hale was more experienced and rougher around the edges for it. She figured that was the reason for his tough exterior, especially if Cade had been bullied when they were little.

"How's your mom doing?" Stevie asked when the brothers were done with their banter. Her words were like pouring ice water over the conversation. She blinked. "Oh, sorry. If you don't want to talk about it . . ."

"No, it's okay," Hale said before Cade could speak up. Once again, Kyra noticed, he was trying to protect his brother, even if it was only from talking about their mom. "She's doing okay. The cancer isn't spreading, which is good, but the chemo didn't really have much effect."

"Besides making her sicker," Cade said under his breath. His eyes were on his plate in front of him.

"We were hoping it might eliminate the cancer, but it only stops its growth for a little while. She gets tired and winded easily, but the pain is manageable, and she can work in her garden some days, which makes her happy."

"That's good," Kyra offered. Hale only nodded, but he leaned his leg over to brush against her knee under the table.

"How about dessert?" Stevie chimed in.

Kyra laughed. "Did you turn on the oven this time?" she asked, making Stevie scowl.

"Did she not turn on the oven last time?" Cade looked delighted.

"No!" Kyra's laughter bubbled inside her mouth. She turned to Hale to explain, but he was already watching her, his eyes on her mouth. The words died away.

"Well," Cade said, coughing. "I'll go with Stevie to make sure there are no other problems."

"I don't need your help," Stevie retorted, but he was already following her.

When they were gone, Hale said, "You look pretty tonight."

Kyra blushed again. "Thanks. So do you."

"I look pretty?" he asked, cocking an eyebrow in question.

She groaned and covered her eyes. "I mean you look handsome."

He reached up and pulled her hand down. It was the wrist with the tattoo. His thumb lightly traced the ink, which felt wonderful because it had been itching her like crazy. "I like you like this," he said quietly.

Her eyes darted back to the house where Cade and Stevie had disappeared. The lights hanging from the pergola sent glittering shadows dancing across the deck. Behind them, the ocean made its turns against the beach, the rhythm so natural and normal to her now that she barely noticed the music. The salt in the air made her hair extra wild tonight. She tucked a piece behind her ear and looked up at Hale through her lashes.

"I like being this way with you," she said.

With his hand skimming up her bare thigh, he leaned in and kissed her. She dug her fingers into the hard muscles of his bicep as his tongue stroked along hers, his teeth finding the flesh of her lip. She shifted in her seat, squirming to get closer to him. Her legs fell open, and Hale stroked his finger along the middle seam of her blue-jean shorts. She groaned as everything beneath his hand tightened and flooded with pulsing heat.

"I want you, Kyra," he growled against her lips.

She wanted to tell him she'd never had sex, but her nerves got the best of her. She didn't know what he would think if she told him she was a virgin. He seemed like the type of guy who liked experienced women, and she wasn't by that particular measure. But his eyes were dark and hooded when he looked at her, waiting for an answer. His hand was on the inner part of her thigh.

She'd opened her mouth to tell him when a crash came from inside the house. She looked up as Hale swiveled around. "What was that?" she asked.

"I don't know."

She jerked up and started toward the house with Hale right

behind her. They crossed the deck quickly, and she slid open the doors leading into the dining room, looking around for signs of Stevie and Cade but saw none. Another crash came from the direction of the kitchen.

Hale swore and took off across the room. Kyra rushed behind him, worried that something bad had happened. Stevie had a lot to drink tonight, and she could've burnt herself or passed out and hit her head.

Hale threw on the brakes, which she wasn't expecting. She crashed into his back. His arm swung out to catch her, but it was too late. She tumbled backward onto the floor, landing with a smack to her tailbone that made her bite her tongue. Blood pooled in her mouth as the pain radiated out from her backside. She groaned, but Hale didn't finish helping her up.

"And we were worried something was wrong," he said with a deep chuckle.

She peered between his legs to see what was going on. Stevie perched on the edge of the kitchen counter with her legs wrapped around Cade's waist, whose pants were down and exposing his bare ass. He jumped back and swung around to cover himself, leaving Stevie to fall back onto the counter with a screech. Her head landed right in the middle of the chocolate cake she'd actually baked for dessert.

It was a train wreck, but Kyra couldn't look away. Stevie sat up, her hands reaching for the back of her head. When she pulled her fingers away, they were coated in sticky chocolate frosting and cake. She stuck them in her mouth. "Yum. It's good at least."

"Oh my god, Stevie!" Kyra managed once she'd recovered from the shock. Hale bent over double with laughter, while Cade turned a million shades of scarlet. Stevie continued tasting the cake from the back of her tousled red hair. She shrugged.

"What?"

"Put your panties on!"

"Oh." She reached down to where her lacy thong was hooked around her ankle. She shimmied off the counter, which thankfully blocked Kyra's view as her best friend pulled her underwear back up. Cade caught the full view though, and his eyes fell downward as Stevie adjusted herself.

"Cade Cooper!" Kyra admonished, making his eyes fly back up. Hale was still too busy gasping for air as he laughed to help her up.

"Thanks for the ride, cowboy," Stevie said in a purr, patting Cade's cheek as she passed. She sashayed through the kitchen, dripping mashed cake from her hair. A glob fell on her shoulder. "I'm going to take a shower. Y'all can leave whenever."

As soon as she left, Cade rocketed from the room, yelling at Hale that he'd be waiting in the truck. Kyra bit back her own laugh and swatted at Hale's leg.

"Quit laughing and help me up. I think I broke my butt."

An hour later, everyone was gone, and Kyra had finished cleaning the kitchen and bringing in all the dishes and leftovers from outside. She checked on Stevie on her way out. Her best friend lay sideways across her bed with a wet towel still wrapped around her body. Her breath whooshed in soft snores from her open mouth, her expression peaceful and soft.

Kyra slipped out of the large, quiet house, making certain to lock the doors behind her. She walked along the edge of the beach and into her back garden, which still looked like a troll haven. Tomorrow she needed to start hacking at the overgrowth before the

Petunia Patrol returned to harass her. Thinking of Hale taking on the nosy old ladies made her shake her head, smiling.

"What are you smiling at?"

She gasped and jumped back from her porch steps. A figure sat on the top stair. He stood and came into the light.

"Hale," she breathed. "You scared me."

"Sorry." The white of his teeth gleamed in the moonlight.

"What are you doing here?" She climbed the steps and looked up at his face. The night cast angular shadows across his jaw and cheekbones so only half his face showed. The moonlight turned his eyes dark and shining, and she could easily imagine him as some fae prince like in her romance books, especially with the wild growth and tall trees of her back garden.

"I told Cade to go on home." He closed the distance between them and ran his rough hand up her arm. "Your skin is so soft, so perfect. Do my hands hurt you?"

"No," she answered quickly, reaching for his other hand. "I like it."

"I couldn't bring myself to leave tonight." He wove his hand around to the back of her neck, setting her nerve endings on fire and pulling her closer, until their foreheads touched. She ran her hand up his chest, marveling at the muscles dancing beneath her hand. She paused over his heart to feel the solid beat beneath the press of her palm.

"Come inside?"

He drew back slightly to look her in the eyes. Deep lines formed between his brows as he studied her face, looking for her honesty. She wondered if she'd pushed her emotions so far down it was impossible to show them anymore. She took a shaky breath and ran her thumb across his lips. Right then she considered telling him she was a virgin, but when her eyes flicked back to his, she saw he had already made his decision.

Still holding his hand, she led him into the house. She didn't bother turning on lights since she knew the twists and turns by heart already. Silently, they walked up the stairs and into her bedroom. Hale closed the door.

He didn't look at the sparse furnishings or the cluttered floor brimming with video equipment, shoes, and makeup. He watched her, his eyes shielded in the unlit room. The only light to guide their hands as they came together next to the bed was the moon shining over the ocean. The breeze fluttered through the open window, sending the lacy curtains brushing across the back of her bare calves.

Hale reached for her hips, skimming the exposed skin above the waistband of her shorts with his calloused fingers. One hand inched up her side, lifting her shirt, while the other trailed up her back, fingers bumping along the notches of her spine. She raised her arms for him to pull off her shirt.

"Wait," she said as he reached for the hem of his shirt. She squatted next to her laptop, which she'd left on to upload another video, and found her favorite folk band and pushed play. The male vocalist's voice immediately crooned through the speakers, filling the room with a haunting lilt that eased her nerves. She stood up in front of Hale and noticed his questioning stare. "Music calms me down."

"You're nervous?"

She looked up into his eyes as her hands went to his stomach. She eased the hem of his shirt up, making his jaw flex. "Yeah," she whispered.

He was too tall for her to take his shirt off, but he finished the task for her. For the first time, she was close enough to his bare chest to see his tattoos.

Kyra traced her finger over the ink of his chest piece. Traditional roses spanned across his chest, all in black and gray. Even their leaves and stems were intricately shaded down to the smallest area. The artwork was impeccable and took her breath away. The detail must have been excruciating, but she already knew he would've handled it with a tight jaw and a stormy expression.

That's who he was. Nothing else. No pretending. It was why she liked him so much.

He eased down the zipper of her shorts and rocked the tight denim material over her hips. She shimmied out of them, letting them fall to her ankles, and kicked them away.

He went to unbutton his pants, but she eased his hands away. Her fingers trembled slightly as she tugged his button undone. When she unzipped his pants, he released a tight hiss of air through his teeth. His breath tickled down the side of her neck, but still he didn't kiss her.

He kicked off his jeans and stood before her in just his briefs. He looked etched in stone, as if he were an ancient creature with all his life's secrets marked across his skin. She blinked to keep the sheen of tears at bay. She didn't know why she started getting emotional, other than the fact that she would lose her virginity tonight.

She reached up and slipped the straps of her bra over her shoulders. Her eyes never left Hale's. She unclasped the band and let it fall to the floor before she hooked her thumbs in the delicate lace of her panties and eased them down.

She'd imagined he'd stripped her down completely before with just his words, but now she stood before him truly naked. With a steady, quiet calmness, he looked at every part of her before his hands found her hips and pushed her gently back onto the bed. Laid out beneath him, feeling only the tiniest suggestion of his weight on top of her, he finally kissed her, his lips and tongue gliding across her skin. Her hands wove up his flexed arms and onto his back. She opened her legs beneath him so he fit between her. The breeze from the window whisked across her fevered skin.

Hale rose above her and tugged off his briefs. The sight of him made her breath hitch, and she began to tremble as the ache built within her. Above her, he licked the tips of his fingers before he stroked them against her. She arched off the bed and moaned, close already. When he pushed his fingers inside, heat pulsed through her body as she came, rocking his fingers deeper inside her.

Her orgasm came in waves of heat, echoing the ocean's waves outside. She was as useless against her climax as the beach was against the water. Only when she could breathe normally again did she open her eyes and see him watching her, his nostrils wide and his eyes narrowed.

She'd never been with someone this way. Not like this. She'd never done anything like this. He pulled her apart piece by piece, and she'd never felt so whole. But she was lying to him.

Hale hooked her leg over his hip and wrapped an arm around her neck. She felt every inch of his skin against hers. Her breath hitched.

Right before he pushed inside, she said, "Wait!"

He froze. "What's wrong?"

"I . . ." She took a shaky breath. He hovered above her, the outline of his jaw illuminated in the moonlight, the sounds of the ocean calling out over her shoulder.

She was fine. She could do this. He needed to know. And she was strong enough to tell him, to be honest when she just wanted to hide behind fake confidence and a sexy smile.

She was more than that.

"I haven't exactly done this before," she said, relieved when her voice didn't tremble.

At least, she was relieved until Hale reared back, his expression horrified.

"You're a fucking virgin?"

14

Kyra's expression must have been answer enough, because Hale swung himself off of the bed and jerked on his briefs.

"I need some air," he growled before storming out of her room.

Feeling numb, she sat up, clutching the thin cotton sheet to her chest. For a long moment, she just stared at the door he'd slammed behind him. She blinked slowly, already knowing she was sinking down, down, down, to a place where even moving was hard, where she felt nothing.

Normally, she would cut right now, to pull herself out of this. Because *this* could be bad. This numbness meant scars and therapists and medication that made her foggy and confused.

The force of will to stand up from the bed nearly made her cry. But walking over to the first bathing suit she found was easier. Scooping it up took hardly any effort. And by the time she wiggled into the bottoms, she moved like normal Kyra.

She flung open her bedroom door and pounded down to the stairs to the back door. The house was quiet. She ignored all of it, letting the screen door slam shut behind her. She grabbed her board from the rack.

If Hale could get some air, so could she.

The moon shined bright over the ocean. The surf was down, but just being in the water would suffice for tonight. She needed to feel it. Her toes sank into the sand while the rough grit of her board scratched against her side.

Immediately the feeling of safety washed over her.

Her hair hung loose across her shoulders, and it twisted around her face in the salty air. Kyra licked her lips to taste the ocean's balm on her skin. It was all comforting, but when the water splashed against her skin, she unspooled.

She lay down on her board and paddled out. There would be no surfing tonight. There wasn't even much of a break to fight through. She dove under just to immerse herself. All the places Hale had scorched with his touch cooled instantly. He slipped farther away as she paddled out. His rejection, his anger, his judgment: all problems for the shore.

When her arms were tired, she sat up on her board, letting her legs dangle into the water. She tilted her head back and closed her eyes, letting her body bob and sway with the current. Her house and the shore became distant things out here. The whole ocean acted as her barrier. Nothing could get to her out here.

"Kyra!"

She groaned and looked around until she spotted Hale hollering from shore. He had one of her larger boards under his arm as he jogged out to the surf in his briefs. Before she processed what he was doing, he'd splashed into the water and started paddling toward her.

As he drew closer, she seriously considered paddling away or splashing the water and throwing a fit, but that would be ridiculous. The ocean wasn't hers. He could come out here if he wanted. On her board. She scowled.

"What the hell is your problem?" he shouted when he was close enough.

"My problem?" she yelled back. She lowered her voice when his board bumped up against hers. "I don't have a problem. You're the one coming out here yelling."

His glare was on a whole new level tonight. "Because you're in the water at night!"

"So?"

"It's dangerous!"

"Look," she said, her anger building, "I do this all the time. You're not going to tell me what I can and can't do."

Hale snarled, his hand snaking out and snagging her wrist in his tight grip. "If you're putting your life in danger, I *will* tell you what to do. Surfing at night is dangerous. Especially alone, Kyra."

She jerked her hand away, which made them both jostle around on top of their boards. "I make my own choices, Hale. Why are you freaking out so much?"

"I'm freaking out because I care about you!" His voice had the tiniest tremor of hurt in it. For him, that spoke volumes on its own, and she finally put the pieces together.

Her anger fell away. Chill bumps spread along her arms, and suddenly she was cold—too cold. Hale was terrified for some reason. "Hey," she said quietly. "It's okay. I was being careful."

With his expression softer, he said, "You scared me."

As he stared at her, Kyra traced the scratch along her board where she'd tanked one day in California and her board had raked across the reef just feet below the surf. It had banged up her knee pretty good too. She shook her head, trying to focus her thoughts.

"I'm sorry, but I come out here to feel better. I needed to clear my thoughts after what happened. I know I should have told you about my," she cleared her throat, "inexperience or something, but we haven't known each other that long, really. And that's really personal."

Hale's fear slowly receded from the deep lines around his eyes, and the tight, rigid tension in his shoulders eased as they bobbed out in the moonlit water. "And what we were about to do wasn't that personal?"

She narrowed her eyes at him. "Hale, I'm going to give you a hint about women. If you want them to be more open with you, maybe you should try yelling and cursing at them less."

His eyebrows rose. For once, he looked speechless. She didn't wait for an answer. Instead, she reached over and flipped his board. He tumbled into the water with a yelp and soft splash. She bent back over her board and paddled to shore, letting the tiny waves pull her in. Maybe she was petty, but it felt good to hear him sputtering and spewing water behind her.

She smiled to herself.

She reached the shore well before he did. Carefully, she placed her board back in the rack before she went inside. Locking the doors behind her would probably only stop him for a minute. With a sigh, she just waited as he paddled in and strode up the beach.

He didn't take the time to put up her board, which irritated her, before he came inside.

He opened his mouth to start talking, but she lifted her hand to stop him. "You don't get to yell at me. Look, Hale, I'm sorry I didn't tell you I was a virgin." She gritted her teeth, because he didn't look like he wanted to yell anymore. He was softening and moving closer to her. She shook her head and backed away. "I chose you," she whispered. "And you just left me up there."

A tremble of that earlier terrifying numbness itched up her spine. She shoved it away. She was fine.

"I came back." He tried to close the distance between them again, clearly torn between his fleeting anger and his passion for her. The emotions warred across his face, his eyes wide and consuming.

"But you left."

"And came back," he insisted again, emphasizing each word.

"My virginity isn't just some fake smile," she said. For some reason, she couldn't help but wonder if her mom had stood like this, like Kyra was now, arguing with a boyfriend in this very house.

"What is it then? You could've told me."

Water rolled down her body in tiny droplets. It dripped from her hair and onto her shoulders. "I know," she said quietly, her eyes meeting his. "But my virginity feels like a mistake. It feels like something dirty, because it's my failure as a human being. Who can't let themselves be touched or loved or even let someone stand that close to them? I'm a virgin because I can't deal with the emotions of letting someone take it from me. But with you . . ." she fought to steady her voice, ". . . I would have risked them."

Hale finally caught her and wrapped his arms around her. He felt salty too, the water still slick against his skin. It soothed her to feel the ocean on their bodies.

"You talk about your feelings like they are dangerous." His words ruffled her hair with their breath, and her eyes drifted closed.

"They are," she said so quietly she barely heard herself.

He hadn't heard. His hands cupped her face as he leaned back to look at her. "Sorry for leaving tonight. I'm not good at handling my temper, and you're so good at setting me off."

She lifted a shoulder, smiling slightly. "Maybe it's a gift."

"I've never been with someone so complicated before," he breathed, dipping his forehead against hers. "I'm a simple guy, Kyra, and you scare the hell out of me."

"I scare myself too." She ran her hands up his broad arms to his neck, where she entwined herself against him. "After we met, I told myself to avoid you. You seemed so dangerous. I've never met anyone who spoke their mind so much."

"I wanted nothing to do with you either."

She laughed softly. "We didn't do a good job of staying away from each other, did we?"

"Not even a little bit," he said, the corner of his mouth dimpling into a crooked grin.

She didn't return the smile. Instead, her eyes trailed down to the floorboards at their feet. She could give everything—every part of herself—to Hale, and, in the end, it might not be enough to make the relationship work. People broke up all the time. But she didn't know if their possible relationship would be worth the pain. She had to weigh things like that, because, for her, pain was different. Her darker feelings were abysses that could suck her in, so she had to be careful how close she toed the line. Her entire life, nothing was worth it compared to the darkness inside her. So she'd played it safe. Until now.

"Tell me what you're feeling," Hale pleaded. "I can't tell and it drives me insane."

She breathed out a long breath, her eyes still examining the floor, like maybe an answer would be scrawled there. *This way to happiness.* "Scared," she whispered.

He took her chin between his fingers and lifted her gaze back to his. "I'm sorry about tonight, Kyra. I'm not good at being understanding, I know. Cade was always the better, nicer brother." He smiled at her, shaky and uncertain. "I wish I was more like him. But I'm not. I'm going to screw up so much with you, but I want to try. You're so complicated beneath your smile, but I'm willing to try if you are."

The anxiety tight in her throat loosened slightly at his words, like they were approaching solid footing again. She ran her hand up his still-wet chest. "I think that's the best compliment you've ever given me."

"So we're going to try? You're going to be honest with me, and I'm going to try to not be such a dick."

She couldn't help but grin at his words, even if the thought of trying terrified her. But she would just have to figure out a way to hold it together, because maybe, just maybe, Hale was worth it. In her heart, it felt right to toe the line between her safe place and the darkness inside her. For him, she would.

"I get to call you out every time you're being an a-hole," she said, smiling softly.

His eyes glinted in the moonlight streaming through her windows. "And I get to say when you're being fake."

"Deal."

"Deal."

With that, he took her hand and led her toward her stairs. "Let's go to sleep. I'm exhausted."

He didn't wait for her answer, but she followed him anyway. They didn't bother with showers or changing before collapsing onto her mattress. Kyra scooted under the covers, and Hale wasted no time wrapping her in his arms. For the second time that night, she sank into his body and let go.

She fell asleep right away.

15

"*Technically*, I have the day off."

Kyra stirred, blinking into the bright light streaming through her bedroom. Hale stood next to her bed with a thermos of coffee in his hand from the organic coffee shop in town. He looked ready for the day, and apparently he'd gotten a head start on her.

"What?" she mumbled, tasting her awful morning breath. Quickly, she reached for the coffee to burn it out. He handed it to her and sat down on the edge of her bed.

"The inside of the house is getting painted today, so I have the day off, since Cade handles the subcontractors." He raked his hand over his head. "And I need a break from this house, and I want to take it with you."

She burnt her tongue, but the coffee tasted like heaven. She moaned her approval. "Where are we going?" she asked a moment later.

"To my favorite spot on the island. So get dressed and wear hiking shoes." He smacked her butt through the thin sheet, which sloshed her coffee, and left the room.

When she went downstairs ten minutes later, Hale appeared from the back of the house and presented her a bag. "Breakfast of champions," he said. She peered inside the bag and discovered a still-warm bagel. "You can eat on the drive over."

"Where's your favorite spot?" she asked as she followed him out the door and locked it behind her. She stole a glance at Stevie's house; the lights were off with no sign of activity.

"It's a surprise," he answered cryptically. His smile was crooked and goofy, but Kyra liked it.

They'd changed last night together in their promise to try, and she was already enjoying this different Hale, who grinned and joked. She only hoped he liked her honesty as much as she liked his understanding side.

His truck roared to life as she climbed into the passenger seat. Judging by Cade's earlier description of how filthy his brother's truck often was, she decided Hale must have cleaned it out this morning. It still smelled like a combination of sweat and dirt and concrete, but the floors were clean. She settled into her seat, buckled up, and started in on her bagel, a delicious blueberry kind, as he navigated through town. They rode in comfortable silence, music playing quietly in the background. Kyra didn't know much about country music, but she recognized some Johnny Cash and George Jones, which surprised her because it was so different from his usual hardcore rock music.

"What are you staring at?" he asked, keeping his eyes on the road.

"How did you know I was looking at you?"

"I can just tell."

The rasp in his voice took on a husky edge that sent chills down her arms. "I thought you only listened to rock."

Hale flipped on his blinker and turned right, heading out of town and toward the northern end of the island with the steep bluffs and rocky beaches. Kyra hadn't had much time to explore more since her tour with Cade, but she knew that part of the island was mostly just a nature preserve.

"My mom used to play this stuff all the time when we were kids. I guess it kind of stuck, because I like it."

"How is she really doing?" she asked carefully, not knowing how far to push him after the group had talked about his mother last night at dinner. She munched on her bagel, taking small bites and watching Hale out of the corner of her eye.

His grip tightened slightly on the wheel, but he said, "She's tough. Maybe too tough. She won't tell us when the pain gets too bad, and she insists on living at her house. It makes it hard to keep an eye on her, but the nurse we hired is really good."

"Is she starting another round of chemo soon?"

"No."

The single word said it all, and she knew when to drop the subject. She turned to the window and marveled at the scenery. All the houses and buildings were bright, cheerful colors, but the buildings became fewer and fewer as they drove farther north, the road narrowing and twisting along the towering bluff. She could just make out the crashing waves far below them as they went around the sharp corners.

"You're really not going to tell me where we're going?" she asked, growing excited.

"Nope." He shot her another grin, once again easing the tension. He looked as excited as she felt.

"Have you always lived on the island?" She neatly folded her bagel bag and put it in one of the cup holders.

"Left for college. Didn't work out, so I came back when Cade started the business." He turned off the main road and headed down a single-lane service road. She bounced in her seat when he hit the massive potholes.

"Why did it not work out?" She reached for the door handle and held on, almost biting her tongue off when they hit another deep rut.

Hale shrugged. "Wasn't for me. I never went to class, and I hated the types of people there. I couldn't find my place with them, so I left."

"And you've found it now?" she asked, raising her eyebrows at his profile. She thought about his gruff and grumpy personality. From outside appearances, he certainly didn't fit in with the typical Canaan crowd.

Confirming her thoughts, he snorted derisively. "I'm the type of person that'll never fit in. People see me and think I should be in jail or doing drugs—or both. Maybe I look like some in that crowd, I guess, but that's not me, and no matter where I am, people are going to judge me. So when Cade started the business, I figured Canaan was as good a place as any. And it keeps me close to Mom, which is good right now." He glanced over at her. "What about you? Did you fit in at college?"

She squished up her nose and looked out the window as they drove. The trees up here were nothing like the pretty, delicate

Magnolia trees in town. These were the scraggier, wind-whipped kind that held onto the earth out of sheer will alone; their beauty was in their ragged, white-knuckled survival.

"I did," she answered, thinking back to those years. "Really well, actually. But by the time college rolled around, I knew how to use my appearance and personality to fit in." She turned her attention away from her reflection and back to Hale, who carefully watched the road, like he didn't want to break the spell of her honesty. "Which I guess is the exact opposite of you. I made sure I fit in, at whatever cost, because to have been on the outside was unthinkable." She laughed and shook her head. "But you know what? I have no friends from college. No one calls me or even emails me anymore. It's just me."

They hit another bump, and her elbow cracked against the door. "But things are different now. You have Stevie and Cade and me."

"That's a good point."

He finally stopped the truck in front of a large metal gate with a crooked, rusty *No Trespassing* sign. He turned off the engine and looked at her. "Thanks for being honest."

His gaze was simple and open. All he wanted was for her to be honest with him too. She took a deep breath. "I'm trying."

He smiled. And it wasn't his crooked, snarky one either. It was a real smile, and it hurt her heart because he looked like a child when he smiled, like a little boy without the harsh judgments of his neighbors. It was a smile he'd probably given his mother countless times when she was healthy and young and he played in the house with a young, gangly Cade while she listened to old country music. It takes a real man to smile so unguardedly like that, Kyra realized, and he was smiling it for her.

Not noticing her dazed, dreamy state, he jumped out of the car, slinging a backpack over his shoulder. She blinked as the door slammed. It took her a moment to recover, and when she did, she rolled her eyes at his back.

"So much for having a moment," she mumbled before she got out of the car and followed him. He headed down the fence line, stepping through tall brush and briars. She went after him carefully, making sure not to snag her bare skin on the thorns.

"Are we doing something illegal?" They passed another warning sign about trespassing.

"So many people come up here, the cops don't care anymore."

Aside from the ugly fence, the area was beautiful. The trees were thick, blanketing her in pine smell, and seagulls squawked above her head. From somewhere up ahead came the slight sound of waves. Hale crunched along the path in front of her until they came to a slit in the fence. He pulled back the metal for her.

"Thanks." She ducked through and watched as he followed just as quickly. He pulled the chain link back into place like an expert. Clearly, this wasn't the first time he'd been up here.

"This is your favorite place on the island?"

"Yep." He adjusted his pack and took the lead once again. "You'll understand in a minute."

The trees opened up some as they climbed a slight hill. The grass scratched against Kyra's thighs as she waded through. A breeze bent the limbs around her, making the trees sing in tune with the birds. Pockets of brightly colored yellow flowers cropped up along the way. And all the while, the ocean smell grew stronger, overpowering the pine scent. The waves grew louder, and their pull ached in her chest.

"Look there."

Kyra followed Hale's finger and saw a tall lighthouse emerging through the trees. It sat atop the hill they were climbing, which she now saw was a large bluff. The lighthouse clung to the very edge, its base surrounded by rocks.

"Oh, wow," she whispered, taking in the sight. They kept climbing, but she slowed to look up at the lighthouse.

Its age and neglect plainly showed, and it obviously wasn't in use anymore. The door at the base was boarded up, and the paint along its curving sides had peeled and crumbled off. It towered into the sky with a narrow railing wrapping around the very top. The glass surrounding the lights up there had long ago broken away, but she could tell it had once been majestic. Now it just looked kind of sad.

"Now you can see why this is my favorite place," Hale said, sweeping his arm to the view in front of her. She hadn't even noticed they'd come to a stop on the edge of the bluff.

The bluff overlooked a small cove with sides made of huge rock outcroppings that the waves bashed themselves against, sending sprays of water as high as the bluff's edge. The wind buffeted against her, causing her ponytail to twist and swish around. Looking down at the battle of water against land, she had the sense of power and war, ageless and unending. It was raw and powerful, consuming and devouring. They could've been the only ones in the world standing up here, except for the lighthouse, which felt like a presence of its own.

Her eyes traveled farther down the bluff's edge, which was miles away from where she and Hale stood, until she saw the abandoned house. From the distance, she only made out its sagging state and how precariously close to the bluff's edge it sat. Like at any moment, one strong breeze could send it into the ocean.

"It's amazing," she said. She couldn't come up with anything else to describe how gorgeous this secret place was. Together they sat down in the grass to overlook the ocean below, and Hale pulled out some water bottles from his pack and handed her one.

"The lighthouse has been here since the late 1700s. It's the oldest one in the South."

"Why isn't it used anymore?"

He finished his water and put the empty bottle back in his pack before he peered up at the lighthouse beside them. "The technology was old and really dangerous. Fires were a big worry back then in lighthouses because the fuel was so flammable. So the town built a new one a few miles away."

"This one doesn't look like it burned," Kyra said. She examined the structure, which still looked pretty solid, just forgotten.

"Nah," Hale said, and she heard the amusement in his voice. "It's just haunted."

Goose bumps spread across her skin; she felt the presence of the lighthouse, as though the building breathed right next to them, looking at them as they looked at it. She forgot to inhale for a second. "Really?"

"It's just legend. It may not even be true," he said with a shrug.

"Tell me!"

He shot her a grin, like that was just what he wanted her to say. "Sometimes on foggy nights, the beam comes on and sweeps across the ocean. You can see it from all over the island, flashing back and forth to warn the ghost ships of sailors long lost."

"That's crazy. I thought you said the technology was too old to be used."

"It is," he said, lowering his voice. "The oil is too old and dried up to ever be used for light. You hear stories of teenagers coming up here for a good time when the beam comes on. They say they saw a White Lady standing out on the bluff with her dress whipping in the wind, crying for her lost lover who never came home."

Kyra's brows rose. "A 'White Lady'?"

"It's a type of ghost dressed in white, hence the name."

"Gosh, Hale." She rubbed her hands over her arms. "And this is your favorite place on the island? That's weird."

"I think it's awesome." She caught a flash of his smile, and she knew the child in him delighted in ghost stories. "Besides, the story of the White Lady is just silly. Everyone knows the ghost is really just Violet Relend standing out on the bluffs at night. She wears old clothes and looks a little weird, so people just jump to assumptions."

Kyra frowned, thinking of the woman she saw in the cemetery when she visited her mother's grave. "Wait, I think I've seen her before."

Hale nodded. "You probably have around town. She lives in that house," he said, nodding toward the abandoned house farther down the bluff. Kyra's mouth fell open.

"Someone actually lives in that? Is that even safe?"

"Not at all. The city's been trying to buy it, but she keeps fighting to stay."

"And people call her a ghost," she said quietly, shaking her head in wonder as she stared at the house. She remembered how the young woman had actually looked rather ghostly, and Kyra herself had wondered if she was a specter when she ran into her in the cemetery. "That seems awful."

"Yeah, it is. But it's hard to shake a reputation in this town."

She turned back to Hale in time to see the flash of hurt in his eyes. Deciding to change the subject from Violet, she asked, "Have you ever seen the lighthouse's beam?"

He instantly perked up at her question. "Not yet. But maybe one day. The old folks in town say it's good luck to see the lights."

"That's so crazy." She reached over and shoved him back. "Why did you bring me here? This isn't romantic at all."

Hale looked at her with his eyebrow cocked, which pulled the piercing in his brow. "You think this was supposed to be romantic?"

"Uh . . ." She didn't know what to say, but he saved her from answering. He stood up and pulled on his pack.

"Come on. Let's hike down to the shore, then we can go back to my place. Is that romantic enough for you?" he asked with a wink.

16

They spent the rest of the day hiking around the lighthouse bluff. Kyra found herself scanning the rocks above them for Violet standing on the bluff, braced against the wind. Of course, she never saw her or the lighthouse beam flashing across the ocean. Hale caught her looking a few times, but he never teased her.

They passed the afternoon talking about the island and her house. Once he started talking about his restoration work and original versus new, she discovered he had a hard time stopping. But his passion was contagious, and she found the subject interesting when he talked about it, which was probably because she liked watching his expressions flare and ebb as he went on, gesturing wildly with his hands. She wondered if she could ever be so open and unguarded.

They spent a lot of time talking about her college years and her career. It was hard to be more than just smiles and laughter after a lifetime of faking it. He expected more, and he didn't settle for a fake grin and some silly comment. He pushed her until she told the truth. It gave her a headache and set her teeth on edge, but he seemed to be able to tell when he was pushing her too far. Their silence was easy, and Kyra let herself unwind in between their words.

Hale only brought some protein bars with him, and when her stomach growled so loudly he heard, he announced it was time to go home. They hiked back to the truck and headed into town. He picked up vegetarian-friendly ingredients for tacos at the store, and they headed back to his house.

On the way, Kyra checked her phone. She had a few texts from Stevie and a missed call from Aunt Carol.

Stevie: Where are you? I knocked on your door but you didn't answer. Did someone murder you?

Stevie: Hey, if you're not murdered, I want to go for drinks. You wanna come?

She'd sent that last one at noon. Kyra really hoped she hadn't gone to a bar so early in the day, but when she read the next text, her fears were confirmed.

Stevie: hy. Whre yu @

She tried to call Stevie, but her phone went straight to voicemail. With a sigh, she sat back against the seat. "What's up?" Hale asked, catching her concern.

"It's Stevie . . ." She didn't know how much to tell him about Stevie's drinking, but he seemed to read her mind anyway.

"She drinks a lot, huh?"

Surprised, she glanced at him. "Yeah. Sometimes it seems like a lot. But it's normal for young people to go out on Fridays."

"It's noon," Hale deadpanned. "That's a little early for pre-gaming."

Kyra cringed. He was right, and if the texts were anyway to judge, Stevie was likely already drunk.

"Do you think she has a problem?"

She shifted in her seat, reluctant to begrudge anyone their ways of coping because hers weren't the healthiest either. "Maybe."

"Have you said anything about it to her?" He turned at a red light and once again headed out of town.

"Not really . . . I never feel like it's my place to talk to her about it. Shouldn't her family do that?"

"That girl's family is shit." The venom was readily clear in his voice, and it surprised her. "Everyone knows they're the reason Stevie is so messed up. No, they would probably encourage her drinking because it would be good for ratings or publicity or what-the-fuck-ever."

"You're probably right . . ."

"You two hang out a lot. If you think she has a problem, it might be better coming from you."

Stevie did drink a lot, and if Kyra was honest with herself, she knew it was something that should be addressed. It just made her feel like a total hypocrite. "I'll talk to her tomorrow. She's already drunk, so it might not go over well today."

"Can it wait until tomorrow?"

She glanced over at him, and he met her eyes briefly before looking back to the road. She hadn't paid attention to where they were going, but once again they were surrounded by trees in the middle of nowhere. "I think so," she said, biting at her nail. "But what if we eat and then we can go find her?"

He pulled off the road and onto a narrow gravel path that cut through the woods. "I think that sounds like a great plan."

Below the thick canopy of leaves and Spanish moss, the bright world of Canaan became all darkness and shadows. Hale didn't turn on his headlights; he had the road memorized. Almost as quickly as it disappeared, the sunlight fractured back across the windshield, temporarily blinding her, when they pulled out from under the tree cover.

When he drove across the grass toward a small airstream trailer, she wasn't surprised. Everything from the grill outside to the workout bench in the corner of the yard screamed Hale. The awning was out and some lawn chairs sat unfolded beneath it.

"Do you expect me to open your door or something?"

She realized he stood on his side of the truck with his door still open, waiting. He stared in at her while he held the grocery bags. She shot him a dirty look. "I'm going."

"Move your ass," he said, grinning widely. "I'm hungry."

She grumbled to herself as she walked to the trailer. He banged open the door and disappeared inside. Instantly, old country tunes rolled out from inside to twang in her ears. After spending the day with Hale, she'd grown accustom to the gravelly voices and crooning lyrics, and she realized it suited him more than the angry rock he often played while he worked.

She ducked under the trailer's door and stepped inside. He stood at the small counter, laying out their supplies for tacos. His broad form took up most of the room, and he had to bend his head to accommodate the low ceilings in the trailer. Craning her neck to see around him, she spotted the bedroom with the bed neatly made. Above a narrow, lumpy couch hung some odd drawings full of lines and shading. To her right was a narrow dinette. She hadn't moved and already she felt claustrophobic.

She opened her mouth to comment on the "coziness" when she realized what the drawings were. "Oh, gosh," she said, completely shocked. "These are amazing, Hale."

She went forward and leaned over the couch to examine the drawings. The pencil marks were light and delicate, each line perfectly straight and precise. She counted nearly twenty drawings hanging above the couch, and each one of them was of her house. Hale had rendered the designs freehand, drawing up his own blueprints since the originals were long gone.

She didn't need to be an expert to see he was amazing at his job. Even from the drawings, she saw his intentions for the house through the detail in his work. One drawing outlined the front of her house, but she barely recognized it. He'd painstakingly drawn in perfect accents for the house custom of a Victorian style. Even the door and windows were done in a manner that suggested he'd done his research. Another drawing showed her garden with each plant labeled. Other drawings were of furniture he clearly planned to build, one being of a giant buffet for her dining room that she already knew would fit the space perfectly.

Gaping, she looked over her shoulder to see him watching her. He shrugged without a comment. "You're really good at this," she said again.

"I like it fine," he said. He turned back to the counter and dumped the vegetables into the miniscule sink for cleaning. With one last look at the drawings, she joined him at the counter.

"Is that what you're going to do to my house?" She turned on the water and held an onion under the stream.

"It's what was original to the house, even if I have to remake it. Everything has its place and it belongs there."

He pulled out a cutting board and a long knife. She handed him the onion, which he immediately started peeling and cutting.

"I think it's great how you try to keep to the original plan for the house."

"It deserves it," he said with a grunt. He sniffed at the aroma coming off the onion.

"When did you start drawing?" she asked, washing more vegetables.

"Before I could write my name."

She elbowed his side, which wasn't hard to do in the small space. "They're really good. Stop being so modest."

"I'm not disagreeing with you. I think they're good too."

She laughed at his answer, which won her a crooked grin. They turned up the music and kept making the tacos. She found herself humming and swaying along to the songs as they worked. They didn't talk, which suited her fine. It was nice just being so close to Hale and doing something she was comfortable with.

When the rice was done, they wrapped up their veggie tacos with hot sauce and settled on the dinette to eat. In between bites, she asked, "Does Cade like the business as much as you?"

Hale frowned down at his taco while he munched. "He likes the number crunching and money side of it, and he's better with the people. So I guess he likes it. We just do completely different things."

"When I first got here, I thought it was so weird that Cade had to talk with clients instead of you. I figured you must be a monster or something."

"And then you met me." Hale smirked.

"And realized that's exactly what you are." She laughed. "Are you so honest that you can't even pretend to be nice sometimes?"

He leaned back in his chair. "I can be nice, but I've found most people don't deserve it. I like to keep to myself because I can't stand when people insist on being polite even though they are going to talk about you behind your back. Your wonderful Petunia Patrol neighbors are a prime example."

Kyra shuddered at the thought of Mrs. Walker and her friends. "Even so, I was raised to be polite no matter what, even if you didn't like that person."

"That's fine on the kindergarten playground, but I think it's bullshit that adults can't honestly tell each other how they feel about the other. Why hide it? Wouldn't it have made you feel so much better those first couple of days just to tell me I was an asshole?"

"I did tell you that."

"Days later when I nearly ran you over, which I still feel awful about by the way. But why wait so long? I clearly pissed you off before then. Yet you smiled and acted all nicey-nicey."

"Nicey-nicey?" She scoffed. "Some people just don't like confrontation. Like, when we first met, I was trying to understand you. I didn't want to judge you because Cade had asked me not to."

The taco paused on its way to Hale's mouth. "He really asked you to be nice to me?" He seemed genuinely bewildered his brother would stand up for him.

"He asked me to cut you some slack, which I did. Not that you noticed. You were awful to me."

"I was mean because you were acting so fake all the time. It pissed me off."

She tossed her taco on the plate and threw her hands in the air. "I was being fake because you gave me no reason to actually, sincerely be nice to you!"

"Would you call me out now when I'm being a jerk?"

"Oh, yeah." She nodded enthusiastically as she picked her taco up and took a bite.

"Then that's what I call progress." He grinned at her.

They talked some more as they finished eating. After quickly doing the dishes, she tried to call Stevie again. She must've been frowning when she hung up because Hale asked, "Still no answer?"

She shook her head at his question. "I think her phone must be dead or something."

"Okay. Let's go find her." He wiped his wet hands on his jeans before heading to the door.

With a sigh, she followed. She wasn't looking forward to this conversation with Stevie. Talking to her about her drinking likely made Kyra the biggest hypocrite in the world, but she didn't want to see her friend struggle. She hoped Hale would stay with her and help her, but she had her doubts about that. Besides, it probably needed to be just between her and Stevie. Hale was right: Kyra was the only one who cared in Stevie's life.

"Hit that light, will ya?" He turned around to point at the light switch over her shoulder, but she was following so closely he bumped into her. He reached out and caught her as she stumbled back.

His hands didn't move away when she righted herself. She twisted around to turn off the light like he asked. The trailer went dark, save for the streams of sunlight coming through the tiny windows. The music was off now, and she heard only the sound of her breathing.

His hands skimmed across her back, pulling her closer and winding up her shirt. The rough, cracked pads of his fingers scraped across her skin and sent chills down her arms. Without even realizing it, she arched her body into his, twining her hands up his neck and into his hair.

He kissed her then, pressing her back against the counter. She couldn't help the quivering, dipping sensation in her stomach as he worked his lips over hers. His tongue threaded into her mouth and took control. When he pressed against her hips, she felt how hard he was through his jeans.

She was panting when he eased back, leaving her lips parted and swollen from his kiss. He unbuttoned her shorts and tugged them off her hips so that they pooled at her ankles. Without pause, he stroked his fingers between her legs, feeling her wetness through her panties. He pushed the material aside and slipped two fingers inside her. With his thumb, he traced lazy circles around her clit while he pulsed in and out of her.

"Has anyone used his fingers on you before me?" He hissed the question into her ear.

She rocked against his fingers, feeling the fullness inside her but aching for more. He was getting her close, but he slowed and waited for her answer. "Yes," she breathed, her voice cracking.

Hale frowned, not liking her answer. He growled and sped his fingers back up until she came. She shuddered against him, letting her head fall back as the orgasm rocked through her. Her muscles clenched around his fingers, her body vibrating with electricity.

"Has anyone made you feel like that before?"

She looked back at him, his expression wild in the darkness as he watched her. "No. Never that."

Hale slipped his fingers out of her. He ran his hands underneath her shirt and cupped her breasts, working his thumbs over her nipples until she felt another ripple through her core.

"What do you want to do, Kyra?"

She swiveled her hips against him, thinking about what she wanted. He seemed to know she was gauging herself so he stayed quiet and still. She pulled her hand away from his neck, where she'd been clinging for dear life, and rubbed her palm down the front part of his jeans. He hissed out a breath when she took him in her hand, measuring his heft. What did she want?

Her eyes flicked up to his. A tiny smirk pulled at her lips. He understood instantly as she went for his jean's button.

His mouth parted slightly, and she knew she'd taken him by surprise. His nostrils flared and he nodded. After pulling up her shorts, she started to sink to the floor just as her phone rang.

"You've got to be fucking kidding me," he growled as she stood back up. He turned away and shoved his hands through his short hair. Seeing how undone he was made her smile secretly behind his back. She picked up her phone.

"Hello?" Her voice surprised her. Even she could tell it was thick with lust.

But all that fell away as she listened to the person on the other end. Hale seemed to notice too. He turned back around and looked at her, his expression changing.

"Who is it?" he mouthed. She listened for a moment longer before she responded.

"The hospital."

17

Kyra spotted the film crew before she saw Stevie. Two burly guys with pit stains held massive, expensive cameras in their oversized hands in the hospital's hallway. If the cameras were here, then Stevie's parents must be. She hurried past cameramen, shooting glares they didn't notice, on her way to the nurses' station with Hale hot on her heels.

"Um . . . excuse me." She cleared her throat. Hospitals made her queasy, as if the sickness could force itself down her throat; her hand locked over her left wrist, wringing her bracelets for all she was worth. A nurse looked up at Kyra's shaky voice. "I need to see Stevie Reynolds. Do you know how she's doing? I, um, don't know who to talk to."

"Her family is in there with her now. You'll have to come back tomorrow." The nurse looked back down at the computer while phones rang around her.

Kyra almost burst into tears. "But can you tell me how she's doing at least?"

The nurse looked up with a bored, dismissive expression. "No. I can't. We called you because you were listed as her emergency contact in her phone, but as you're clearly not family, we can't disclose patient information."

"But—"

"Is Dr. Faraday here?" Hale stepped from around Kyra. He towered over the nurses' station. Something about the way his muscles tightly corded beneath his shirt or the way he loomed over the partition or even the spark in his eye set the nurse into motion. She blinked.

"Yes."

"Can you page him?"

"I can't just—"

"Page him."

"Yes, sir." The nurse turned away and picked up a phone to page the doctor.

"Who's Dr. Faraday?" Kyra asked quietly, so only he would hear.

"Mom's doctor. Bit of a hippie, but a good guy," he said. Now that he wasn't talking to the nurse, she noticed the paleness of his face and the way his shoulders slumped slightly. Without thinking, she took his hand and squeezed.

They had to wait only a moment before a tall, lanky guy in a white coat that nearly swallowed him came down the hall. His hair was too long and flopped into his eyes, but he smiled when he saw them. Before he was even close enough, he stuck out his hand to shake Hale's.

"Hey, man. How's it going?"

"Good," Hale said, shaking the doctor's hand. "Ethan, this is Kyra. Kyra, this is Ethan."

"Good to meet ya, Kyra." Ethan Faraday nodded at her before he flipped his hair out of his face with a jerk of his chin. "What's up?"

"Kyra's friend was brought in earlier. Car accident."

Ethan ran his hand over his face. "Oh, yeah. I did a consult on that one. She's pretty banged up, but she's stable. The ER doc took care of her. She bruised some ribs and knocked her head pretty good, but other than that, she'll be fine."

Kyra grimaced, forcing the pool of hot saliva back down her throat. "Can I please see her?"

Ethan thought for a moment before he nodded. "Sure. Let me get her parents out of there and check on her. Come by in five."

"Thanks, Ethan." Hale shook the doctor's hand again before he walked away. She watched him disappear into a room she could only assume was Stevie's. The tears were stirring again when she looked back at Hale.

"I should've gone to find her earlier," she said, her voice cracking. "I should've talked to her sooner about this, but I kept convincing myself it wasn't my place."

"Maybe," he said with a shrug. "But that's not how it happened. We just have to deal with what did."

She would've preferred a hug, but he was right. She couldn't change what had happened no matter how much she wanted to. Just then, a well-dressed man and woman left Stevie's room. The woman was shockingly skinny with dry, bleach-blonde hair and too-full lips. Her makeup was flawless and her clothes expensive. The man had flashy tattoos and wild hair that was obviously painstakingly styled. As they walked out, the cameramen snapped to attention and hustled behind the couple, filming them as they walked away from their daughter's room.

"That's disgusting," Kyra said, balling her fists at her sides. "How could they bring cameras into a hospital?"

"How did they get down here so fast?" Hale asked.

"I have no idea. Don't they live in Los Angeles?" She watched Stevie's parents walk around the corner of the hall. If she wanted to see Stevie, now was her time. "Come on, let's go."

She slipped down the hall to Stevie's room and knocked softly on the door before she went in. The room was dark, with only a small light on so that Ethan could read Stevie's vitals. He nodded when they walked up.

"Oh, Stevie," Kyra said, reaching for her best friend's hand.

"That bad, huh?" Stevie asked. She tried to grin, but the motion pulled at the stitches lining the side of her mouth. Another gash stretched vertically down her left eyebrow. Scratches were scattered across her pasty skin where the glass had broken around her.

"No, it's not bad at all." Kyra squeezed her hand as she settled softly down on the bed beside her.

"You're an awful liar." She snorted, but it only dislodged the oxygen tubes under her nostrils. Before she could reach up and readjust it, Hale stepped forward and helped her, handling the delicate tubes like a pro. "Thanks, Hale."

"No problem."

Stevie looked so small in the hospital bed. Her red hair was a tangled mess behind her, and her gown was crooked. Smudged makeup amplified the bruises on her face. Even with her tan, she still looked too pale.

"I'm so glad you're okay," Kyra whispered, her throat thick.

"I'm gonna have to agree with you on that one." Stevie shifted in bed, grimacing when the movement caused her pain.

"What happened? Why didn't you get a cab?"

Her eyes fell to the thin, scratchy sheet covering her legs. "I thought I had it under control. I feel like a piece of shit. What if I had hit someone? How would I have dealt with that?"

"But it didn't happen," Kyra said quickly before her friend could start crying. "So let's focus on that."

"Always so optimistic," Stevie mumbled.

"We make a good pair since you're so doom-and-gloom." Kyra was the only one who tried to laugh at her joke.

"The size of the ticket the cop gave me is pretty doom-and-gloom worthy. But he could've put me in jail, so there's that. I can just picture my parents' glee if they got to film bailing me out of jail. Would've been great for ratings," Stevie mumbled.

"What are they even doing here?"

Stevie met Kyra's eyes, and the sadness there shocked her. "That's why I went to the bar. They called me yesterday to say they were flying in to discuss another show."

"That's awful," Kyra said quietly.

Stevie lifted a shoulder then grimaced when the movement hurt. "I didn't know how else to deal with it and all I wanted to do was drink. I thought just one would help me get my head clear again."

Kyra took a deep breath, her nerves making her hands clammy. She needed to talk to Stevie about her drinking, and now was as good a time as any. But she felt like she'd failed her friend by not doing it sooner. And she felt like a fraud.

"Stevie, I think you need to go to rehab. You need help before you hurt yourself worse."

Stevie's eyes flickered away to look toward the window where the bright afternoon sun had dimmed behind thick gray clouds. A drizzle of rain slicked down the glass. "Have you been talking to my parents?" she asked with a halfhearted laugh. "They said the same thing."

"They want to make sure you're healthy and safe," Kyra said, regretting her earlier judgments; Stevie's parents couldn't be so awful if they had wanted what was best for their daughter.

As if Stevie read her thoughts, she said, "Oh, please. They want to make a buck. As soon as they found out what happened, they were on the phone with the network to pitch a new show. They told me I had to go to a rehab they picked and bring the cameras for a reality show spinoff about my recovery and our reconciliation."

Kyra's regrets vanished just as quickly as they'd appeared, and she bristled. "That's horrible and awful. And, like, really, really . . . just . . . *bullshit.*"

"They said they would stop sending me money and all that," Stevie mumbled. Her fingers pulled at the thin bed sheets. "Not that they send me much anyway because they're completely broke. But I think the network was going to pay for my rehab if I agreed to the show."

"Screw that," Kyra growled. Stevie looked up at her in surprise. "I'll pay for it. We'll pay for it. I don't give a crap who pays for it as long as it's not them. But don't let them make you do a show because you're worried about money. You can live with me."

"Really?" Stevie's voice trembled slightly. It was a tone Kyra had never heard before. It was weak, like a little girl on the verge of tears. And even now, Stevie's big green eyes brimmed with them. Something in her expression told Kyra that her life had been full of fake friends and bad relationships. She'd probably never been offered something out of pure love.

And it infuriated Kyra. She didn't know much about parents. Actually, she didn't know anything besides the stilted kind of love her aunt and uncle had shown her, even though Aunt Carol really tried to be a mother to her. But Stevie's parents were alive, and she should've had better.

"Yes," Kyra said, her voice strong. "Whatever it takes. We can pick a place together and work out the cost. Then you can live with me if they take your house." She leaned forward, gripping Stevie's hand and feeling a determination to help her friend that she'd never felt for her own health. "But *fuck* them."

"Fuck who?"

"And who are you?"

Kyra looked over her shoulder as she pushed to her feet. Stevie's parents walked in the door and flipped on the lights, making Stevie cringe. Without thinking, Kyra shielded Stevie behind her as she fully turned to the couple in the room.

"I'm Kyra Aberdeen, Stevie's best friend. And this is Hale Cooper." She gritted her teeth, seconds away from going off on someone.

Mrs. Reynolds scoffed. "Only family is allowed in here. So I think you should leave. Now."

"I want them to stay," Stevie said weakly from behind Kyra.

"Stephanie, you need your parents right now." The woman looked back at Kyra and Hale. "If you two don't leave now, you will be forcibly removed." As if she could sense drama brewing, she leaned back out the door and motioned in the cameramen. When Kyra realized Stevie's mom wanted to catch all this on film, she lost it.

"Are you fucking serious?" she hissed. Her words were borderline yelling. "Get those fucking things out of here!"

"Excuse me?" Mrs. Reynolds gasped, but she motioned for the crew to start recording.

"I'll have you watch your language around my daughter and wife," Stevie's dad said, pointing his finger at Kyra.

"Oh, really?" she snapped. "I think you both are disgusting people. How could you bring those things in here when your daughter is in the hospital? So, no, I won't watch my language. And actually, I'll add that you're both fucking pieces of shits that don't even deserve to be crapped out of a dog's ass!"

Mrs. Reynolds gasped. "What did you just say to me?"

"You heard me," Kyra growled.

"Security!" Mr. Reynolds yelled out the door.

"Turn those off right now," Hale said, stepping around Kyra and blocking her. She peered around his massive shoulders and saw the closest cameraman had raised his camera and started recording.

The man didn't lower the camera or turn it off. Hale advanced, and Stevie's mom quickly backed out the room. Hale wrenched the camera out of the crew guy's hands. With a grunt, he brought the thing down on his knee, shattering it with a symphony of cracks and splinters.

"You'll pay for that!" the man stuttered.

"Perfect," Hale said, tossing the camera calmly aside. "Send me the fucking bill."

Kyra heard footsteps rushing down the hall. She quickly turned to Stevie and kissed her cheek. "Sorry, Stevie. I'll text you."

"Don't apologize. This made my day so much better."

The rent-a-cops came in the room, their eyes darting between the broken camera and Hale's formidable size. They advanced toward Kyra until Hale shot them a seething look. "Touch her, and I'll break you like that camera right there. We can walk out just fine."

He took Kyra's arm and guided her through the crowd of bodies and out the door. The cops followed them closely. As they left, Ethan smiled and gave them the thumbs-up sign.

"I'll have you arrested for destruction of property!" Stevie's dad called down the hall.

"Sounds like fun!" Hale hollered back.

The security guys walked them all the way out of the hospital and to Hale's truck. He opened Kyra's door for her before he went around to his side. The tires spun as he rocketed out of the parking lot.

"I can't believe we just got kicked out of a hospital," Kyra said, groaning. She was crashing back down from her anger high, which at the time, had felt amazing. She always felt guilty after standing up for herself against people like the Reynolds or her neighbors. But standing up for Stevie made her feel proud, if not exhausted.

"They deserved it."

"I just feel bad that we left Stevie alone with them."

"She can handle it." He turned out onto the main road that led back to Kyra's house. "And Ethan will make sure they don't hassle her."

"Yeah. You're right."

He glanced at her before he reached over and took her hand. With a squeeze he said, "Have I mentioned it turns me on when you curse?"

18

Kyra didn't sleep after Hale dropped her off. She tossed and turned all night, seeing Stevie's cut face and her big, scared eyes staring up at Kyra from the hospital bed every time she closed her eyes.

Finally, at four in the morning, she gave up on sleep. It was too early to go to the hospital, so she did a brutal circuit training workout on the beach. When she came back inside, she dripped sweat and sand. Her hands and feet were raw, and tendrils of her hair were plastered to the side of her neck. She took the stairs slowly, as her muscles wavered and buckled beneath her.

By the time she'd showered and drank her protein shake, it was almost a decent hour to go to the hospital. On her way, she picked up some blueberry scones from Maggie's Sweets to take to Stevie. The bag was warm and oozing delicious smells as Kyra walked to the double sliding doors at the hospital's entrance.

When she walked into a gust of cold air, a lady sitting at the front desk looked up and frowned instantly. Kyra's stomach twisted. "Ma'am," the lady called before she could duck past.

"Yes?" she asked, redirecting herself to the front desk. Tall green plants along with neutral-colored paint tried to cheer up the place, but the decorations couldn't do anything about the typical hospital smell hanging in the air, no matter how many plants littered the entrance.

"Please state your name," the lady said, her eyes on a clipboard in front of her.

"I'm just here to see my friend." Kyra held up the bag of scones, plastering a sugary-sweet smile on her face. "Would you like a scone?"

"Ma'am, your name please."

"Kyra Aberdeen," she said with a sigh.

"Ms. Aberdeen, you've been temporarily banned from the hospital," the lady said with a sniff. Her hair was teased and hair sprayed within an inch of its life. She wore a shirt buttoned all the way up to her throat and had a neat cardigan draped over her shoulders. She looked like Kyra's fifth-grade teacher, which meant Kyra had a better chance of getting past a fire-breathing dragon than this woman.

"Okay," she said with a small smile, feeling defeated. "I'm sorry for the hassle. Have a good day."

The lady harrumphed when Kyra's back was turned. The doors whooshed open, and the morning sun tickled her skin. The parking lot was empty besides her Jeep and a beat-up Honda that sputtered and jerked when it turned off. She wasn't surprised when Dr. Ethan

Faraday stepped out wearing rumpled scrubs and crooked sunglasses.

She wasn't in the mood to talk, but when he recognized her and waved, she stopped. "Hey, Dr. Faraday," she said, adjusting her grip on the bag of scones.

"Bleh. Call me Ethan." He shoveled his hair out of his face. "Did you come to hang with Stevie?"

She smiled at the doctor, but even she could tell it was a bad attempt. "Apparently I'm banned from the hospital."

"I'm not surprised. The Reynolds put up quite a stink when you two left yesterday. I considered sedating myself because they were getting so annoying."

"That bad, huh?" she asked, feeling a real smile tugging at her lips.

"Pretty killer." He shrugged, dragging out the word for a few extra syllables and making her giggle. "I can't let you into the hospital, but she rested well through the night. She just needs to stay until tomorrow afternoon, and then she can go home." He patted her arm awkwardly for a second, like he was trying to comfort her. "Anyway, I better scoot."

"Thanks for the information, Ethan." She remembered the bag in her hand. "Can you take these to Stevie? There's plenty in there for you too."

Ethan grinned and took the scones she offered. "Oh, yeah. From Maggie's?"

"She baked them fresh this morning."

"Man, she's the best. I'd marry that woman if I could. Thanks!"

"You're welcome," she said and waved.

Driving back to her house, she couldn't stop yawning. Her lack of sleep the night before was catching up to her, so she stopped at a gas station and filled up the Jeep and bought some coffee. By the time she got back to her house, the hammering was in full swing since Hale had called the crew into work on a Saturday.

Kitchen cabinets were being reinstalled since all the walls were up and the rooms were painted in the sea-blue palette Kyra had picked out. The cabinets were Hale's custom design, but a local cabinetmaker had built them. Even though he could make them himself, he'd insisted on using local shops for everything he could.

By the end of the day, she would have her kitchen almost ready. Her new appliances would be plugged in, and she could finally start using a real refrigerator and stove, which meant she could try out a vegan cookie recipe she'd been waiting to try.

Hale wasn't in the front room when she entered, but she waved to Chevy and the other guys and went upstairs. Since she was staying in here, they'd left this room unpainted, but it had been in better condition to begin with anyway, and she'd grown to like the simple, bright-white paint. With the gauzy curtains fluttering in the ocean breeze and a clammy sheen of salt coating every surface, her room felt right. She plugged in her phone and texted Stevie.

Kyra: Hope you're feeling better. Sorry I can't be there :(

Later in the day, she tried yet again to make the moor mud mask sponsored video. After her disastrous first attempt, she'd emailed them and asked for another sample, which had arrived in the mail yesterday while she was out with Hale. But as she stared at her mud-caked, stinking face in the camera's viewfinder, her overly perky, fake voice trailed off. She couldn't talk another moment about how great the mask was. It actually really sucked. And her subscribers should know, even if it meant she didn't get paid.

For once, she didn't stop and retake certain parts of her video. She just talked about why she didn't like the mask before she lost her nerve. She went straight through, in one continuous take, and when she was done, she stopped the video and started the uploading process.

Something in the act of making that video and posting it had eased the tension stretching across her chest. She took a full breath for the first time all day. Hale had been right; it felt good to be honest.

Before her eyes even landed on the ocean, she wanted to go surfing. But then she saw her back garden and sighed. She needed to get the weeds pulled and the bushes hacked down to size before the ladies of the neighborhood came by again.

She put on old work clothes and sunscreen. On her way out her bedroom door, she pulled on a baseball cap, tucking her hair through the back. Downstairs, the construction effort remained in the kitchen, so she went outside unnoticed.

She started in the front since it was the worst and more visible to everyone passing on the street. Once she set about the task, it didn't take her as long as she thought, since she'd already worked on it once before. She dumped countless loads of weeds in the big dumpster in her driveway, but when she was done, there was actually a clear path to her front porch. The garden almost looked bare without all the overgrowth. She stood on the porch to admire her work as she wiped the sweat from her eyes.

From across the street, Mrs. Harrison came out of her house and crossed the road. It was clear she'd seen Kyra in her garden and wanted to talk, but Kyra seriously considered turning around and hiding inside her house. Instead, she sighed and stood her ground.

"Hello, Mrs. Harrison," she called, not bothering to sound welcoming. She knew what the old lady wanted.

"Kyra." Mrs. Harrison drew out her name like it was a reprimand. "I'm glad to see you finally got around to fixing your garden." She paused as she came to a stop on the other side of the newly exposed fence. "After our garden club pictures, I might add."

"I had to wait until the construction crew finished all their repairs to the outside." She flashed an overly sweet smile.

Mrs. Harrison clucked her tongue, not believing Kyra for one second, even though it was technically the truth. "I came over to ask about dear Stephanie. How is she doing after her . . . *accident*?"

Kyra's eyes narrowed, and all the fear and anger she'd felt since yesterday surged back. "She's doing well."

"That's good to hear. But of course, if you play with fire, you're going to get burned, and all that boozing she does is playing with fire."

"Excuse me?" Kyra sputtered.

"Looking good, Mrs. Harrison," Hale called from behind Kyra. He put his hand around her waist, and to her ear, he said, "Calm down. It's okay."

"Mr. Cooper," the older woman drawled, her eyes settling on his hand on Kyra.

"It's awfully hot out here today," he said. "You better get inside and get cooled off. You don't want to have a stroke or something."

Kyra snorted as Mrs. Harrison's eyes threatened to bulge out of her head. Hale didn't wait for her response. He pulled Kyra inside and slammed the front door shut.

"I thought you wanted me to be more honest about how I feel? I was about to give her a piece of my mind," she said, taking a deep breath to calm down.

"I do, but I don't want you to give Mrs. Harrison a heart attack if you say she's not worth being crapped out of a dog's ass."

"Okay, fair point."

"Garden looks good though. I can order some mulch and topsoil for you. You can pick out the flowers you want to add in." Hale thought for a moment before he went on. "I could even build you some window boxes if you're nice to me. It would help brighten up the porch if you added some plants up here too."

"Will you do all the planting and mulching as part of the job?" she asked hopefully.

He let out a bark of laughter and clapped her on the shoulder. "You're funny."

"I wasn't trying to be," she said, mumbling the words under her breath.

"The kitchen should be done soon," he went on as if he hadn't heard her. "You could cook tonight if you want."

"Are you inviting yourself over?" Only now did she notice the sheen of sweat making his thin, worn shirt cling to his chest. He smelled of musk and man, and it was enough to have her insides tightening. He noticed her staring; he leaned in and ran his hand across her lower back.

"Yeah, I am. Is that a problem?"

"No." She let out a whoosh of air when his fingers found the bare back of her thigh. He hooked a finger underneath the hem of her shorts.

"Good." Blushing, she looked around to make sure none of the crew had seen before she hurried off to shower.

him. The pain subsided to allow for some pleasure.

She squeezed her breasts again and sped up slightly. As she started to move faster, so did his thumb. The pain was still there, but her body reacted to his touch. Then he started tapping his finger against her.

It undid her. She stopped moving up and down his length and just rocked her hips against him, feeling as if she were rocketing down a steep hill with her heart rising up her throat. He grabbed her hips as she came and pressed into her harder. He followed almost immediately after, his entire body flexing and straining beneath her as he forced himself not to move too much. The muscles along the side of his face pulsed with every clench of his jaw. "Oh, fuck," he growled.

Finally, he relaxed back against the bed and looked up at her. Her expression must have been as glazed over as she felt, because he grinned in satisfaction.

"Is anything on fire?" he asked.

She looked over her shoulder, pretending to look around the trailer before she turned back to him. "I think we actually had sex without something awful happening."

"How about you make me a sandwich while I stretch out my butt muscles, and we'll test the theory one more time."

24

The light in the trailer flared to life. From within the cocoon of downy blankets and pillows, Kyra groaned. It took effort and her sore body protested, but she managed to peek above the mound of blankets covering her to glare at Hale.

"Dude . . ."

"Time to get up and go to the job site!" He kicked the bed so hard her teeth rattled.

"The job site is *my* house."

"Exactly. And if you want to roll up on your house with the entire crew watching as you climb out of my truck and make your walk of shame inside, by all means, wait a few more minutes." He checked his watch. "They should be getting there in, oh, ten minutes."

She swore and flung the covers off her naked body. She sprawled across the bed and started gathering up her clothes from where they'd been tossed the night before. All the while, Hale laughed and sipped his coffee as he enjoyed the show.

By the time they reached her house, the crew was just arriving, having had a day off yesterday. She managed to slink down the side alley and go in through the back door before anyone saw her. The door to her bedroom clicked shut just as the front door opened and the rowdy crew piled in.

She plugged in her phone to charge. While she waited, she took a long bath, letting the heat ease her sore muscles. When the water cooled, she got out and opened her medicine cabinet. Inside, her eyes flickered to where she could just see the tip of her blade poking out. It was a tiny thing, meant to be used as a replacement blade for a knife she had.

Her eyes shifted back to her reflection in the partially opened door. She examined her eyes for any change, any sign that she'd changed overnight, but she found nothing. She looked the exact same. Like nothing had happened. She felt okay too. Last night hadn't broken anything, like she'd expected.

Quickly, she grabbed her lotion and closed the mirrored door.

As she dried off, Kyra checked her phone. She had a text from Stevie.

Stevie: Visitation hours tomorrow. Sheez. That sounds like it's for my funeral. Anyway, come. Or don't. Whatever.

Kyra: You know I'll be there.

With her phone still in her hand, Kyra slowly went through her past calls and hit dial on the new therapist's number. She quickly canceled her appointment for today and hung up. Things were better now; she felt good, solid.

Feeling buoyant, she dove into work.

The next day, Kyra drove out to The Lodge. A handful of cars were already parked along the circular drive, so she parked the Jeep at the end of the line. Before she even reached the front door, it opened and someone in a white uniform greeted her with a smile.

"Good morning! Welcome to The Lodge," the greeter said cheerfully. "Who are you here to see today?"

"That would be me." Stevie strolled up and examined Kyra carefully, sniffing the air like a dog. "You got laid."

"Uh . . . I'll leave you two to it. Have a wonderful day!" The greeter quickly darted away.

"Stevie!" Kyra hissed, looking around. Some of the other visitors sitting in the front room with their family or friends had looked up at Stevie's exclamation.

She shrugged. "Was it at least good?" Kyra shifted uncomfortably and glared at her friend. "Fine. You can tell me in a minute. Let's go out to the deck."

She followed Stevie down the hall. Almost every room had a massive fireplace and a huge bank of windows overlooking the lake. The wooden walls were warm, making the entire place smell like cedar. She passed a gym and a game room. Inside a moderately sized theater, she heard strains of a movie playing in the flickering darkness.

"This is nice, Stevie. Even better than the website made it sound," she said, marveling at the landscape paintings lining the hall.

"Yeah, it's cool." Stevie opened the French doors at the end of the hall and stepped out onto a large deck.

"Oh, wow," Kyra said, taking in the view of the lake, where people were swimming or canoeing. The air was clean and brisk, the breeze shifting through the loose strands of her hair as she watched people splash around in the crystal-clear water.

"It's like the best summer camp I never got to go to," Stevie said with a snort as she sat down, reclining in one of the chairs.

Kyra sat beside her. She studied her friend's face, which wasn't so pale and sickly anymore. The cuts had started healing more and the garish stitches were gone. Everything on the outside seemed okay, but she couldn't tell how Stevie really felt through her snarky humor. "So how is it going?"

Stevie's eyes stayed on the activity down at the lake. "It's going, I guess. I was imagining more of *One Flew over the Cuckoo's Nest*, but it's actually decent here. I like my therapist."

"That's good!"

"I think you would like her too," she said, the tone of her voice changing.

Kyra's smile slipped. "As long as you like her, that's what matters."

"I mean," Stevie said, fiddling with the hem of her shirt now, "maybe you could talk to her too."

"Uh, well . . ." The familiar stab of fear returned at the thought of therapy.

Stevie looked up. "I talk about you some in our sessions. She knows about you." She shrugged. "Like I said, she's good and I like her. Maybe you would like her if you talked to her."

"It's worth a shot, I guess."

"It was just a suggestion," she said quickly, but any embarrassment she felt fell away as she narrowed her eyes on Kyra. "Tell me about the sex."

Kyra groaned and ran her hands over her face. "It was okay, I guess," she said, the sound muffled.

"Ah, I see." Stevie nodded in understanding. "He couldn't get it up."

"What?" Kyra jerked, mortified. She looked around the deck. Thankfully, they were alone. "No. He could. I mean . . . it was just good. It was fine. Stop asking questions!"

"How big is he?"

"That's a question!"

Stevie sighed. "Do you know how bored I am? All I do is talk about my feelings and how much I want to drink and how much everyone *feels* all the time. It's annoying as shit. So tell me, please, before I waste away in here and go crazy, how big is he?"

"You," Kyra said, rolling her eyes, "are so dramatic."

"Have you met my parents? You should be glad I landed on dramatic and not batshit bananas."

"True," she said, pretending to think about it too long. Stevie swatted at her arm until she laughed. "Fine. He's big."

Stevie tapped her chin in thought. "Like hoagie sandwich big or like hotdog bun big?"

"Um . . . I don't understand the difference. Can we talk about something else?"

"How are you feeling after sleeping with him?"

"Exactly how much time have you spent in therapy?" Kyra asked with a nervous laugh.

"I'm serious," Stevie said, meaning it. "Are you okay?"

"I think so. Should I not be? I mean, I feel like he should talk to me or look at me more or something. I feel like he's just being normal or something when this isn't just *normal* anymore. Like we had sex and everything is different now, but he's just so calm about it."

"So you want more attention from him?"

She straightened off the chair. "You're freaking me out. You have to stop."

"I'm just saying." Stevie held up her hands in surrender. "Have you watched the weather lately?"

"Oh, you mean the storm?" Kyra floundered at the unexpected subject change.

Nodding, Stevie said, "Could you ask Hale to put up my storm shutters? They're in the garage. I'll pay him when I get back."

"Sure thing. But do you think it'll actually hit us?"

"Maybe."

They talked for a while after that, but Kyra couldn't stay long. Guests were only allowed for a couple hours. Stevie showed her out, walking her back to the front door. When they got there, a willowy woman was saying goodbye to some other guests. She looked up when they approached.

"Hey, Stevie," she said, her voice bright and crisp as the breeze around them. She smiled sweetly. "And you must be Kyra. I've heard a lot about you. I'm Dr. Clemens."

She reached out and shook Kyra's hand. "Nice to meet you," she said politely.

"Kyra, this is the therapist I was telling you about," Stevie said, sounding sheepish. "Anyway, thanks for coming to see me. I have to go so they can put me back in my straightjacket and padded room."

Dr. Clemens laughed. "Very funny, Stevie."

Stevie pulled Kyra into a fierce hug, which surprised her. She was even more shocked when Stevie kissed her cheek. "Talk to her," she whispered. And then she left, leaving Kyra alone with the therapist and feeling effectively maneuvered when she turned back to the doctor.

"So, uh, Stevie said she enjoys your sessions with her."

Dr. Clemens's smile broadened. "She's a good person. She has a smart head on her shoulders."

"Oh, she's smart all right," Kyra said, grinning.

"I don't want to keep you too long. Here's my card in case you would like to contact me about anything. I do more than just addiction counseling."

She took the card the doctor offered her, wondering exactly how much Stevie had told Dr. Clemens about her. "Um, thanks," she said, swallowing to alleviate the dryness in her mouth. "I'll be in touch soon. I, uh, recently moved, so I haven't had time to talk with anyone lately."

"Understandable," Dr. Clemens said, still smiling. The perfume she wore reminded Kyra of fresh linens flapping in a summer breeze. "But you don't want to wait too long."

"Right. I better get going." Kyra stepped outside and pulled on her sunglasses.

"Kyra?"

She turned and looked back at the doctor, who stood framed in the doorway. "Yeah?"

"Thanks for getting Stevie help. I don't think she would've

come if it weren't for you."

"She's a smart woman, like you said. I'm sure she would've figured it out," she said, shrugging. From the entrance, she could hear people calling and splashing in the lake. The front drive was empty except for her Jeep.

"That might be true, but sometimes we need to take the advice of others because we get in our own way." Dr. Clemens waved. "Have a safe drive."

"Thanks," she mumbled. She hurried down the stairs to her car. She didn't breathe again until she was inside and the music was loud enough to drown out any sounds from outside the car. As she pulled away, she looked in the rearview mirror. Dr. Clemens was gone, and The Lodge stood gleaming in the sun as she drove on.

25

"*Like* this?"

Kyra rocked back on her heels and wiped the sweat off her brow with the back of her gloved hand. A bug buzzed beside her ear, and the pollen-laden fragrance of blooming flowers turned the air thick and heavy. Annabelle sat on the garden bench wearing a big straw hat while she supervised Kyra.

"Make the water basin a little deeper. It'll help hold in the water to keep the roots moist," Annabelle advised. Kyra pressed on the dirt more, forming a deeper bowl around the newly transplanted flower bush.

"I'm happy you stopped by today," Annabelle said, sitting back and sipping her water.

Kyra flushed. "I still feel bad for just barging in on you. I probably should have called first."

"Oh, bah. You never have to call ahead to visit me." Annabelle flapped her hand at Kyra. "Now the compost. Just sprinkle it evenly over the top and add some mulch."

Kyra pulled over the bag of compost. The dirt was fine and loamy, slipping through her fingers like sand. She breathed in the rich, healthy smell of it. "What about the storm?" she asked. "Will this plant survive if it gets bad?"

"If it's strong, and you've given it a good start," Annabelle said with a smile. "Hale mentioned you were visiting your friend today. Do you miss her?"

"Yes, ma'am," Kyra said, focusing on the compost. "I visited, but I think I miss her more than she misses me." She laughed. "Stevie would get along fine no matter where she was."

"She sounds like she's a strong girl then."

"She's overcome a lot," Kyra agreed. She set the compost bag aside and scooped out some mulch from the wheelbarrow beside her. The breeze cooled the sweaty tendrils of loose hair at her neck. "I'll be glad when she's back home though."

Annabelle nodded thoughtfully. "It does a soul good to be where it belongs. Do you feel like you belong on Canaan?" Annabelle suddenly laughed, the sound bright and crisp in the humid air. "See? I ask too many questions."

Kyra smiled up at the woman. "I don't mind at all." Peeling the gardening gloves off her hands, she straightened off the ground and sat in the vintage metal chair across from Annabelle. "And to answer your question, I do think I belong. Or at least I hope I do, but my grandmother seems to have other ideas."

"Ah, Florence." Annabelle's eyes clouded over as if she was lost in thoughts. "I remember when your mother was little. I used to see her and Florence in town. Your grandmother was so happy then, so free. A lot like you, maybe." Kyra cringed at the words, which made Annabelle smile kindly. "She didn't always used to be this way, you know. But now I think she hides a world of hurt behind her icy demeanor because she doesn't want anyone to see the cracks running through her."

With Annabelle's words, the jagged, sharp piece in Kyra's life that was Florence Aberdeen finally made sense. Florence was a faker, just like Kyra. While Kyra hid behind smiles and laughter, her grandmother used cruelty and condescension to keep people at a distance. To keep her broken heart safe. She'd never healed after Lila. Just like Kyra.

"Maybe you're right," she said, murmuring the words but feeling the rightness of them somewhere deep in her chest.

"Anyway! On to lighter subjects," Annabelle piped up. Just then, Nancy brought out a tray of sweet tea and fruit. The ice in the glasses clinked together. "Thank you, Nancy. Would you like to stay out here and visit with Kyra for a bit?"

Nancy smiled, taking Annabelle's wrist to make sure she wasn't getting too hot. "Maybe next time. I have pies in the oven."

Annabelle sighed. "All she does is bake pies. She's trying to make me fat."

"We'll get those curvy hips back so we can catch you a man," Nancy said.

"Humph." Annabelle fussed with the brim of her hat, her cheeks flushing slightly.

Nancy winked at Kyra before she went inside. "How long were you and Mr. Cooper together?" Kyra asked, smiling.

"Oh, goodness. All our lives. We fell in love in high school. Lord, he was the dorkiest thing. You wouldn't ever look twice at him. But something about him spoke to me, and I knew he was the one." Annabelle's smile was faraway, her memories of her husband clearly touching her heart. "He was a good man. I miss him every day," she added.

"You both did wonderful jobs raising Hale and Cade. They are good men," Kyra said, making Annabelle smile even wider.

"They will always be my boys to me." She leaned forward, cupping her chin in her hand. Her eyes were sharp and clear now as they focused on Kyra. "I saw how Hale watched you the other day. He's never brought a girl to see me before."

Kyra choked on her sweet tea. "Really?"

"Really."

"Oh, um," she said, trying to recover. "We're not really that serious or anything. Or, I mean," she fumbled, thinking Annabelle would assume she'd meant they were just sleeping together, "we haven't known each other very long."

"I get it." Annabelle shook her head with a sigh. "Hale can be a crotchety old bastard, just like his father."

Kyra didn't just choke on her tea this time. She spewed it. Thankfully, Annabelle was out of the line of fire. She looked up to see Annabelle's mischievous glint in her eyes, and she burst out laughing. "He really can be!" she managed, still coughing.

She thought about the night before and how pissed Hale had been about the mosquitoes and sex. She blushed as Annabelle said, "He doesn't mean anything by it, though. It's just who he is. Like I said, he took after his father."

"He can be so funny and lighthearted sometimes. And then he

gets all grumpy." Kyra wiped under her eyes and took another drink, the condensation making her hand slick.

"Never said he was consistent."

Kyra reached for some fruit to munch on. She felt so at home with this woman, like she'd known Annabelle her whole life. "I like that about him. He's always honest about how he feels."

A shadow flittered over Annabelle's face, and Kyra instantly worried if she'd said something wrong. "Hale may have taken after his father, but Cade took after me. You probably know Cade was bullied when he was younger?" Annabelle asked, and Kyra nodded in answer. "It bothered him a lot, but we never knew how bad it was until one day, Hale caught him holding his breath in the bathtub. He'd been under so long that he was turning blue. Hale pulled him out, but it scared him, scared us all. None of us really understood the depth of Cade's pain. Since then, Hale's been the protector, the one who always makes sure we're okay. He insists on being honest."

Kyra could only nod in agreement. She thought about that evening when Hale had raced to the ocean and paddled out to her, yelling that she was putting herself in danger. He'd been wild with a deep-rooted fear that she finally understood. It was why he always pushed her so hard to be real and open. He needed that from those around him because he was terrified of losing them.

She and Annabelle visited for a while longer until Kyra noticed the woman growing tired. Almost as if on cue, Nancy appeared with Annabelle's afternoon medicine and an update on the building storm. It was then that Kyra noticed Hale had already been to his mother's house earlier in the day to put up her storm shutters. With a smile, she hugged each of them goodbye and walked through the gardens to her Jeep.

It was late in the afternoon, and the car was stuffy when she got in. Checking her phone, she noticed a text from Stevie.

Stevie: Cade is coming to see me tmr. So you can't since only one visitor is allowed. #conjugalvisit. Looks like the storm is getting closer!

Kyra: Gross, Stevie. Have fun. We will get your storm shutters up.

She also had a text from Hale.

Hale: I'm waiting.

Two simple words made her heart hammer.

When she pulled in the drive, she noticed all the house lights were on. It was the first time she'd ever had the sensation of coming home to someone. Her smile stretched wide as she walked to the front door.

Inside, Hale had his radio turned up so loud that she heard it from the entry. She threaded her way through the work supplies and walked to the back of the house. There, she found Hale bent over a sawhorse, cutting precise lines through old pieces of wood they'd taken off the house. He never let anyone throw anything away that had come from the house, especially if it was wood or something that could be repurposed. He said if it had been with the house this long, he was going to ensure it stayed with it for the next hundred years.

"What are you making?" she asked. She settled her hand against his back, pressing her palm into the swells of his muscles. Without a word, he turned and kissed her until she'd forgotten what she asked.

"A new buffet. The original one is long gone, so I'm going to replicate it from the old pictures we have."

"Pictures?"

"The ones upstairs in the extra bedroom," he said, frowning.

"Oh, right." Her throat constricted. It hadn't occurred to her that he would return to the bedroom to look at her mother's pictures. "I've been looking through them too."

"Is it okay that I looked at them?"

"Yeah. Of course." She shrugged, smiling, which made him narrow his eyes. "I just mean," she went on, "that I didn't realize anyone else had seen them. My aunt and uncle had a few pictures of Mom, but nothing like what I've found here."

His expression relaxed. "I understand. I won't look at them anymore."

"What? No. I didn't mean that. You can look at them too," she said, her voice too high-pitched.

"How about if you find some pictures of the house or any old furniture, you can show it to me if you want?"

A little spot in her chest eased at his patient words. She hadn't realized she would be so protective of the pictures. Hugging him, she murmured against his neck, "Thank you."

"You're welcome. Now let's go order takeout. I'm not eating that tofu shit again."

She called for some Thai takeout while he listened to the radio. "It'll be here in thirty minutes. What's going on?" she asked when she hung up the phone.

"That storm is building up pretty good, and its aiming straight for us. We could get hit by the end of the week," Hale answered, switching the radio to a channel playing rock music.

"How bad is it?" She'd never been through a hurricane before. The worst she'd experienced in California were earthquakes and sunburn.

"They're saying it could be a Category 3 when it hits land, which could get pretty intense."

"Stevie asked if we could put up her storm shutters," Kyra said, remembering her friend's request.

"Already done. We have to delay painting the outside of your house until after the storm passes. I don't want anything to nick the paint."

She didn't know what to say. He seemed to think of everything to take care of those around him. "Thank you," she said.

"You're welcome." His eyes brightened. "A storm means some nice swells though. Good surfing for the next few days."

"That sounds awesome. Let's go out there now before the food comes!" She was already moving toward the back door when his voice stopped her.

"We can play in it tomorrow," he said. "I have plans for right now."

She narrowed her eyes. "What plans?"

"Ones that don't involve me puking everywhere." His expression was mischievous, and she practically read his dirty thoughts.

Later that evening when the Thai takeout boxes were in the trash, Hale said, "I have a surprise for you."

"Is it a furniture magazine?" Kyra asked, groaning as she rose from the floor. "Cause I really need to get some."

"I can take you to some salvage places tomorrow to pick some stuff out if you want. The crew will have the floors stripped by then, and by the time the furniture is delivered later in the week, everything will be dry from the polyurethane."

"That would be great." She stretched out her back. "So what's the surprise?"

"Follow me."

They went to the back porch and turned on the outside light. Kyra gasped.

The entire back garden was pruned and weeded. New plants with fragrant, white blooms had been added with fresh mulch. A hammock stretched between the two large magnolia trees.

"Hale! How did you do all this in one afternoon?"

"You did most of the work, and I don't have the patience for stripping floors, so Chevy took the lead with the guys. So I had some free time, and most old houses like this always had a white garden in the back. The flowers only bloom at night, and they have the sweetest smells."

She went down the stairs and examined her new garden. Something about the delicate, white blooms opening up only at night swelled her heart. They were hidden, precious gems with the nicest perfumes.

"This is . . . it's amazing. Thank you, Hale." She looked back up at him where he still stood on the porch. In the warm light from the porch and with the moon illuminating his face, he looked like the man she wanted to keep for all her life. She needed this, to see him standing on her porch smiling down at her. Tears brimmed along her eyes. This was what she wanted, what she yearned for.

Suddenly, she just needed his hands on her. She needed to feel him close to her, to claim him while he was hers. When she pulled her shirt over her head, his eyes went wide with understanding. He was down the porch steps by the time she reached for the button on her shorts.

"I think we should break in that hammock," she whispered, letting her shorts fall to the ground. Hale bowed over her, his hands reaching for her face to pull her into a kiss. Their lips met, and she knew she was falling in love with him.

He picked her up and carried her to the hammock. He sprawled out on it, pulling her down on top of him. "You're so beautiful," he said, removing her bra. His hand closed over her breast. "I couldn't stop looking at you that day we met. It pissed me off."

"I could tell." Her laugh turned into a gasp when he rolled her nipple between his fingers.

"I wanted you then. I knew I would need to get my hands on you."

She couldn't respond as he kissed her neck, his hands rasping across her skin. They came together beneath the night sky to the sounds of the ocean crashing against the beach right behind them. If her neighbors looked out their windows right then, they probably would've gotten a shock, but Kyra had never felt so at peace with herself.

26

"If I'd known you had such horrible taste in furniture, I never would have asked you to come."

Hale's brows lifted, twisting his piercing. "Volunteered to help, actually. And I don't have awful taste. This is a really functional table."

The table was plain and uninspired, with flat white paint and straight lines. Kyra blew a loose strand of hair out of her eyes. They had left early that morning, once Hale had given the crew instructions to get the house prepared for the storm. Now it was almost dinnertime, and he'd taken her to three salvage and antique stores. So far, she'd found some awesome things to fill her house, but she really needed a great dining room table so her friends wouldn't have to sit on her porch's rough floorboards when they came over for dinner.

"I can't even imagine what Stevie would say about it," she said with a smile.

"Fine. We'll keep looking. Have you heard from her today?" He inspected every piece of wood they passed, which was a lot. Their going was slow.

"She texted me earlier. I guess she and Cade had a good time together yesterday. They went swimming."

"Huh."

She looked over her shoulder. Hale had a purposefully neutral expression on his face. "He likes her, doesn't he? Has he mentioned it to you?"

"Not getting in the middle of that crazy train. What about this?"

She barely glanced at the table he'd stopped in front of. It was falling apart and appeared to be slightly rotten. She crinkled her nose, opening her mouth to tell him how ugly it was, but then she saw it.

"Oh!" she gasped. She shoved by Hale and made her way over to a table propped up on its edge in the corner. "Look at this one! It's amazing!"

It was huge enough to fit ten people around it. The legs were carved into angels with their wings holding up the top planks of the table's surface. Their faces were heartbreakingly sad, their expressions turned upwards to the sky, as if longing to go home. The ancient wood was a little banged up in the corners, but Kyra thought it added character. She couldn't imagine all the people who'd likely sat around this table. The stories it would tell, she thought. She turned to Hale, grinning like a fool.

"I would tell you that it doesn't match the era of the house, but since you've already picked out a pink zebra-print chair, an early-nineteenth-century gargoyle, and a sixties-era shag rug, I'm not wasting my breath." Running his hand down the wood, he shrugged. "Nice table, though. Solid. Probably hundreds of years old. Look at the wood. Those rich, undulating colors aren't from a stain. That's just time. Time and age. You can't recreate that."

His eyes glazed over as he ran his hand back and forth over the planks. She snapped her fingers in front of his face. "Tag it. I want it."

"You don't even know how much it is." He twisted the price tag over. "Never mind. It's a steal." Shaking his head, he added, "These people don't know what they have in here."

"It's amazing," she said, still in awe of the beautiful angels.

"Yeah. You got lucky with that one."

"I always get lucky." She called the words over her shoulder as she walked away, looking for chairs to go with the table. She'd found a lot of great things today, even if Hale had made fun of every one. If it were up to him, her house would be full of stuffy, uncomfortable furniture that was true to the time period of the house. Her tastes were a little eclectic and all over the place, but she could tell he was having a good time trying to teach her about the different time periods' styles. As if she was paying attention.

"Look at these chairs, Kyra." She doubled back to where he was standing. "Before you say it, I know they are plain. But they're well made, and they won't distract from the table. You could get the cushions reupholstered and they would look good as new. And, little Miss Lucky, there are plenty of them here to fit around the table."

She snapped her fingers. "Tag 'em."

"You get bossy when you shop," he grumbled.

She picked out a an outdoor dining set, a few lamps, mirrors, and knickknacks she deemed she couldn't live without before they left an hour later. Hale arranged for the larger pieces to be delivered tomorrow while Kyra toted her smaller gems out to his truck. Its entire bed was filled to the brim. She checked the sky, hoping it wouldn't start raining early. All people had been talking about was the storm coming in.

It was evident in the clouds over the ocean. Miles and miles away, they were building, dark and foreboding. She shivered and looked away.

"Do you want to stop at the art gallery? They always have cool, local art," Hale said when he'd joined her outside.

"Nope." She hopped in the tall truck. "I already have art for the house."

"Oh, really? What?"

"You're going to frame your drawings of the house. I want them signed too," she added, speaking over the rumble of the truck.

He pulled out of the parking lot. "Those aren't art. You don't want to hang them in your house."

"Yes, I do." He was about to complain some more, but she held up her hand. "No more arguments. I'm getting them framed."

"Not if I don't give them to you." He maneuvered through the traffic. It seemed like everyone was in town getting supplies for the storm.

She smirked, crossing her arms over her chest. She knew how to get him. "I'll withhold sex until you do."

He barked out a laugh. "Like you could. One look from me and you'd strip in the streets."

"Oh, please. You're not that good."

"Funny. That's not what you said this morning."

The heat spread up her neck and fanned out to her cheeks. She was certain she'd begged for it, praising him with each stroke. With one glance, Hale confirmed that she was blushing. "I . . ."

"Exactly." He parked the truck outside of her house. "Looks like the crew got a lot done today."

Recovering from her embarrassment, she asked, "Are those my storm shutters?"

Solid aluminum panels covered every one of her new windows. They made the house look like a grinning old man with silver teeth. Overall, the shutters didn't add much to the aesthetic of the house, but if they worked, she was okay with them.

"Yep. You have storm-resistant windows that shouldn't break, but the shutters are good precautions," Hale said.

"Oh, okay." She shielded her eyes against the setting sun and peered up at her house. It was coming together, even if the outside looked like hodge-podge of old wood and new replacements. Hale had promised it would all look the same when the house was painted, but Kyra had her doubts.

She turned away and helped carry in her smaller purchases, making multiple trips and joking with each other as they passed. Hale complained about her ruining the aura of the house with her incorrect-era pieces, but she knew he liked her taste, even if he wouldn't admit it.

"What are you going to put up in the front bedroom?" he asked, sprawling out on the stairs.

She set the last two lamps down in the front hall. "Uh . . . " She hesitated. "Probably nothing," she said, muttering the words as she bent down and pretended to dust off the lamps.

"Why not?" He sat up straighter, his eyes like lasers on her.

Even before she'd gone shopping, she knew she wasn't going to put anything in the room. She couldn't confirm it, but she just knew it had been her mother's room. And she didn't want to tarnish the memories in there by masking it with new furniture that wouldn't match what had been in there before. The only bed that belonged in there was the one her mother had slept on, but it was long gone now.

"It just doesn't feel right," she said when she met his gaze.

He thought about her words for a moment before he nodded. "Was it her room?"

"Yeah."

"I get it." He rose from the steps and pulled her in for a kiss. It was deep and passionate and over far too quickly. He pulled away and looked down at her. "Want to surf for a bit?"

Kyra didn't answer. Instead, she bounded up the stairs and raced into her bedroom. She was already naked when she heard Hale chuckle from downstairs. "Guess that's a yes," he called out.

By the time she was downstairs, he was in his trunks, which he kept in his truck, and had taken a larger board from her back porch. Together, they walked to the water where the swells peaked much higher than normal, which made Kyra's heart pound with excitement. She couldn't bear it any longer, so she started running toward the waves. Hale followed at a more leisurely pace.

They surfed until they were worn out. Then, surprising Kyra, Hale made dinner. He'd found a vegetarian recipe that he was willing to try, and it was one he could cook. She taste tested and smiled her approval. They ate and laughed from the kitchen floor until they were stuffed.

He laid back and beckoned her over. Without thinking twice about it, she crawled over to him, tucking her body along his side. His arm cushioned her head, and she could've fallen asleep in seconds.

With a contented sigh, she wiggled closer, wrapping her arm around his chest. "I lo—" she choked off the word, her body going tense. She'd almost told Hale she loved him. The words had practically spoken themselves. She cringed.

"What?" he murmured, clearly not understanding what had almost happened.

But it was an eye-opener for her. She had no clue how he felt about her besides that he liked sleeping with her, but she wasn't the type of girl who could just have sex or even just have a casual relationship. She felt herself opening up to him, but it also meant she was experiencing wild swings in emotions. She couldn't handle that; her throat closed. She didn't know how she would deal with things if he broke her heart.

She hated herself for thinking it, but she already had before she could stop herself: how many times would she have to cut herself to deal with the pain when he left? Even once was too much. Even thinking about it wasn't okay. She resolved to call Dr. Clemens tomorrow. And she wouldn't let herself cancel it this time.

She shouldn't ask him, but she couldn't stop herself. "Hale?"

"Hmmm?" He stirred next to her, his eyes closed and his breaths deep.

"What are we doing?"

He grunted and shifted against the hard floor. "Giving ourselves back problems."

"No, I mean, like, what are we doing together?" She propped up on her elbow and looked down at him. He opened his eyes and instantly narrowed them.

"Thought we were just enjoying each other's company," he said carefully. Too carefully, she thought.

"But you hated me when you first met me," she said. She stood up from the floor. Behind her, he sat up, crossing his legs and running his hand through his hair.

"You have to admit, the overly perky attitude was pretty hate-worthy."

She spun around. "Don't make a joke right now. I'm serious." She sighed. "I need to know."

"Why?" he asked. "Does it matter? Does it make a difference?"

"Yes!"

He scowled at the floor before he looked back up at her. "It shouldn't. If we both like each other, why should it matter what this is? Shouldn't we be able to just have fun and experience things as we come to them? 'Cause that's life, or at least how I understand it to be. If my answer changes that for you, then I don't think you're living life the way it should be lived."

But his answer *did* change things for her. It had to. This was the way she protected herself. He mistook her distress. "Come here," he said, opening his arms.

She crossed the room and climbed into his lap, threading her legs around his waist. He tucked a loose piece of hair behind her ear. His other hand settled against her hip bone. "Don't worry so much," he said quietly. "We'll figure it out, okay?"

"Okay," she breathed.

He leaned forward, weaving his fingers into her hair, and kissed her. His tongue slipped inside her mouth, and she sighed. His lips worked over hers, his tongue stroking along her lips.

Rocking against him, she could already feel his growing hardness. His hand on her hip slid around and down her backside until he was between her legs. Through her shorts, he stroked her. He pressed hard, ensuring she could feel every flick of his thumb through the material of her shorts.

She couldn't believe how turned on she was with all her clothes still on. He watched her as she moved with his hand, encouraging more from him. Already she could feel the steady thrum between her legs. She hummed her pleasure, letting her head fall back.

"Doesn't this feel good, Kyra?" he asked. His fingers caressed up the middle of her backside, making her gasp. The thrumming quickened as she drew closer to her climax.

"Yes."

"Then why question it?" He sounded almost as if he was growling. He rubbed his fingers faster and harder against her.

Because something was wrong with her, she thought, but didn't say the words aloud. Even through the haze of pleasure, even when she was so close, she sensed the bottomless black hole inside her, waiting and preparing to pull her in. If she gave in to it, she would fall forever.

She rocked against him one last time before she came. Gasping, she opened her eyes and watched him as her hips bucked into his hand. The pleasure rolled through her, flaring her insides until she felt like she'd been set on fire and left to burn.

When it was over, she settled against him, her limbs numb. Easily, he rose from the ground, picking her up as well. She wrapped her legs around his waist as he carried her from the kitchen and up the stairs.

"Stay with me, baby. We're not finished yet," he murmured. He opened her bedroom door with his foot. She was still too hazy to do much besides nod against his neck. Gently, he laid her down on the bed.

She looked up at him, watching as he pulled off his shirt and pants. The moonlight streamed in from the window and etched every line of his body, every dark curve of ink. He lowered himself over her, and she arched up against him, thinking eventually this man would break her heart apart without even knowing.

"Be careful with me, Hale," she whispered, not meaning it the way he thought she did.

"Always."

27

Kyra was up early the next morning. Before Hale woke up, she'd gotten in a punishing workout, shower, and breakfast. When he finally stirred, just as the sun was fully rising, she was back in bed, working. She pulled out her earphones and looked over at him with a smile.

"I'm tired," he said, sounding half asleep.

"You worked hard last night."

"Could probably conjure that strength now," he said, the corner of his mouth twitching.

"Ha!" She snorted. "Is the crew coming today?"

"Nah." He pulled the sheet back up to his shoulders and burrowed deeper into the pillows. "Gave them today off to prepare their houses for the storm this weekend."

"That was nice of you," she commented, tucking one of her

earphones back in and jigging her foot in time to the lilting beat.

He grunted in response. Just when his breathing turned to the slow, deliberate breaths of sleep, a loud honk sounded from outside. She chuckled as he reared up in bed.

"What the fuck?"

"Furniture." She slapped his arm, springing from the bed. "You get to help."

As she passed by the bed, she ripped off the sheets, exposing the length of his hard, naked body. She didn't bother paying attention to his string of colorful curse words as she pounded down the steps and swung the front door open before the furniture guys even had a chance to knock.

"Morning!" She beamed up at the surprised man. His beard was bright red and his belly protruded nearly a foot in front of him.

"Ma'am," he said gruffly with a nod. "We've got some furniture for you today."

She clapped her hands together in excitement. "Awesome! Let's get to it then." She swiveled around and hollered up the stairs, "Hale! Hurry up!"

"Uh . . . I'm Dusty."

"Nice to meet you, Dusty. I'm Kyra." She shook his offered hand quickly before stepping around him onto the porch. A floor lamp was being lowered from a large truck in front of her house. She already knew the neighborhood ladies would complain because the truck had blocked most of the street. But Mrs. Harrison could suck it because her house was finally getting furniture.

She practically danced down her front walk to the back of the truck. Inside, she recognized her wrought-iron bed frame with gilded roses. The old sixties record player sat right in front, and her mouth watered at finally being able to play all the records she'd kept carefully packed away.

Hale finally came downstairs after Dusty and his helper had muscled in a heavy coffee table. Together, the four of them got everything inside and in the right rooms. By the time it was all done, Hale was wiping beads of sweat off his brow and Kyra was flitting from room to room, trying to figure out how to arrange everything. She stopped long enough to tip the guys from the salvage store before they left. Hale collapsed onto her pink zebra chair, which happened to be the only comfy seat she had in her living room. She pulled out her phone to take notes. Her first one: *couches*.

"You know," he said, "this isn't what you pay me to do. I'm a contractor, not a mover."

Distracted, she looked up. She'd already opened an app on her phone and started shopping for cute couches. "What?"

"I don't arrange furniture either. And I certainly don't rearrange furniture fifty million times."

"I'm not going to ask you to rearrange it fifty million times," she said, frowning.

He gestured toward her. "I see what you're doing. The crazy is brewing in your eyes right now. You have that *fifty million* look on your face."

She sniffed. He might have a point. She really had no clue where she wanted everything. "So you're not going to help me?"

"I'll help you." He crossed his legs at the ankle, stretching his arms over his head. His shirt lifted, revealing a swath of tan skin and patch of dark hair below his belly button. She knew that spot on him well by now, but her mouth still pooled with warm saliva. "But it'll cost you."

"You're going to charge me?"

"In many ways. Later tonight. Maybe even during all this furniture arranging if I get bored or you piss me off extra good."

"Okay, whatever, Fabio. Let's get going."

Later that night, after she had asked him to rearrange everything numerous, but not quite fifty million, times, she realized he really did intend on charging her.

He took her hand and tugged her from the kitchen and up the stairs. They'd put her new bed up here, in addition to some other pieces, so it looked completely different now that it was organized. Hale spun her around so her back was to the bed before he pushed her down.

Laughing, she landed on the soft blankets. The iron frame rattled against the wall as he climbed on top of her, his face drawn into serious lines. He jerked her shorts down her legs, taking her panties down with them. He didn't bother with her top.

He reached between her legs, testing her. She was more than ready. His voice was rough with pleasure when he said, "I'm figuring out that I'm enjoying being the only one you've had."

She pressed herself into his hand as she hooked her leg over his hip. "What about me being with guys after you? Does that make you mad?" Her growl almost matched Hale's. He shoved his fingers deep into her. Kyra groaned, spreading her legs wider.

"Do you really want to talk about this right now?"

"Why not?" She pulled his length out of his jeans and positioned it against her.

"Fine," he hissed. "And yeah, it fucking pisses me off."

Before, he had eased into her, letting her adjust to his width. Not this time. She cried out as he shoved himself inside her all at once, her hands reaching behind her to hold on to the wrought-iron rods of the bed as he slid out slightly, only to slam back inside her, making the headboard bang against the wall.

It surprised her to learn she liked it rough. She hooked her other leg around him and just held on as he hammered into her. Her mouth gaped open, head pressed into the mattress as Hale filled every inch of her. He destroyed her, tore her apart. But she loved the punishment.

After a moment of his grinding pace, he slowed but didn't ease off the intensity. He reached between them and worked his finger over her. It was all she needed. She cried out, not worrying about being quiet. Too late, she realized the windows were still open, but she didn't care as her body writhed under Hale.

Deep lines formed between his heavy brows. The tattoos along his neck twisted and bulged. He emptied into her, pumping himself against her until his hips finally grew still. Then he collapsed on her.

His weight was crushing, but he rolled, pulling her on top of him. She was too exhausted to do anything but sprawl on top of him. Already, the soreness built between her legs.

"Do you not want me to be with anyone else?" she asked quietly.

She thought Hale must have fallen asleep, it took him so long to respond. "It would be a nice fantasy."

His words gave her the tiniest flicker of hope. And courage. She told herself she needed to be honest. "Why does it have to be a fantasy?" she asked. She twisted her head to look at him, but his gaze was lost somewhere outside.

"Do I really seem like the marrying type? In case you haven't noticed, I'm a little rough around the edges."

Her heart pulsed with fear. She was losing him. He was going to say something wrong, say something that sent her skittering back behind a fake smile. But she didn't want to do that with him. She wanted . . .

"I love you," she blurted out the words, expelled them from her body, before she told herself not to.

Hale froze. With every passing second, she felt like a hole might open up beneath her and swallow her whole. Slowly, carefully, like he was talking her off a ledge, he said, "You love what's not good for you."

He didn't know how close he was to the real, darkest truth of her. She stood abruptly, tugging at the hem of her shirt. It was easier for her to tell him she loved him than it was for her to show him the raw, scarred truth.

Hale sat up, not bothering to cover himself. "Come on, Kyra. Look at you." He gestured broadly in her direction. "You're not the kind of girl who settles down with someone like me. You shouldn't love me."

The anger building inside of her was welcomed. She grabbed onto it instead of the gaping black hole of sadness welling at his rejection. "Oh, really? Am I the same girl you called fake? Or is this the goody two-shoes Kyra? I'm getting confused with all your judgments of me."

He sighed, raking his hand roughly through his hair. "You know that wasn't what I meant."

"No, you think you know better than I do about what I want. You think you have it all figured out, huh?"

Maybe he did know her, but the thought infuriated her. How could he know when she constantly had no idea? She knew she loved him, or, at least, she thought she did. She wanted to be with him, but he didn't want her.

"I just want to protect you."

"You didn't even try," she accused. "We made a deal to try."

This was exactly what she'd feared during that moment weeks ago, when she decided to toe the line of darkness inside of her for him. With one kick, he could send her falling down into the abyss of her depression, her dark thoughts, her bad days. It terrified her.

She'd done this. She'd given him this power over her.

"When we said that, I didn't think we were talking about love."

"I know that," she fired back. And she did. She knew they hadn't been talking about love or commitment or marriage, but she thought they'd been talking about *more*.

Something more than this, because this wasn't enough for her.

"Come here. I don't want to fight."

She went to him, but she knew.

It wasn't enough.

28

Hale didn't even stir when Kyra got up the next morning. He'd stayed, even after all they'd said to each other. Maybe he knew more about her darker truth than she thought. Because if he'd left, she knew what she would've done. She would have cut to punish herself for being so stupid. So idiotic. Even now, she craved the pain. She wanted to control something, since everything else seemed to be spiraling out of her hands.

Mindlessly, she tidied the kitchen and tinkered with the furniture some more. Too restless to shop and too distracted to work, she meandered through the house and out to the back porch. Any thoughts of surfing were nixed at the sight of the ocean; the waves were massive and crashing, the sky dark with roiling clouds. Gusts of wind buffeted against the house and bent the trees. The first few raindrops hit the back porch as she stood in the doorway, sipping on her coffee.

With nothing else to do, she drifted up the stairs and into the front bedroom. By the time she'd picked up a new album and sat in the window seat, the rain pattered against the storm shutters in splattering drops that rattled the aluminum. She wondered how many times her mom had been stuck inside, sitting where Kyra sat now, when the weather turned bad.

These kinds of questions plagued her. Lately it seemed like she compared everything she did to her mom. She had come to Canaan Island to fill the hole left behind after her mother's death, and she had found more than she thought she would with all these albums, but they hadn't helped. If anything, the hole inside of her was widening.

"Morning."

Hale stood in the doorway, but he didn't come any farther. Kyra had been so consumed staring down at the pictures of her mom, she hadn't even heard him go downstairs and get a cup of coffee.

"Hey," she said.

"You okay?" His words were careful as he took a slow drink of his coffee.

"I am."

"What are you going to do with all these books?"

She lifted a shoulder. "Maybe put them downstairs on the bookshelf in the living room."

"If it means I don't have to move it again, I think it's a great idea." His joke fell flat; something was off between them. She didn't have the energy to smile, even though she felt his eyes on her face. Setting aside his coffee in the hall, he picked up a stack of books.

An envelope slipped loose from the stack he held. They both watched as it fluttered to the floor. Kyra frowned. "What's that?"

"It came out of one of these . . ." Hale shifted his arm load.

Ignoring him, she bent and picked it up. She flipped the letter over. In slightly slanting, curving script was her name. She didn't recognize the handwriting. Actually, she'd never seen it before in her life. And that fact alone told her who it was.

"It's from Mom," she whispered.

Everything seemed to fade away in that moment. For the first time all morning, she felt herself winding up, like an old clock coming to life once again. She forgot about Hale and last night and how stupid she was. Everything melted away except for the letter in her hand—at least she hoped it was a letter. She closed her eyes and prayed it was a letter.

This could make everything okay, she thought. This could heal her.

"I'm going to go downstairs and let you read it in private." Hale took their coffee cups and left.

When the door shut softly behind him, she sank to the floor. She held the letter in her arms like it was a newborn baby.

Before she talked herself out of it, she opened the letter. The sealant was long gone, so she pulled out the folded paper without damaging the envelope. Opening the page, it smelled like time long past and mildew, but she caught the softest strains of perfume wafting from it.

Lila had been the last person to ever hold this letter. This was the closest she'd ever come to her mother in her adult life. She took a deep breath and began to read.

Sweet Kyra,

Happy Birthday, baby girl! You're turning one year old today, and, for me, it's been a blessed year knowing you're in the same world I live in.

I can't give you a present this year, so I wrote you a fairy tale. I hope your aunt and uncle will read this to you as a bedtime story. And one day, I hope you will read it for yourself. When you do, I pray you'll understand why I have to leave you. I also pray you know how happy you made me the day you were born.

So here goes . . .

Once upon a time, there was a young princess. She had a good life, a fortunate life, high up in her castle. The king and queen gave the princess everything she ever wanted. She had ponies, dolls, and all the friends a girl could ask for.

But the kingdom was cursed. There was a darkness in the lands that only certain people saw, including the princess. Some nights it would slip in her window and stifle her cries. Sometimes she would see it when she played with her friends or took a nap. Its inky depths terrified her; its shadowed tendrils chased her. She thought if she looked too long at the black depths that it would suck her in and she would never see the king and queen ever again.

Years passed and the young princess grew up, but she saw the darkness more and more. And then one day, a handsome prince rode into to the kingdom on a mighty black stallion, and he told the princess he saw the shadows too. She cried with relief because someone was finally like her.

The prince rescued her and took her away from the darkness. He had magic potions to make the shadows go away. The princess drank the potions to make the kingdom pure and light and bright again. But the potion only lasted for a short while. And when the blackness came back, it would always come back worse than before.

Soon the princess realized she had her own little princess baby growing inside of her. It was the most exciting day of her life. She raced across the kingdom to tell the king and queen, but they were not happy. They sensed the prince's magic on her, and they banished her from the kingdom. Magic was not allowed, but it was a rule the princess had been sheltered from. She'd never known hate, and she never knew love could be broken.

Sad and destroyed, the princess went back to her prince. He fed her more and more of the magic potions to keep the darkness away. All the while, the baby grew inside the princess. She would hold her stomach and feel the little baby saying hello, and she knew that some love was strong enough to never break.

But the magic started to not keep the blackness away completely. The princess couldn't run away anymore, and men came and took her away from the prince and locked her in a forgotten, dark tower far away from anywhere she'd ever known. The magic was gone, and all she had was the baby inside her for comfort.

And when the baby was born, the princess was the happiest she'd ever been. Her baby was better than any of the rich, lavish presents the king and queen had ever given her. Her baby was the greatest magic potion in the world. It was the best day of the princess's life. But then the men from the tower took her baby away, and the princess was alone once again.

She had no protection from the darkness now. She had no one to comfort her. The prince was far away and had found a new princess to save. All the happiness the princess had felt when she held her baby princess was long gone.

So she dreamed of sleep, a sleep so deep the darkness would never find the princess ever again. The sleep would take her to a kingdom so perfect it could never be tarnished by shadows. It would have jeweled castles and white horses and knights in shining armor. The princess would be loved and cherished and protected forever. There, in that perfect kingdom, the princess would wait for her happiness again. One day, she would find her little baby princess. It would be perfect.

So the princess went to sleep. She went to that perfect place to free herself from the binds of the darkness. Her knights in shining armor would protect her. She would ride around on fancy white horses. But all the while, she would wait for her baby to come to her. And when they were together again, they would live happily ever after.

The end.

I love you baby girl,
Lila

Kyra's grip on the letter wrinkled the pages. She wasn't breathing. Tears fell in torrents down her face. She swayed in her seat, feeling dizzy and overcome with emotion. Setting the letter aside to keep it from getting wet, she bowed her head and sobbed.

Her mom had written her a fairy tale for her first birthday. She could have grown up falling asleep to the words of her mother. She would have cherished this letter, this story. It could have been the bridge over the dark hole inside of her.

Her mother had felt the same darkness she did. She wouldn't have felt so alone. She wouldn't have wondered what was wrong with her.

Maybe she could have fallen asleep with dreams of princesses and kingdoms instead of crying into her pillow because she was a little girl who missed her mommy.

When the tears stopped and she was just hiccupping into her hands, she stood on shaky legs. She didn't know if she was going to vomit or pass out. Her eyes drifted back to the letter.

She didn't understand why she'd never gotten it if her mother had intended for her to have it. Instead, it was here, lost amongst forgotten pictures. Like the photo albums, the letter had been left behind as trash for the next person to clean out, which meant there was only one person who knew the albums and letter had been left behind.

Florence had done this. Florence had ruined Kyra's life like she'd ruined her daughter's life. That selfish, evil bitch had driven her daughter to suicide and left Kyra with no memories of her mother.

A strangled sound ripped from her throat. After snatching up the letter, she launched herself at the door. She would settle this. She would end this today.

She rocketed down the stairs, her feet barely touching the treads. She hit the door at full speed, banging it open on the hinges. It crashed against the wall, rattling the windows.

"Kyra?" Hale called from somewhere inside the house. She leapt from the porch, her knees buckling when she hit the ground. "Kyra!" he shouted again, and from a corner of her mind, she heard the fear in his voice.

The rain came down harder now, plastering her hair to her face, but she didn't go to her Jeep. She raced out to the road and took off for Florence's house, her bare feet splashing through the growing puddles of Gardenia Street. Her breathing came in pants as she pumped her arms, racing down the middle of the street, likely appeared like a crazy person to anyone who looked outside. Her clothes clung to her body. Rain dripped into her eyes. Or tears. She couldn't tell.

The building wind made her stumble as it blustered about. The trees whipped above her, and all the houses were closed up and prepared for war. No one walked the streets and no cars passed her. It was a ghost town; she was the only one crazy enough to venture out into the weather.

She leapt over the front gate of the large, white house two streets over from her own. The house she'd driven by a few times, but never knocked on the door. She'd been too scared then.

She wasn't now.

She jumped up the steps and pounded on the front door. When it opened and Florence stared down at her with wide, shocked eyes, Kyra reared back and slapped her grandmother as hard as she could.

29

Florence screamed.

Kyra screamed louder.

"How could you?" She waved the soaked, sloppy mess of a letter in front of her grandmother's face. "How could you do this to me?"

"Florence?" Garlan came from the kitchen holding a newspaper in his hands. He looked between Florence and Kyra, understanding instantly.

"Get her out of here! Call the police!" Florence shrieked, stumbling back as Kyra advanced farther into the house.

Kyra threw the letter at Florence, who ducked in time. The paper sailed straight past her like a lumpy ball. "You kept her letter from me! It was the only thing I had, and you didn't give it to me!"

"I don't know what you're talking about!"

"You know exactly what I'm talking about." She stalked closer.

Garlan bent to pick up the letter from the floor. He didn't look like he was calling the cops anytime soon. "But how could you do that to your daughter? To your granddaughter?"

"You are *not* my granddaughter. She is *not* my daughter."

"Yes, we are!" Kyra screamed inches from Florence's face. "No matter how many times you say it or how cruel and vicious you are, it doesn't change the fact that we are your family. And you killed us. You destroyed us. You tore everything we had from us!"

"She deserved to have nothing!" Spit flew from Florence's mouth. "You weren't wanted, just like she wasn't wanted."

"How can you say that? She was your child!"

"Florence," Garlan started, but she shouted above him.

"She was dead to me the day she walked out of my house. I mourned my baby then, long before she hanged herself in that disgusting prison."

Kyra recoiled, vomit rising in her throat. She'd never known how her mother had killed herself, but hearing it now only fueled her trembling rage. "You should have loved her through it. You should have done something to help her! She just needed help!"

Her words were jagged, guttural shrieks. She could barely understand herself. Garlan came farther into the room, his eyes dancing between the two women.

"Nothing could save her. She was on her own. That's the way she wanted it, so I gave it to her." Florence sniffed, tilting her chin as if she'd only deigned to give Lila her greatest wish.

Kyra wanted to hit her grandmother so hard that she lost any memory of her daughter, which, sadly, was probably exactly what Florence wanted too.

She leapt forward and grabbed the material of Florence's linen shirt. The woman screeched and flailed, but Kyra held on. The sound of material ripping filled the house. "You could've saved her! She needed her mom, and you just kicked her down further! What kind of person are you? You're horrible and ugly and filthy and . . ." She petered out, her words turning into a garbled mess. She began to shiver, began to see shadows building in the corner of her vision. Her hold on Florence slackened.

Florence's face looked stricken; she stumbled away from Kyra's grip and began to cry. "You're crazy. *You're crazy*. Get out of my house. Garlan, help me!"

"You broke her heart, you know that? And you broke my fucking heart . . . I *needed* that letter. I *needed* to know she loved me, but you took that from me too . . ."

"You're just like her! You're selfish and hateful! You probably take those evil drugs and spread your legs for any man who walks by. You're despicable. Just like her. She burns in Hell, just like you will."

"Florence!" Garlan bellowed. "That's enough!"

Everyone quieted. Exhausted, Kyra looked at her grandfather, who'd finally had enough. Florence cringed away, her face paling and her tears falling harder. She sniffled, looking between her husband and Kyra.

"That's enough. I can't take this anymore," he said, shaking his head and looking as if the weight of his wife's bitterness had aged him more than time. He walked past Florence and handed the tattered, soaked letter to Kyra. "I'm sorry. I didn't know about the letter. If I had, I would've made sure you got it. I hope one day you can forgive us for what we did to you and your mother." Garlan turned his head to his wife, his expression loathing. "If we ever deserve your forgiveness."

Kyra looked down at the letter. It was completely ruined. The water had turned the paper into shredding clumps of goo. The ink bled and blurred into an unreadable mass. The only link she had to her mother was ruined. She'd ruined it.

Like she ruined everything.

The line between her and her mother was blurring. She felt the darkness inside her open its gaping maw and devour her. She was cracking apart, right there, in the house of her enemy.

A sob escaped her throat, and she turned and ran. The door was still open where she'd barged in. She didn't bother closing it. Halfway down the steps, she fell, wrenching her ankle to the side. Sobbing, blinded by her tears, she tried to stand. She would've fallen if not for strong hands wrapping around her waist.

"I've got you," Hale said.

She looked up at him. Water dripped down his face, but his eyes were full of real love and compassion. She wilted against his arms, sobbing even harder. "It's ruined," she said over and over.

He tucked her into his truck. He must have followed her over and waited outside for her. The thought tore through her harder than the wind that gusted around them, tugging at the truck and rattling the windows. The windshield wipers beat back and forth, not able to keep up with the torrent of rain. The storm was upon them, but she had already been through one.

She was destroyed. Everything was gone. All that remained was a skeleton.

30

"*Please* just go!" Kyra howled.

Hale hovered in the door to her bedroom. "I don't think you should be alone like this . . ."

He was right, she thought. If she'd told him about the cutting, he would know not to leave her. He would know the only thing she wanted in the whole wide world right then was a shiny metal blade. He should stay, but the rational part of her wasn't strong enough to tell him that, to tell him that she needed help right now. She was too lost, too ravaged, to speak the words. She'd told no one but Stevie that she was broken. No one else knew. And Stevie didn't know what was happening right now.

She didn't know Kyra had fallen into a hole so deep she couldn't feel anything but the hollow echo of her silent screams around her as she plummeted down and down and down.

"I don't want you here!" she shouted. "Leave me alone!"

She needed that blade against her skin so badly her mouth watered.

Hale still hesitated. He was torn between going and staying. "Kyra . . ."

"Get out of my fucking house!" She threw her laptop at him. It bounced off the wall and landed on the floor, cracking apart like a split fruit. She screamed in frustration. Nothing was working to make him leave, and she needed to feel that cutting pain before her heart exploded inside her chest. He advanced toward her once again, his hands stretched out, reaching for her.

She snapped.

"I bet Cade tried to drown himself just to get away from you!"

He jerked as if she'd slapped him. The compassion that had been in his eyes moments before iced over. She'd done the trick.

"You know what, Kyra? Fuck you!" he shouted, his rage twisting his face. He slammed her bedroom door hard enough to make a picture hanging on her wall fall to the floor and shatter. She hadn't even noticed it. Seeing it broken on the floor, she understood it for what it was: an apology for last night. A sign that he was trying. That he wanted to try.

He'd framed one of his drawings for her.

She'd ruined that too.

31

Kyra didn't know what time it was. It was so dark outside she couldn't tell if it was night or day. The storm rocked around the house, making the old structure howl and screech like a banshee. She covered her ears and screamed until her head threatened to split apart.

She felt nothing but her own pain. The darkness ate itself around her and bore down on her like a monster with snapping jaws and dripping drool. This was it, she thought. This was where she'd finally go crazy.

Her eyes flickered to the bathroom. The door was open. Inside the medicine cabinet, the razor blade waited for her. She couldn't hold off the desire any longer.

She didn't want to kill herself. This wouldn't be a suicide attempt, she told herself. She was in control. She just needed one cut, one little slash to control the pain. To punish herself for ruining the letter, for yelling at Florence, for breaking Hale's heart.

She just wanted some relief from the loathing she felt burning through her insides. Relief from the howling inside of her. Relief from the everlasting fall through the darkness. Relief from the pictures of her mother that played across her mind in an endless loop.

Tutus and dance recitals. Birthday cake crumbs and melting candles. Lila on Garlan's shoulders, laughing and clinging to his head. A whole life. A good life. A short one too.

Something banged against the side of the house and Kyra fell out of bed.

She crawled to the bathroom.

This had to end.

32

Deeper. Deeper this time. This time, you'll feel in control. Deeper to make it hurt. Deeper to punish. Don't be scared. Make it deeper to feel. Make it deeper to float away.

Deeper and it'll take away those bad feelings.

Kyra whimpered at the searing fire stretching across her skin. The tears pressed against the back of her eyes. But the pain . . . the pain was the most intoxicating relief. It drowned out the black hole writhing inside her.

Even if only for a moment. And then she had to cut again.

Like the princess and the magic potion that didn't last long enough. A laugh bubbled from her mouth. She choked on it, gagged, and cut again.

The blood trickled down the bone of her wrist from a cut carefully in alignment with two other shallower marks next to year-old scars. The blood cooled against her feverish skin. Shivering on the bathroom floor, she watched its inching path down her thumb. There it hovered, curling into itself until it fell ever so slowly to the floor. There it splattered, sending tiny droplets over the beautiful white tile. There it lay, waiting for company.

As more drops fell, Kyra wondered if her blood would stain the grout.

Hale would hate that.

33

They kept coming back. Kyra couldn't keep them at bay. The tsunami of emotions gave her no relief. She felt them all, the entire gamut. They were relentless, battering against her.

The darkness. The princess. A kingdom of white horses and knights in shining armor and castles that glinted in the warm, summer sunlight. There, just there, in a sleep so deep that not even the sadness could reach her.

She shook her head. No, not the sleep. Just relief. She only wanted relief. So she kept cutting. She kept thinking she was in control, only to feel it slip away more and more with every passing moment.

"Please," she prayed. "Please."

The cuts didn't line up anymore. They ran in hashing, crooked lines across the entire length of her arm. Blood pooled like a magic lake around her.

She couldn't stop. She prayed to stop. She'd lost control. Lost herself.

34

She crawled out to her bathroom, her palms slipping in the blood, stopping once because her body was shaking too badly to move. Her vision slanted horribly, but she managed to make it. She threw her hand up to the night stand, fumbling about until she found her phone. The glass lamp tumbled off the table and crashed to the floor beside her. It shattered inches from her face. She ripped her phone from the wall where it had been charging.

Blood streaked across her phone as she fought to pull up a text to Stevie. Tears coursed down her cheeks, knowing she'd finally done it. She'd finally broken herself beyond repair.

"Hello? Kyra?"

She blinked down at the phone. She'd called Stevie instead of texting her. She hadn't meant to do that. Her brain was too sluggish to keep up. Another course of shivers cascaded through her body.

Cold. So cold. So tired.

"Kyra? Dude, what's up?"

"Stevie?" Her voice cracked, and she choked over the dusty dryness of her throat.

"Kyra? Kyra, what's wrong?"

"Stevie, I . . ." She looked down at her arms. Gashes spread across them. There was no pattern, no method. It was just a gruesome checkerboard of a girl who needed relief, a girl who'd lost control.

She couldn't cover these marks. There would be no hiding now.

"Kyra! Talk to me!"

Stevie sounded frantic. She sounded scared to death. Looking at her arms, Kyra thought her friend might have a right to be scared. She couldn't remember what she'd said.

"She told me a story about a princess and the magic that kept the darkness away, but it doesn't work." She sniffed, feeling lightheaded. She looked away from the blood and swallowed loudly. "It never works."

"What the fuck are you talking about? Did you cut yourself, Kyra? Did you hurt yourself?"

She couldn't help it; she looked back down at her arms. "No."

She hadn't hurt herself. She'd broken herself.

"Oh," Stevie said, sounding confused. "Dude, are you drunk? Cause you should hear yourself right now. You really had me freaked out."

She laughed, the sound making Kyra laugh too. The storm was getting worse. The banging on the side of her house grew louder.

"I didn't hurt myself."

"That's good. You know it's not too nice to call your friend who's in alcohol rehab when you're drunk."

"I couldn't feel it anymore," she mumbled. She fell back to the floor, cracking her head against the wood. The phone fell from her hand, but she still heard Stevie's reply.

"Couldn't feel what? Wait . . . Kyra?"

She picked the phone up. She had to try a couple times because her hands were slick with blood. "The cuts. I couldn't feel them anymore. So I cut deeper to feel it. To feel something besides all the . . . the pressure in my head. Hale framed this picture for me and I broke it. He hates me. I ruined the letter too. I hate me. So I got the blade. But . . . but I think I did too much."

"What?" Stevie shrieked. She started screaming to someone in the background for help. "Kyra, what happened? Are you at your house?"

"I didn't feel it, I swear. That's why I kept cutting. I wasn't trying to kill myself. I just needed relief. I just needed to breathe." Kyra sobbed. "She's dead, Stevie."

"Who?"

"My mom. She's dead, and I have nothing."

"Listen here, you have everything, you bitch. Now get a towel and wrap up your arms. Do it now. Wrap them fucking tight or I swear I'll kill you myself."

"I love you," she said, her voice garbling thick in her throat.

35

"*Kyra!*"

Something stung across the side of her face. Blurrily, she blinked, looking up to see a figure shrouded in shadows looming above her. She tried to cringe away, but the figure held her tight.

"Damnit, Kyra, stay awake!"

The figure sounded a lot like Hale, but she thought it was more likely the prince from the fairy tale had come with some magic potion. She was lifted into the air rather indelicately. The prince kept slapping her and shaking her until she bit her tongue.

"I should've known . . . I should've . . ." The prince choked on his sobs as they bounced down the steps. Before they were even outside, she felt the drops of water like rain dripping down onto her face, but she didn't understand how it was raining inside her house.

"Please, be okay. Be okay. I love you. Kyra, I love you."

36

The first time Kyra woke, she was in a hospital. Slow, continual beeping filled the room. She was too weak to move, but she couldn't if she wanted to. She felt the restraints tight around her bandaged wrists.

Outside her room, through a large glass window, Cade had his arms wrapped tightly around Hale, whose massive shoulders wilted over and shook with tears. The sight was wrong, off somehow. Hale was the protector, the fist around all those he loved. He was supposed to be the one who held instead of the one who was held. But he looked small and broken. Cade's long, lanky arms were the perfect length to envelope the broad, bowed form of his brother.

Both protectors. Both perfectly molded to weather the storms for each other.

Cade met her eyes through the window, glaring as if he hated her.

Kyra understood. She hated herself too. She turned her head away and went back to sleep.

37

Three weeks later, Kyra returned to her house. She'd spent a few days in the hospital while her wounds healed. She'd suffered bad blood loss and shock, and if it hadn't been for Hale returning to her house and Stevie sending help after the phone call, she probably would've died. The hospital released her into the care of Dr. Clemens. She'd spent the next couple of weeks healing at The Lodge.

Her aunt and uncle had come to see her many times. Stevie too, after she'd completed her own rehabilitation. Cade came with her, following her around like, but she was committed to her sobriety first and foremost, she'd told him. Then she would roll her eyes at Kyra. Hale never came. Kyra made the mistake of asking about him once, but Cade had looked so uncomfortable she didn't ask again.

Never again did she catch Cade glaring at her. She wondered

what had changed.

Stevie didn't offer to carry her bags as they got out of Stevie's car, but Kyra took the lack of an offer as a good sign. For weeks, everyone had been tiptoeing around her as if she was a cracked porcelain doll. But now she must look well enough for Stevie to deem her fit to carry her own luggage. Luckily, it wasn't much. She tossed the backpack over her shoulder and looked up at her house.

The exterior was finally done. The mint-green paint thrilled her. It looked inviting and cheerful—everything that she needed right then. The shutters were a deep purple, which complemented the green perfectly. All the delicate scrolls and twisted wood were painted in white to set them off against the house.

"I feel like I'm walking into Willy Wonka's Chocolate Factory. I can't believe I'm going to have to live next to this for the rest of my life."

She wrapped her arm around Stevie. "Oh, come on. It's awesome, and you know it."

"Whatever."

Stevie helped her get settled, but Kyra could tell she was lingering. When she offered to help dust, Kyra knew she was worried about her. "Go on, Stevie. I'm fine. Seriously. It's okay."

"Are you sure?" Stevie frowned. She looked around. "Will anything in here trigger you?"

"If it does, I'll call Dr. Clemens."

"Okay . . ." Stevie bit her lip. "Remember, no surfing until the stitches are out."

Kyra looked down at her arms, but they were covered by her hoodie. Some of the cuts were so deep that they were still wrapped in bandages to cover the stitches holding the flesh of her arm together. "I remember."

"Good. I'm coming over for dinner, and we're eating meat. You need your strength."

"Fine," she said, smiling at her friend. She pulled her in for a hug. After a quick moment, she tried to step away, but Stevie clung to her.

"Never again," she whispered. Kyra couldn't see her friend's tears, but she heard them in her voice. "Don't ever do that again. You're all I got, and you're supposed to be the good one, okay? Leave this shit for me to do."

Kyra hugged Stevie back, squeezing her tight, even though it made the wounds pull in her arms. "How about neither of us do anything like this again?"

"Sounds good. But I'm still entitled to some small form of meltdowns. Just nothing Chernobyl-scale like this."

Kyra laughed. "Okay, fine. I'll agree to those terms."

"I love you," Stevie whispered into the side of Kyra's hair.

"I love you too."

Finally, she released Kyra. When she stepped back, she looked cool and collected as always. She pulled her sunglasses down onto her face. "See ya later, alligator."

When Stevie left, Kyra was once again alone. She walked through her house, opening windows to air out the stuffy smell. Hale had finished all the custom furniture, which meant the renovation was officially over. She noticed he'd put all her mother's albums on the bookshelf in the living room. Upstairs, her bed was neatly made, the lamp replaced. She trailed a finger down the side of her chin, where a small scar had been left behind by the shattering glass.

She pulled her phone out of her pocket. Her finger hovered over the text button. All she wanted to do was text Hale, but she wasn't sure. When she closed her eyes, she saw him in Cade's arms that night in the hospital after he'd found her with her arms cut up like Christmas ribbons. Like she needed to heal and restore herself, he probably needed time for the same after what she'd done to him. Plus, she had a lot of therapy in front of her, and she doubted he wanted a part of that.

A knock came from downstairs. Instantly, she hoped it was Hale, but she knew better. Knew him better. He needed time, like she'd needed time, and when he was ready, he'd reach out. She accepted that. With a sigh, she walked back downstairs.

She opened the door and found Florence standing on her porch. If her vision could've turned red with anger, it would have. She tried to slam the door in her grandmother's face, but Florence put her hand on the door.

"Wait, please," she said, stammering.

"What do you want?" Kyra hissed. She was trembling. Tears pricked in the back of her eyes, which only made her angrier.

Florence cleared her throat. She looked as nervous as Kyra was angry. When she finally met Kyra's eyes, she saw the normal hostility wasn't there. "I heard about your . . . your accident." Kyra snorted at Florence's words, but the woman hurried on. "But I came over to say I'm sorry about that day you came over. You caught me off-guard, and I . . . I just . . ." Florence looked away, taking a deep breath. "It's just so hard."

"If you're looking for sympathy or something from me, you've come to the wrong house," Kyra said, refusing to feel sorry for this woman. "Have you ever thought maybe it's hard because disowning your daughter and granddaughter was the wrong thing to do? Maybe it weighs heavily on your conscious because it was a bad fucking decision."

Florence cringed at her language, but she didn't mention it. "I think you're right," she said so quietly Kyra had to lean forward to hear. The words surprised her.

"Then why did you do it?"

Florence's light-blue eyes swam with tears when she looked up. She held a small wooden box in her hands. "I was so angry with her. You can only be that angry with someone you love the most. You know exactly the right way to cut someone down when you love them like that. So, I cut her down." Her voice cracked and the tears streamed down her wrinkled face. "I cut her down and kicked her out. When she needed love the most, I only gave her hate, just like you said. I still loved her, but I thought anger was the best response. So I broke her. And I . . . I think . . . I think I killed her."

Kyra didn't hate her grandmother so much that she didn't feel the slightest bit of empathy for her. She was glad Florence had some remorse for her actions, but she still didn't invite her in. This was her mother's house, and only love for her was allowed inside. "She killed herself, Florence. You didn't do that."

She shook her head. "She died of a broken heart. I did that to her. I broke her."

Kyra couldn't hold back the tears anymore. But they weren't angry tears or tears of forgiveness. She stepped out of the shield of her house and embraced Florence. The box her grandmother held pressed into Kyra's abdomen, but she didn't care. Florence seemed to wither in her arms. She couldn't wrap her arms around Kyra because of the box, but she put her head on Kyra's shoulder and cried softly, delicately.

"I was . . ." Florence's words hitched and cracked around her tears. "I was her mother. I was the only one who could love her through it, and I broke her down instead. I was her *mother*."

"Shhh," Kyra said, rubbing Florence's back. "She knew you loved her."

"You can't know that," she whispered.

"You were her mother. Of course she knew you loved her. And she loved you."

"I said awful, horrible things. Things a mother should never say to her daughter. I told her she would die young and alone."

Kyra stiffened at the words. Florence was right; those were words that should never be spoken to daughters. Actually, Florence was right about a lot. As a mother, she was supposed to love her daughter through the hard times. A mother's love should be the only kind of love that never faltered. Kyra didn't understand Florence, and she knew she would be angry with her for a long time, but she pitied her.

Her grandmother's remorse soaked Kyra's shirt. It was years too late, and the woman was crying on the wrong daughter's shoulder, but it was still remorse. She kept consoling Florence until she could straighten and wipe underneath her eyes where her careful makeup had run.

She sniffed. "I'm sorry. I didn't come over here to be a blubbering mess. I just wanted to give you some of her things." She held up the box, offering it out to Kyra.

It was a little cedar chest with tiny flowers drawn onto the lid. She took it from Florence and clutched it tight in her grip. "Are you sure?"

"I don't feel right keeping them anymore."

"Thank you." The silence stretched out, and Kyra shifted awkwardly. She didn't know what else to say, and no matter what, the woman wasn't coming into her house.

But Florence needed to say something else. She visibly steeled herself before she met Kyra's eyes again. "I know this is probably the last thing you want to do, but would you come to her grave with me on Sunday?"

Kyra clenched her jaw. Everything in her screamed to say no, but Florence looked so raw, like she'd been split open before Kyra. "Sure."

Florence's smile was shaky. "Thank you, Kyra."

"You're welcome."

She turned to leave, making her way carefully down the steps. Kyra stood on her porch. On the road, Garlan sat in the car. He turned it on as Florence approached and lifted his hand in a silent greeting. Kyra waved back, offering her grandfather a tiny smile. She knew he'd been a big part in Florence's reformation.

She paused halfway through Kyra's front garden and turned back around, shielding her eyes against the sun. "You're a lot like her, you know." Kyra tensed at the words, thinking Florence was going to add something hateful, but instead, she said, "You have all her best parts, and I can see you struggle with the same depression. Don't let it take you like it took her." Florence was crying again. She swiped at the tears as if she was frustrated with them. "If you need any help or need anyone to talk to, I'm here. I'm here," she repeated mostly to herself before she turned back to the car.

Kyra didn't wait for her to leave. She went inside and closed the door. With the box in her hands, she slid down the door onto the floor, feeling as if she'd been wrung from the inside out. With a deep breath, she opened the box.

There wasn't much inside, which she was thankful for. She had Dr. Clemens's number pulled up and ready to hit send in case something upset her. But the box contained just a few pieces of jewelry, a medal from a science fair, and a diary.

Kyra knew better than to try and read it now. She closed the lid on the box and set it beside her. There was plenty of time for that later. After a few minutes, she stood and went into her living room. She put the box next to the albums. It looked good there, she thought. And it could stay there until she was ready.

38

That evening, Kyra heard another knock on the door, followed by Stevie tromping in. "Hey, dork," Stevie called out, her voice ringing off the walls of the house.

"I'm in the kitchen!" Kyra shouted back, smiling at the familiar comfort of her home and Stevie's humor. She finished planting the last little herb container. She'd purchased a kit today along with some new plants. Stevie had tried to water her flowers while she was gone, but Stevie would be Stevie, in all her forgetful glory.

"I hope you're ready to swallow some meat," Stevie said in a sing-song voice as she came into the kitchen. "'Cause I brought pepperoni!"

"Very funny, Stevie," Kyra said, rolling her eyes. She looked over her shoulder as Stevie deposited the pizza on the counter and hopped up next to it. Cade walked in the door behind her.

"Hey, Kyra. I hope you don't mind . . ." Cade's voice had never sounded so shy and unsure around her, even when they'd first met, but he clearly had to work not to stutter now. She still didn't know how he felt about her, but she thought it was a good sign that he'd come over.

"No!" Kyra said, walking over to hug him. "It's totally fine."

"You sure about that?"

Kyra froze, her eyes darting back to the kitchen door. It was Hale who'd spoken.

Hale . . .

He stood in the doorway, hesitating and even more uncertain than his brother had been. His hair was a bit longer, and Kyra spotted some new tattoos covering the tops of his hands. He looked tanner, as if he'd been in the water more lately. Somehow, it looked as though his muscles were even bigger. But his beautiful eyes watched her and waited.

"Of course," she said. She had to clear her throat. "Thanks for coming."

"Oh, shitballs. I left the . . . uh . . . the water over at my house." Stevie hopped off the counter. "Cade, come with me to get it."

"But I am sure Kyra has—"

"Her water is gross! I said come with me." She grabbed his arm and propelled him out of the house.

Just like that, Kyra was alone with Hale. Her eyes drifted back to him. "Hey," she said again, almost whispering.

"Hey."

She took a deep breath. "Hale, I'm sorry."

"Why are you sorry?" he asked, his expression dark as he slowly walked into the kitchen.

"Because you had to find me like that. I know how badly that must have hurt you," she said. She knew from her therapy she shouldn't apologize for hurting herself. She just had to accept what she'd done and move on with forgiveness, but that included righting the wrongs of those she'd hurt.

"I'm glad I did." He stopped a foot away from her.

"Me too. Thank you."

He reached out and lightly touched her arm, the one hidden beneath a baggie hoodie and bandages. "Why didn't you tell me? I could've helped."

"You can't fix me, Hale. I have to do that myself."

"I know, but . . ." He stopped himself, clearly struggling, and took a deep breath. "Do you feel better now?"

"Some days are hard, but I'm taking some medicine now to help. And Dr. Clemens is really great. I'll see her twice a week for a while."

"That's good." He nodded his approval. "You need to get better."

"I will," she whispered. She closed the distance between them and hesitantly put her hand on his chest. "Hale, I . . ."

"No, wait." He took her hand off his chest and held it. She felt it coming, his rejection. She'd expected it, but her heart cracked a little. "Kyra, I love you. I did when you said it to me first. But I can't go through something like finding you again. When I saw you on the floor with your arms like that, it was . . . it was unbelievable. I don't understand why you couldn't just tell me. Why did you think you had to carry that yourself?" He didn't give her a chance to answer. "I can't do that again. I didn't come see you because I needed some space to figure out if I could be the right man for you.

I still don't know. And I didn't know if I should even come tonight, but I had to tell you. I do love you. I love you so much, Kyra, but you scared the hell out of me. I don't know if I'm a strong enough man for you."

She closed her eyes. His words burned her. He thought he had to be strong for her. But she could understand his fear and uncertainty. She focused on the fact he'd said he loved her.

"I can be strong enough for myself," she said, giving the words strength and meaning. She repeated them silently to herself. She may not believe it completely now, but she would with time. "You don't have to be that for me."

"I want to love you," he said quietly. His expression was wide open and raw, always honest, always true. "But I'm scared."

"I love you too," she said, smiling at him. She had an idea. "But what if we forget that we love each other?"

"Wait, what?" His brows drew together in deep, worried lines. His eyes snapped with fear, and he stepped even closer to her. "No."

"I mean, what if we just date for a while? We can get to know each other even better, and I can work on my therapy. We won't go too fast, and we can just heal together without all the extra pressure. And then, when we're ready, we can go back to where we were, letting ourselves love each other once we're certain everything else is okay."

Hale quietly thought about it for a moment. He was silent for so long that her stomach began to flip with nerves. It was a solution she'd been proud of, but now she doubted herself. Taking a deep breath to calm her nerves, she told herself she could handle whatever he decided; she was strong.

Slowly, he smiled, flooding her body with relief. He lowered his head to hers until his lips were an inch away from hers. "You're asking me to fake it? You know I hate people who do that."

She laughed, but he caught the sound with his mouth. He kissed her deeply and clearly with all the love he felt in his body. She pulled back slightly.

"Just for a little while," she murmured, their lips still grazing.

"For you, I'll be the biggest faker this world has ever seen. I'll have you convinced I don't love you. I'll fake it so good that you'll wonder if I'll even call the next day."

"Okay," she said, laughing again. "Let's not get carried away."

He kissed her again. "Tell me one last time to carry me through."

"I love you," she whispered.

Hale smiled, lowering his forehead against hers. He seemed to breathe in her words, absorb them into his soul. Finally, as Stevie and Cade clambered up the porch steps, making as much noise as possible, he stepped away from her.

"Eh. I think I probably just like you, but I'll give it a shot, I guess."

He flashed the cheesiest, fakest grin she'd ever seen in her life, but she loved it the most.

About The Author

Meg Collett is from the hills of Tennessee where the cell phone service is a blessing and functioning internet is a myth of epic proportions. She and her husband live in a tiny house with three dogs and not enough couches. She's the author of the bestselling Fear University series, the End of Days trilogy, and the Canaan Island novels. For more information and to sign up for her newsletter, go to www.megcollett.com.

Enjoyed *Fakers*?
Please consider leaving a review!

Made in the USA
Coppell, TX
31 March 2020